# GOSLINGS

# GOSLINGS

*by*

**J.D. BERESFORD**

*introduction by* **ASTRA TAYLOR**

—

**HiLoBooks**
*powered by* **Cursor**
**Boston, MA** *and* **Brooklyn, NY**
**2013**

**HiLoBooks**
**RADIUM AGE SCIENCE FICTION**

**The Scarlet Plague**
*Jack London*
*Comment by Matthew Battles*

**With the Night Mail** *and* **"As Easy as A.B.C."**
*Rudyard Kipling*
*Comments by Matthew De Abaitua & Bruce Sterling*

**The Poison Belt**
*Arthur Conan Doyle*
*Comments by Joshua Glenn & Gordon Dahlquist*

**When the World Shook**
*H. Rider Haggard*
*Comments by James Parker & J.R. Bickley, M.R.C.S.*

**People of the Ruins**
*Edward Shanks*
*Comment by Tom Hodgkinson*

**The Night Land**
*William Hope Hodgson*
*Comment by Erik Davis*

**Goslings**
*J.D. Beresford*
*Comment by Astra Taylor*

**The Clockwork Man**
*E.V. Odle*
*Comment by Annalee Newitz*

**Theodore Savage**
*Cicely Hamilton*
*Comment by Gary Panter*

**The Man with Six Senses**
*Muriel Jaeger*
*Comment by Mark Kingwell*

# TABLE *of* CONTENTS

## BOOK III: WOMANKIND IN THE MAKING



## EPILOGUE

This edition of *Goslings* follows the text of
the 1913 edition published by W. Heinemann,
which is in the public domain.

Library of Congress Control Number: 2013932536
ISBN: 978-1-935869-62-7


Cover design by Tony Leone, Leone Design
Page and text design by Colleen Venable

PRINTED IN THE UNITED STATES OF AMERICA

The mission of HiLoBooks is to serialize and
otherwise popularize forgotten Radium Age
science fiction via the website HiLobrow.com, and
to reissue some of these texts as paperback books.
Both HiLobrow.com and HiLoBooks are edited
by Joshua Glenn, and published by KING MIXER.

For more information, visit HiLobrow.com/HiLoBooks
Follow us on Twitter: @hilobrow

HiLoBooks is grateful to Richard Nash for his vision
and publishing acumen.

POWERED BY CURSOR

DISTRIBUTED BY PUBLISHERS GROUP WEST
10 9 8 7 6 5 4 3 2 1

## RADIUM AGE SCIENCE FICTION

*Series Foreword by* **Joshua Glenn**

SEVERAL YEARS AGO, I read Brian Aldiss's *Billion Year Spree*—his "true history of science fiction" from Mary Shelley to the early 1970s. I admire Aldiss tremendously, and I found his account of the genre's development entertaining and informative... but something bothered me, after I'd finished reading the book. Something was missing.

*Billion Year Spree* is terrific on the topic of science fiction from *Frankenstein* through the "scientific romances" of Verne, Poe, and Wells—and also terrific on science fiction's so-called Golden Age, the start of which sf exegetes date to John W. Campbell's 1937 assumption of the editorship of the magazine *Astounding*. However, regarding science fiction published between the beginning of the Golden Age and the end of the Verne-Poe-Wells "scientific romance" era, Aldiss (who rightly laments that Wells's 20th century fiction after, perhaps, 1904's *The Food of the Gods*, fails to recapture "that darkly beautiful quality of imagination, or that instinctive-seeming unity of construction, which lives in his early novels") has very little to say.

Aldiss seems to feel that authors of science fiction after Wells but before the Golden Age weren't very talented. He certainly doesn't think much of the literary skills of Hugo Gernsback, sometimes called the "Father of Science Fiction," who founded *Amazing Stories* in 1926 and coined the phrase "science fiction" while he was at it. He's right: Gernsback's story-telling abilities were as primitive as his ideas were advanced. But does that justify skipping over the 1904-33 era? (By my reckoning, Campbell and his cohort first began to develop their literate, analytical, socially conscious science fiction in reaction to the 1934 advent of the campy *Flash Gordon* comic strip, not to mention Hollywood's "sci-fi" blockbusters that sought to ape the success of 1933's *King Kong*. In other words, sf's Golden Age began before 1937; if I had to pick a year, I'd say 1934.) Is Aldiss's animus against that era due solely to style and quality? I suspect not.

Aldiss's book is hardly alone in sweeping pre-1934 science fiction under the rug. During the so-called Golden Age, which was given that moniker not after the fact, but *at the time*, as a way of signifying the end of science fiction's post-Wells Dark Age, Campbellians took pains to distinguish their own science fiction from everything that had been published in the genre (with the sole exception of 1932's *Brave New World*) since 1904. In his influential 1958 critique, *New Maps of Hell*, for example, Kingsley Amis noted that mature science fiction first established itself in the mid-1930s, "separating with a slowly increasing decisiveness from [immature] fantasy and space-opera." And in his introduction to a 1974 collection, *Before the Golden Age*, editor Isaac Asimov apologetically notes that although it certainly possessed an exuberant vigor, the pre-Golden Age science fiction he grew up reading "seems, to anyone who has experienced the Campbell Revolution, to be clumsy, primitive, naive."

We should be suspicious of this Cold War-era rhetoric of maturity! I'm reminded of Reinhold Niebuhr's pronunciamento, at a 1952 *Partisan Review* symposium, that the utopianism of the early 20th century ought to be regarded as "an adolescent embarrassment." Perhaps Golden Age science fiction's stars—Asimov, Robert Heinlein, Ray Bradbury, and so forth—were regarded as an improvement on their predecessors because in their stories utopian visions and schemes were treated with cynicism. Liberal and conservative anti-utopians who point out that pre-Cold War utopian narratives often demonstrate a naive and perhaps proto-totalitarian eagerness to force square pegs into round holes via thought control and coercion are not wrong. I wouldn't want to live in one of those utopias. However, I strongly agree with those who argue that the intellectual abandonment of utopianism since the 1930s has sapped our political options, and left us all in the helpless position of passive accomplices.

Sure, some 1904-33 science fiction—Gernsback, Edgar Rice Burroughs, and E.E. "Doc" Smith, for example—is indeed fantastical and primitive (though it's still fun to read today). But many other authors of that period—including Olaf Stapledon, William Hope Hodgson, Karel Čapek, Charlotte Perkins Gilman, and Yevgeny Zamyatin—gave us science fiction that was literate, analytical, socially conscious... and also utopian. Utopian in the sense that whatever their politics, Radium Age authors found in the newly named "science fiction" genre a fitting vehicle to express their faith, or at least their hope, that another world is possible. That worldview may have seemed embarrassingly adolescent from the late 1930s until, say, the fall of the Berlin Wall. But today it's an inspiring vision.

*—Joshua Glenn*
*Cofounder, HiLobrow.com & HiLoBooks*
*Boston, 2012*

## An Un-Cozy Catastrophe

*Introduction by* **Astra Taylor**

I FIRST READ *Goslings*, J.D. Beresford's long-forgotten novel, in a little cabin by flashlight, the power knocked out by Hurricane Sandy as she roared over upstate New York. I had gathered provisions that would last about four or five days: non-perishable goods, bottled water, flashlights, batteries, and firewood. When Sandy finally hit the trees bent, arcing almost to the ground. The sound of trunks and branches snapping echoed through the night. That evening, before my phone died, I saw photos shared by those who had stayed in New York City. Lower Manhattan had gone dark and flooded. Cars were floating in parking garages like apples in a barrel. People were wading down Avenue C. Subway stations had morphed into filthy aquariums.

For the next few days New Yorkers were alerted to the long-repressed fact of their city's fragility. Buildings that had seemed immutable the day before, gleaming as part of Manhattan's famous skyline, were dark and waterlogged, uninhabitable and abandoned. Locals reported of getting lost in neighborhoods in which they had lived for years, familiar intersections made eerie by quiet and lack of light. In hard-hit regions—lower Manhattan, the shorelines in Brooklyn, Queens, Staten Island, and New Jersey—thousands were homeless while others, elderly or infirm, were trapped in their homes. Traffic tunnels were impassable and commuter trains stuck. Gasoline was soon rationed, the lines for fuel snaking for blocks.

Though the situation was unprecedented in recent memory, people kept remarking that the experience felt oddly familiar. Sandy opened an uncanny window onto an apocalyptic future that we have already seen at the movies, and read about in books like *Goslings*, which is a relatively early example of the apocalyptic science fiction genre.

Slavoj Žižek, riffing off of Fredric Jameson, has been known to say that it is easier to imagine the end of the world than a modest alteration of the current political and economic order—and no doubt this has something to do with the stories we tell ourselves. That we are better able to envision a giant asteroid hurtling towards Earth or an alien invasion than even a subtle transformation of our social system may say something about the comparative lack of science fiction films or novels exploring the impact of things like free higher education or healthcare in the United States. Nonetheless, Žižek's insight glosses over the fact that many people—particularly those of a progressive bent—implicitly assume that the threat of end times is *the only viable route* to social change. Crisis is too often regarded by progressives as an unpleasant but necessary stop on the way to a better world: something terrible and unprecedented will have to happen to snap us out of our collective apathy so we change course and save ourselves. This buried utopianism—the underlying fantasy of the human race awakened at last by catastrophe—explains part of the unflagging appeal of apocalypticism.

Hurricane Sandy, even before it hit, was heralded in progressive circles as just such a wake-up call, and this possibility suffused my first reading of *Goslings*, which is threaded by a similar optimism. Fallen pines blocked the country road to the cabin; phones had gone dead; my power, heat, and running water were off; and my adopted city was unrecognizable. With few distractions, I made swift progress on the novel, fully immersed in Beresford's gripping tale of what happens when the planet's male population is nearly decimated by an uncontainable plague. As the vast majority of men perish, modern civilization slowly ceases to function. London, the bustling metropolis around which the story is set, shuts down: factories no longer churn out merchandise, farms no longer produce food,

Parliament empties, laws go unheeded, and nature begins to reclaim stone and steel. Women and a handful of male survivors persevere, trekking to the countryside to scratch out a life on the land. It's a tale of devastation, to be sure, but also one of tenacity and triumph. As civilization crumbles Beresford's main characters discover hidden strength and talent and the freedom to articulate criticisms of the old social order they never would have uttered otherwise. A resilient minority represents hope for a radically transformed and improved future.

While Beresford takes a novelist's pleasure in describing the pandemic's arrival and the adventure that ensues (it's that pleasure that makes the novel so absorbing) long passages are devoted to more conceptual reflections, the kind of philosophical asides that would likely derail a lesser work. The plague opens a space for the expression of new ideas about how to live—ideas that overlap with the progressive values Beresford personally espoused. On a plot of land in the English countryside a group of women, aided by one thoughtful man, put some of these ideas into action, forming a sort of agrarian commune informally organized around principles of self-reliance, cooperation, and even vegetarianism.

Seen through the eyes of Beresford's protagonists, the plague was an atrocity, yet it's not clear they would turn back the clock if they could. Viewed from a certain perspective, the epidemic produced desirable social effects not easily achieved through other means: freeing women to break out of prescribed habits and social roles (smashing patriarchy by all but eliminating men), for example. This perspective was heightened for me as I read the novel in the immediate aftermath of a "Frankenstorm" many imagined might serve a similarly rousing purpose, however painful the process may be. We had placed hope in disaster, and done so out of despair: despite overwhelming evidence that climate change is real—the acidification and rising of the oceans, the melting of glaciers and permafrost, the record levels of $CO_2$ in our atmosphere, and so on—it remains a remote, abstract phenomenon for the vast majority of Americans, and thus incredibly difficult to organize around politically and collectively address. For a brief moment it seemed Hurricane Sandy's flattened homes and flooded streets were the taste of potential destruction needed to spur awareness and action: even *Businessweek* blared, in a cover story, "It's global warming, stupid."

It's a dark thing to put your faith in catastrophe. Though disasters do occasionally serve as turning points—the Cuyahoga River fire is one example—more often they do not. Yet we continue to cling, all the same, to the twisted logic that things have to get worse in order to get better. In some political circles well-meaning people can be heard discussing things like peak oil or unemployment or financial collapse in almost wistful tones, as though social change only results from a kind of chemical reaction precipitated by a high dose of suffering. It's evident from reading *Goslings* that Beresford felt the tug of similar sentiments but rightly resisted them, for the tale he tells is hardly one of straightforward redemption. The plague he invents creates an opening but offers no promises, and that's why the novel is so interesting.

The ambiguity and depth of *Goslings* hit me more fully upon a second reading. By that time it was vividly clear that—even when preceded by a summer of raging forest fires, dying forests, and vanishing ice sheets—Hurricane Sandy was not the clarion call we had been hoping for. Those who profit from climate change had not been sanctioned in any way; meanwhile, the lives of regular people had been turned upside down. In Staten Island a month after the storm thousands of residents were still living in shelters or their cars. "The vultures are circling our community," one woman told me. "They see valuable beachfront property, not a place where families live."

There are vultures in Beresford's novel too, before and after the plague, like the head of the Gosling family who urges his firm to make financial investments based on the disease's imminence; the wealthy politicians who stampede to America in an attempt to outrun fate; and the male survivors who become libertines, taking advantage of the scarcity of competition for female attention. Women too, are complicated characters, though it appears Beresford generally preferred them to their masculine counterparts: some hoard, some steal, and some even kill. While the hero and heroines of *Goslings* embrace the opportunity to build the foundation of a new society from scratch, many of the women they encounter cling to the old ways and outmoded beliefs. They judge and persecute and conform almost as if the plague had never happened.

It doesn't give away much to say that Beresford's novel ends with an inspiring disquisition on the future by a fearless young woman. Though he's an unconventional and enlightened fellow, typically loquacious and opinionated, her male companion is comparatively silent, apparently dumbstruck by the force of her vision, her "great plan," as she calls it: a world without class and sex division, without forced labor and forced marriage. It's gender equality she craves most of all, and she details new arrangements for love and child-rearing. Almost a century later, it's remarkable how many of the principles she outlines have become commonplace. Though the society we live in is far from perfect, it has undoubtedly improved by Beresford's measure, and we didn't have to witness the extermination of half of the human race to get here. How those improvements happened is a story worth retelling ourselves of as we face new challenges.

# BOOK I

## THE NEW PLAGUE

# CHAPTER 1

*The Gosling Family*

## 1

"WHERE'S THE GELS gone to?" asked Mr Gosling.

"Up the 'Igh Road to look at the shops. I'm expectin' 'em in every minute."

"Ho!" said Gosling. He leaned against the dresser; the kitchen was hot with steam, and he fumbled for a handkerchief in the pocket of his black tail coat. He produced first a large red bandanna with which he blew his nose vigorously. "Snuff 'andkerchief; brought it 'ome to be washed," he remarked, and then brought out a white handkerchief which he used to wipe his forehead.

"It's a dirty 'abit snuff-taking," commented Mrs Gosling.

"Well, you can't smoke in the orfice," replied Gosling.

"Must be doin' something I suppose?" said his wife.

When the recital of this formula had been accomplished—it was hallowed by a precise repetition every week, and had been established now for a quarter of a century—Gosling returned to the subject in hand.

"They does a lot of lookin' at shops," he said, "and then nothin'll satisfy 'em but buyin' somethin'. Why don't they keep away from 'em?"

"Oh, well; sales begin nex' week," replied Mrs Gosling. "An' that's a thing we 'ave to consider in our circumstances." She left the vicinity of the gas-stove, and bustled over to the dresser. " 'Ere, get out of my way, do," she went on, "an' go up and change your coat. Dinner'll be ready in two ticks. I shan't wait for the gells if they ain't in."

"Them sales is a fraud," remarked Gosling, but he did not stop to argue the point.

He went upstairs and changed his respectable "morning" coat for a short alpaca jacket, slipped his cuffs over his hands, put one inside the other and placed them in their customary position on the chest of drawers, changed his boots for carpet slippers, wetted his hair brush and carefully plastered down a long wisp of grey hair over the top of his bald head, and then went into the bathroom to wash his hands.

There had been a time in George Gosling's history when he had not been so regardful of the decencies of life. But he was a man of position now, and his two daughters insisted on these ceremonial observances.

Gosling was one of the world's successes. He had started life as a National School boy, and had worked his way up through all the grades—messenger, office-boy, junior clerk, clerk, senior clerk, head clerk, accountant—to his present responsible position as head of the counting-house, with a salary of £26 a month. He rented a house in Wisteria Grove, Brondesbury, at £45 a year; he was a sidesman of the church of St John the Evangelist, Kilburn; a member of Local Committees; and in moments of expansion he talked of seeking election to the District Council. A solid, sober, thoroughly respectable man, Gosling, about whom there had never been a hint of scandal; grown stout now, and bald—save for a little hair over the ears, and that one persistent grey tress which he used as a sort of insufficient wrapping for his naked skull.

Such was the George Gosling seen by his wife, daughters, neighbours, and heads of the firm of wholesale provision merchants for whom he had worked for forty-one years in Barbican, E.C. Yet there was another man, hardly realized by George Gosling himself, and apparently so little representative that even his particular cronies in the office would never have entered any description of him, if they had been obliged to give a detailed account of their colleague's character.

Nevertheless, if you heard Gosling laughing uproariously at some story produced by one of those cronies, you might be quite certain that it was a story he would not repeat before his daughters, though he might tell his wife—if it were not too broad. If you watched Gosling in the street, you would see that he took a strange, unaccountable interest in the feet and ankles of young women. And if many of Gosling's thoughts and desires had been translated into action, the Vicar of St John the Evangelist would have dismissed his sidesman with disgust, the Local Committees would have had no more of him, and his wife and daughters would have regarded him as the most depraved of criminals.

Fortunately, Gosling had never been tempted beyond the powers of his resistance. At fifty-five, he may be regarded as safe from temptation. He seldom put any restraint upon his thoughts, outside business hours; but he had an ideal which ruled his life the ideal of respectability. George Gosling counted himself—and others counted him also—as respectable a man as could be found in the Metropolitan Police area. There were, perhaps, a quarter of a million other men in the same area, equally respectable.

## 2

As he was drying his hands, Gosling heard the front door slam and his daughters' voices in the passage below, followed by a shrill exhortation from the kitchen: "Now, gels, 'urry up, dinner's all ready and your father's waitin'!"

Gosling trotted downstairs and received the usual salute from his two girls. He noted that they were a shade more effusive than usual. "Want more money for fal-lals," was his inward comment. They were always wanting money for "fal-lals."

He adopted his usual line of defence through dinner and constantly brought the subject of conversation back to the need for a reduction of expenses. He did not see Blanche wink at Millie across the table, during these strategic exercises; nor catch the glance of understanding which passed between the girls and their mother. So, as his dinner comforted and cheered him, Gosling began to relax into his usual facetiousness; incredibly believing, despite the invariable precedents of his family history, that his daughters had been convinced of the hopelessness of approaching him for money that evening.

The credulous creature even allowed them to make their opening, and then assisted them to a statement of their petition.

They were talking of a friend's engagement to be married, and Gosling with an obtuseness he never displayed in business remarked, "Wish my gels 'ud get married."

"Talking about us, father?" asked Blanche.

"Well, you're the only gels I've got as I know of," said Gosling.

"Well, how can you expect us to get married when we haven't got a decent thing to put on?" returned Blanche.

Gosling realized his danger too late. "Pooh! That don't make any difference," he said hastily, adopting a thoroughly unsound line of defence; "I never noticed what your mother was wearing when I courted 'er."

"Dessay you didn't," replied Millie, "I dessay most fellows couldn't tell you what a girl was wearing, but it makes just all the difference for all that."

"Of course it does," said Blanche. "A girl's got no chance these days unless she can look smart. No fellow's going to marry a dowdy."

"It does make a big difference, there's no denyin'," put in Mrs Gosling, as though she was being convinced against her will.

"And now the sales are just beginning—"

Poor Gosling knew the game was up. They had made no direct attack upon his pocket, yet; but they would not relax their grip of this fascinating subject till they had achieved their object. Blanche was saying that she was ashamed to be seen anywhere; and procrastination would be met at once by the argument—how well he knew it—based on the premise that if you didn't buy at sale-time, you had to pay twice as much later.

It was quite useless for Gosling to fidget, throw himself back in his chair, frown, shake his head, and look horribly determined; the course of progress was unalterable from the direct attack: "Do you *like* to see us going about in rags, father?" through the stage of "Well, well, 'ow much do you want? I simply *can't* afford—" and the ensuing haggles down to the despairing sigh as the original minimum demanded—in this case no less than five pounds—was forlornly conceded, and clinched by Blanche's, "We must have it before the end of the week, dad, the sales begin on Monday."

At the end of it all, he received what compensation they had to offer him; hugs and kisses, offers to do all sorts of impossible things, assistance in getting his armchair into precisely the right position, and him into the chair, and the table cleared and the lamp in just the right place for him to read his halfpenny evening paper which was fetched for him from the pocket of his overcoat. And, finally, the crux of Gosling's whole position, a general air of complacency, good-temper and comfort.

Gosling was an easy-going man, he hated rows.

"Mind you, you two," he remarked with a return to facetiousness as he settled himself with his carpet slippers spread out to the fire—" mind you, I look on this money as an investment. You two gels got to get married; and quick or I shall be in the bankrup'cy Court. Don't you forget as these 'fal-lals' is bought for a purpose."

"Oh, don't be so horrid, father," said Blanche, with a change of front; "it sounds as if we were setting traps for men."

"Well, ain't you?" asked Gosling. "You said just now—"

"Not like that," interrupted Blanche. "It's very different just wanting to look nice. Personally, I'm in no 'urry to get married, thank you."

"You wait till Mr Right comes along," put in Mrs Gosling, and then turned the conversation by saying: "Well, father, what's the news this evening?"

"Nothin' excitin'," replied Gosling. "Seems this new plague's spreadin' in China."

"They're always inventin' new diseases, nowadays, or callin' old ones by new names," said Mrs Gosling. The two girls were busy with a sheet of note-paper and a stump of pencil that seemed to require frequent lubrication; they were making calculations.

"This one's quite new, seemingly," returned Gosling. "It's only the men as get it."

"No need for us to worry, then," put in Millie, more as a duty, some slight return for benefits promised, than because she took any interest in the subject. Blanche was absorbed; her unseeing gaze was fixed on the mantelpiece and ever and again she removed the point of the pencil from her mouth and wrote feverishly.

"Oh, ain't there?" replied Gosling. He turned his head in order to argue from so strong a position. "And where'd you be, and all the rest of the women, if you 'adn't got no men to look after you?"

"I expect we could get along pretty well, if we had to," said Millie.

Gosling winked at his wife, and indicated by an upward movement of his chin that he was astounded at such innocence. "Who'd buy your 'fal-lals' for you, I should like to know?" he asked.

"We'd have to earn money for ourselves," said Millie.

"Ah! I'd like to see you or Blanche takin' over my job," replied her father. "Why, I'll lay there's 'alf a dozen mistakes in the figurin' she's doing at the present moment. Let me see!"

Blanche descended suddenly from visions of Paradise, and put her hand over the sheet of note-paper. "You can't, father," she said.

Gosling looked sly. "Indeed?" he said, with simulated surprise. "And why not? Ain't I to be allowed to judge of the nature of the investment I'm goin' in for? I might give you an 'int or two from the gentleman's point of view."

Blanche shook her head. "I haven't added it up yet," she said.

Gosling did not press the point; he returned to his original position. "I dunno where you ladies 'ud be if you 'adn't no gentlemen to look after you."

Mrs Gosling smirked. "We'll 'ope it won't come to that," she said. "China's a long way off."

"Appears as there's been one case in Russia, though," remarked Gosling. He saw that he had rather a good thing in this threat of male extermination, a pleasant, harmless threat to hold over his feminine dependents; a means to emphasize the facts of masculine superiority and of the absolute necessity for masculine intelligence; facts that were not sufficiently well realized in Wisteria Grove, at times.

Mrs Gosling yawned surreptitiously. She was doing her best to be pleasant, but the subject bored her. She was a practical woman who worked hard all day to keep her house clean, and received very feeble assistance from the daughters for whom her one ambition was an establishment conducted on lines precisely similar to her own.

Millie and Blanche had returned to their calculations and were completely absorbed.

"In Russia? Just fancy," commented Mrs Gosling.

"In Moscow," said Gosling, studying his *Evening News*. "'E was an official on the trans-Siberian Railway. 'As soon as the disease was identified as a case of the new plague,'" read Gosling, "'the patient was at once removed to the infectious hospital and strictly isolated. He died within two hours of his admission. Stringent measures are being taken to prevent the infection from spreading.'"

"Was 'e a married man?" asked Mrs Gosling.

"Doesn't say," replied her husband. "But the point is that if it once gets to Europe, who knows where it'll stop?"

"They'll see to that, you may be sure," said Mrs Gosling, with a beautiful faith in the scientific resources of civilization. "It said somethin' about that in the bit you've just read."

Gosling was not to be done out of his argument. "Very like," he said. "But now, just supposin' as this 'ere plague did spread to London, and 'alf the men couldn't go to work; where d'you fancy you'd be?"

Mrs Gosling was unable to grasp the intricacies of this abstraction. "Well, of course, every one knows as we couldn't get on without the men," she said.

"Ah! well there you are, got it in one," said Gosling. "And don't you gels forget it," he added turning to his daughters.

Millie only giggled, but Blanche said, "All right, dad, we won't."

The girls returned to their calculations; they had arrived at the stage of cutting out all those items which were not "absolutely necessary." Five pounds had proved a miserably inadequate sum on paper.

Gosling returned to his *Evening News*, which presently slipped gently from his hand to the floor. Mrs Gosling looked up from her sewing and put a finger on her lips. The voices of Blanche and Millie were subdued to sibilant whisperings.

Gosling had forgotten his economic problems, and his daring abstractions concerning a world despoiled of male activity, especially of that essential activity, as he figured it, the making of money—the wage-earner was enjoying his after-dinner nap, hedged about, protected and cared for by his womankind.

There may have been a quarter of a million wage-earners in Greater

London at that moment, who, however much they differed from Gosling on such minor questions as Tariff Reform or the capabilities of the then Chancellor of the Exchequer, would have agreed with him as a matter of course, on the essentials he had discussed that evening.

## 3

At half-past nine the click of the letter-box, followed by a resounding double-knock, announced the arrival of the last post. Millie jumped up at once and went out eagerly.

Mr Gosling opened his eyes and stared with drunken fixity at the mantelpiece; then, without moving the rest of his body, he began to grope automatically with his left hand for the fallen newspaper. He found it at last, picked it up and pretended to read with sleep-sodden eyes.

"It's the post, dear," remarked Mrs Gosling.

Gosling yawned enormously. "Who's it for?" he asked.

"Millie! Millie!" called Mrs Gosling. "Why don't you bring the letters in?"

Millie did not reply, but she came slowly into the room, in her hands a letter which she was examining minutely.

"Who's it for, Mill?" asked Blanche, impatiently.

"Father," replied Millie, still intent on her study. "It's a foreign letter. I seem to remember the writing, too, only I can't fix it exactly."

"'Ere, 'and it over, my gel," said Gosling, and Millie reluctantly parted with her fascinating enigma.

"I know that 'and, too," remarked Gosling, and he, also, would have spent some time in the attempt to guess the puzzle without looking up the answer within the envelope, but the three spectators, who were not sharing his interest, manifested impatience.

"Well, ain't you going to open it, father?" asked Millie, and Mrs Gosling looked at her husband over her spectacles and remarked, "It must be a business letter, if it comes from foreign parts."

"Don't get business letters to this address," returned the head of the house, "besides which it's from Warsaw; we don't do nothin' with Warsaw."

At last he opened the letter.

The three women fixed their gaze on Gosling's face.

"Well?" ejaculated Millie, after a silence of several seconds. "Aren't you going to tell us?"

"You'd never guess," said Gosling triumphantly.

"Anyone we know?" asked Blanche.

"Yes, a gentleman."

"Oh! tell us, father," urged the impatient Millie.

"It's from the Mr Thrale, as lodged with us once," announced Gosling.

"Oh! dear, our Mr Fastidious," commented Blanche, "I thought he was dead long ago."

"It must be over four years since 'e left," put in Mrs Gosling.

"Getting on for five," corrected Blanche. "I remember I put my hair up while he was here."

"What's he say?" asked Millie.

"'E says, 'Dear Mr Gosling, I expect you will be surprised to 'ear from me after my five years' silence—'"

"I said it was five years," put in Blanche. "Go on, dad!"

Dad resumed "…'but I 'ave been in various parts of the world and it 'as been quite impossible to keep up a correspondence. I am writing now to tell you that I shall be back in London in a few days, and to ask you whether you can find a room for me in Wisteria Grove?'"

"Well! I should 'ave thought he'd 'ave written to me to ask that!" said Mrs Gosling.

"So 'e should 'ave, by rights," agreed Gosling. "But 'e's a queer card is Mr Thrale."

"Bit dotty, if you ask me," said Blanche.

"'S that all?" asked Mrs Gosling.

"No, 'e says: 'I can't give you an address as I go on to Berlin immediately, but I will look you up the evening after I arrive. Eastern Europe is not safe at the present time. There 'ave been several cases of the new plague in Moscow, but the authorities are doing everything they can—which is much in Russia—to keep the news out of the press, yours sincerely, Jasper Thrale,' and that's the lot," concluded Gosling.

"I do think he's a cool hand," commented Blanche. "Of course you won't have him as a paying guest now?"

Gosling and his wife looked at each other, thoughtfully.

"Well—" hesitated Gosling.

" 'E might bring the infection," suggested Mrs Gosling.

"Oh! no fear of that," returned her husband, "but I dunno as we want a boarder now. Five years ago I 'adn't got my big rise—"

"Oh, no, father; what would the neighbours think of us if we started to take boarders again?" protested Blanche.

"It wouldn't look well," agreed Mrs Gosling.

"Jus' what I was thinking," said the head of the house. " 'Owever, there's no 'arm in payin' us a friendly visit."

"O' course not," said Mrs Gosling, "though I do think it odd 'e shouldn't 'ave written to me in the first place."

"He's dotty!" said Blanche.

Gosling shook his head. "Not by a very long chalk 'e ain't," was his firm pronouncement....

"Well, girls, what about bed?" asked Mrs Gosling, putting away the "bit of mending" she had been engaged upon.

Gosling yawned again, stretched himself, and rose grunting to his feet. "I'm about ready for *my* bed," he remarked, and after another yawn he started his nightly round of inspection.

When he returned to the sitting-room the others were all ready to retire. Gosling kissed his daughters, and the two girls and their mother went upstairs. Gosling carefully took off the larger pieces of coal from the fire and put them under the grate, rolled up the hearthrug, saw that the window was securely fastened, extinguished the lamp and followed his "womenfolk."

As he was undressing his thoughts turned once more to the threat of the new disease which was devastating China.

"Rum thing about that new plague," he remarked to his wife. "Seems as it's only men as get it."

"They'd never let it spread to England," replied Mrs Gosling.

"Oh! there's no fear of that, none whatever," said Gosling, "but it's rum that about women never catching it."

The attitude of the Goslings faithfully reflected that of the immense majority of English people. The faith in the hygienic and scientific resources which were at the disposal of the authorities, and the implicit trust in the vigilance and energy of those authorities, were sufficient to allay any fears that were not too imminent. It was some one's duty to look after these things, and if they were not looked after there would be letters in the papers about it. At last, without question, the authorities would be roused to a sense of duty and the trouble, whatever it was, would be stopped. Precisely what authority managed these affairs none of the huge Gosling family knew. Vaguely they pictured Medical Boards, or Health Committees; dimly they connected these things with local government; at the top, doubtless, was some managing authority—in Whitehall probably—something to do with the supreme head of affairs, the much abused but eminently paternal Government.

## CHAPTER 2

*The Opinions of Jasper Thrale*

### 1

"LORD, HOW I do envy you," said Morgan Gurney.

Jasper Thrale sat forward in his chair. "There's no reason why you shouldn't do what I've done—and more," he said.

"Theoretically, I suppose not," replied Gurney. "It's just making the big effort to start with. You see I've got a very decent berth and good prospects, and it's comfortable and all that. Only when some fellow like you comes along and tells one yarns of the world outside, I get sort of hankerings after the sea and adventure, and seeing the big things. It's only now and then—ordinary times I'm contented enough." He stuck his pipe in the corner of his mouth and stared into the fire.

"The only things that really count are feeling clean and strong and able," said Thrale. "You never really have that feeling if you live in the big cities."

"I've felt like that sometimes after a long bicycle ride," interpolated Gurney.

"But then the feeling is wasted, you see," said Thrale. "When you feel like that and there is something tremendous to spend it upon, you get the great emotion as well."

"Like the glimmer of St Agnes' light, after you'd been eight weeks out of sight of land?" reflected Gurney, going back to one of Thrale's reminiscences.

"To feel that you are a part of life, not this dead, stale life of the city, but the life of the whole universe," said Thrale.

"I know," replied Gurney. "To-night I've half a mind to chuck my job and go out looking for mystery."

"But you won't do it," said Thrale.

Gurney sighed and began to analyse the instinct within himself, to find precisely why he wanted to do it.

"Well, I must go," said Thrale, getting to his feet, "I've got to find some sort of lodging."

"I thought you were going to stay with those Gosling people of yours," said Gurney.

"No! That's off. I went to see them last night and they won't have me. The old man's making his £300 a year now, and the family's too respectable to take boarders." Thrale picked up his hat and held out his hand.

"But, look here, old chap, why the devil can't you stay here?" asked Gurney.

"I didn't know that you'd anywhere to put me," said Thrale.

"Oh, yes. There's always a room to be had downstairs," said Gurney.

After a brief discussion the arrangement was made.

"It's understood I'm to pay my whack," said Thrale.

"Of course, if you insist—"

When Thrale had gone to fetch his luggage from the hotel, Gurney sat pondering over the fire. He was debating whether he had been altogether wise in pressing his invitation. He was wondering whether the curiously rousing personality of Thrale, and the stories of those still existent corners of the world outside the rules of civilization were good for a civil servant with an income of £600 a year. Gurney, faced with the plain alternatives, could only decide that he would be a fool to throw up a congenial and lucrative occupation such as his own, in order to face present physical discomfort and future penury. He knew that the discomforts would be very real to him at first. His friends would think him mad. And all for the sake of experiencing some high emotion now and again, in order to feel clean and fresh and be able to discover something of the unknown mystery of life.

"I suppose there is something of the poet in me," reflected Gurney. "And I expect I should hate the discomforts. One's imagination gets led away..."

## 2

During the next few evenings the conversations between these two friends were many and protracted.

Thrale was the teacher, and Gurney was content to sit at his feet and learn. He had a receptive mind, he was interested in all life, but Uppingham, Trinity Hall, and the Home Civil had constricted his mental processes. At twenty-nine he was losing flexibility. Thrale gave him back his power to think, set him outside the formulas of his school, taught him that however sound his deductions, there was not one of his premises which could not be disputed.

Thrale was Gurney's senior by three years, and when Thrale left Uppingham at eighteen, he had gone out into the world. He had a patrimony of some £200 a year; but he had taken only a lump sum of £100 and had started out to appease his furious curiosity concerning life. He had laboured as a miner in the Klondike; had sailed, working his passage as an ordinary seaman, from San Francisco to Southampton; he had been a stockman in Australia, assistant to a planter in Ceylon, a furnace minder in Kimberley and a tally clerk in Hong Kong. For nearly nine years, indeed, he had earned a living in every country of the world except Europe, and then he had come back to London and invested the accumulation of income that his trustee had amassed for him. The mere spending of money had no fascination for him. During the six months he had remained in London he had lived very simply, lodging with the Goslings in Kilburn, and, because he could not live idly, exploring every corner of the great city and writing articles for the journals. He might have earned a large income by this latter means, for he had an originality of outlook and a freshness of style that made his contributions eagerly sought after once he had obtained a hearing—no difficult matter in London for anyone who has something new to say. But experience, not income, was his desire, and at the end of six months he had accepted an offer from the *Daily Post* as a correspondent—on space. He was offered £600 a year, but he preferred to be free, and he had no wish to be confined to one capital or country.

In those five years he had traversed Europe, sending in his articles irregularly, as he required money. And during that time his chief trustee—a lawyer of the soundest reputation—had absconded, and Thrale found his private income reduced to about £40 a year, the interest on one of the investments he had made, in his own name only, with his former accumulation—two other investments made at the same time had proved unsound.

This loss had not troubled him in any way. When he had read in a London journal of his trustee's abscondence—he was later sentenced to fourteen years' penal servitude—Thrale had smiled and dismissed the matter from his mind. He could always earn all the money he required, and had never, not even subconsciously, relied upon his private fortune.

He had now come back to London with a definite purpose, he had come to warn England of a great danger....

One other distinguishing mark of Jasper Thrale's life must be understood, a mark which differentiated him from the overwhelming majority of his fellow men—women had no fascination for him. Once in his life, and once only, had he approached and tasted experience—with a pretty little Melbourne *cocotte*. That experience he had undertaken deliberately, because he felt that until it had been undergone one great factor of life would be unknown to him. He had come away from it filled with a disgust of himself that had endured for months....

## 3

Fragments of the long conversations between Thrale and Gurney, the exchange of a few germane ideas among the irrelevant mass, had a bearing upon their immediate future. There was, for instance, a criticism of the Goslings, introduced on one occasion, which had a certain significance in relation to subsequent developments.

Some question of Gurney's prompted Thrale to the opinion that the Goslings were in the main precisely like half a million other families of the same class.

"But that's just what makes them so interesting," said Gurney, not because he believed it, but because at the moment he wanted to lead the conversation into safe ground, away from the too appealing attractions of the big world outside the little village of London.

Thrale laughed. "That's truer than you guess," he said. "Every large generalization, however trite, is a valuable contribution to knowledge—if it's more or less accurate."

"Generalize, then, *mon vieux*," suggested Gurney, "from the characters and doings of your little geese."

"I've seen glimmerings of the immortal god in the old man," said Thrale, "like the hint of sunlight seen through a filthy pane of obscured glass. He's a prurient-minded old beast leading what's called a respectable life, but if he could indulge his ruling desire with absolute secrecy, no woman would be safe with him. In his world he can't do that, or thinks he can't, which comes to precisely the same thing. He is too much afraid of being caught, he sees danger where none exists, he looks to all sorts of possibilities, and won't take a million-to-one chance because he is risking his all—which is included in the one word, respectability."

"Jolly good thing. What?" remarked Gurney.

"Good for society as a whole, apparently," replied Thrale, "but surely not good for the man. I've told you that I have seen glimmerings of the god in him, but outside the routine of his work the man's mind is clogged. He's not much over fifty, and he has no outlet, now, for his desires. He's like a man with choked pores, and his body is poisoned. And in this particular Gosling is certainly no exception either to his class or to the great mass of civilized man. Well, what I wonder is whether in a society which is built up of interdependent units the whole can be sound when the greater number of the constituent units are rotten."

"But look here, old chap," protested Gurney, "if things are as you say, and men rule the country, why shouldn't they alter public opinion, and so open the way to do as they jolly well please?"

"Because the majority are too much ashamed of their desires to dare the attempt in the first place, and in the second because they don't wish to open the way for other men. They aren't united in this; they are as jealous as women. If they once opened the way to free love, their own belongings wouldn't be safe."

"What's your remedy, then?"

"Oh! a few thousand more years of moral development," said Thrale, carelessly, "an evolution towards self-consciousness, a fuller understanding of the meaning of life, and a finer altruism."

"You don't look far ahead," remarked Gurney.

"Do you think anyone can look even a year ahead?" asked Thrale.

"There have been some pretty good attempts in some ways—Swedenborg, for instance, and Samuel Butler...."

"Yes, yes, that's all right, in some ways—the development of certain sorts of knowledge, for example. But there is always the chance of the unpredictable element coming in and upsetting the whole calculation. Some invention may do it, an unforeseen clash of opinions or an epidemic...."

For a time they drifted further away from their original topic till some remark reminded Gurney that he had meant to ask a question and had forgotten it.

"By the way," he said, "I wanted to ask you what you meant when you said you had seen a god in old Gosling?"

"Just a touch of imagination and wonder, now and again," replied Thrale. "Something he was quite unconscious of himself. I remember standing with him on Blackfriars Bridge, and he looked down at the river and said: 'I s'pose it was clean once, banks and sand and so on, before all this muck came.' Then he looked at me quickly to see if I was laughing at him. That was the god in him trying to create purity out of filth, even though it was only a casual thought. It was smothered again at once. His training reasserted itself. 'Lot better for trade the way it is, though,' was his next remark."

"But how can you alter it?" asked Gurney.

"My dear chap, you can't alter these things by any cut-and-dried plan, any more than you can dam the Gulf Stream. We can only lay a brick or two in the right place. We aren't the architects; the best of us are only bricklayers, and the best of the best can only lay two or three bricks in a lifetime.

Our job is to do that if we can. We can only guess very feebly at the design of the building; and often it is our duty partly to pull down the work that our forefathers built...."

Presently Gurney asked if his companion had ever seen a god in Mrs Gosling.

Thrale shook his head. "It didn't come within my experience," he said. "Don't condemn her on that account, but she, like all the women I have ever met, has been too intent upon the facts of life ever to see its mystery. Mrs Gosling hadn't the power to conceive an abstract idea; she had to make some application of it to her own particular experience before she could understand the simplest concept. Morality to her signified people who behaved as she and her family did; wickedness meant vaguely, criminals, Sarah Jones who was an unmarried mother, and anyone who didn't believe in the God of the Established Church. Always people, you see, in this connexion; in others it might be things; but ideas apart from people or things she couldn't grasp. Her two daughters thought in precisely the same way...."

## 4

One Saturday afternoon Thrale came into Gurney's chambers and burst out: "Just Heaven! why you fools stand it I can't imagine!"

"What's up now?" asked Gurney.

Thrale sat down and drew his chair up to the table. The pupils of his dark eyes were contracted and seemed to glow as if they were illuminated from within.

"I was in Oxford Street this morning, watching the women at the sales," he said. "All the biggest shops in London are devoted to women's clothes. Do you realize that? And it's not only that they're the biggest—there are more of them than any other six trades put together can show, bar the drink trade, of course. The north side of Oxford Street from Tottenham Court Road to the Marble Arch is one long succession of huge drapers and milliners. And what in God's name is the sense or reason of it? What do these huge shops sell?"

"Dresses, I suppose," ventured Gurney, "and stockings, underlinen, corsets, hats, and so on."

"*And* frippery," said Thrale, fixing his brilliant dark eyes on Gurney. "And *frippery*. Machine lace, ribbons, yokes, cheap blouses, feathers, insertions, belts, fifty thousand different kinds of bits and rags to be tacked on here and there, worn for a few weeks and then thrown away. Millions of little frivolous, stupid odds and ends that are bought by women and girls of all classes below the motor-class, to make a pretence—gauds and tawdry rubbish not one whit better from the artistic point of view than the shells and feathers of any half-naked Melanesian savage. In fact, meaningless as the Melanesians' decorations are, they do achieve more effect. And what's it all for, I ask you?"

Thrale paused, and Gurney offered his solution.

"The sex instinct, fundamentally, isn't it?" he said. "The desire—often subconscious, no doubt—to attract."

"Well, if that is so," said Thrale, "what terribly unintelligent fools women must be! If women really set out to attract men, they must realize that they are pandering to a sex instinct. Do you think any man is attracted by a litter of odds and ends? Doesn't every woman sneer when they see some Frenchwoman, perhaps, who dresses to display her figure instead of hiding it? Don't they bitterly resent the fact that their own men-folk are resistlessly drawn to stare at, and inwardly desire, such a woman? Don't they know perfectly well that such a woman is attractive to men in a way their own disguised bodies can never be?"

"Yes, old chap; but your average middle-class English girl hasn't got the physical attractions to start with," put in Gurney.

"Look at it in another way, then," replied Thrale. "Doesn't every woman know perfectly well—haven't you heard them say—that a nurse's dress is very becoming—a plain, more or less tightly-fitting print dress, with linen collars and cuffs? Don't you know yourself that that attire is more attractive to you than any befrilled and bedecorated arrangement of lace, ribbons and gauds? Why are so many men irresistibly attracted by parlourmaids and housemaids?"

"Yes," meditated Gurney, "that's all true enough. Well, are women all fools, or what is it?"

"The majority of women are *sheep*," said Thrale. "They follow as they are led, and don't or won't see that they are being led. And the leaders are chiefly men—men who have trumpery to sell. Why do the fashions change every year—sometimes more often than that in matters of detail? Because the trade would smash if they didn't. New fashions must be forced on the buyers, or the returns would drop; women would be able to make their last year's clothes do for another summer. That must be stopped at any cost. Those vast establishments must maintain an enormous turnover if they are to pay their fabulous rents and armies of assistants. There are two means of keeping up the sales, and both are utilized to the full. The first is to supply cheap, miraculously cheap, rubbish which cannot be made to last for more than a season. The second is to alter the fashions which affect the more durable stuffs, so that last year's dresses cannot be used again. This fashion-working scheme reacts upon the poorer buyers, because it compels them to do something to imitate the prevailing mode, if they can't afford to have entirely new frocks. That is where all these bits of frilling and what-not come in; make-believe stuff to imitate the real buyers—the large majority of whom don't buy in Oxford Street, by the way.

"Mind you, there is a limit to the sheep-like docility of women in this connexion. They refused, for instance, to return to the crinoline, and they refused the harem skirt—one of the very few sensible devices of the fashion-imposers. And this in the face of the prolonged, strenuous and expensive methods of the fashion ring. With regard to the crinoline, I think that failure was due to over-conceit on the part of the fashion-imposers. They had come to believe that they could make the poor fools of women accept anything, and on the two marked occasions on which they attempted to introduce the crinoline, the contrast to the existing mode was too glaring. If the fraud had been worked more gradually by way of full skirts and flounces, some modification of the crinoline to the necessities of 'buses and tubes might have been foisted upon the buyers."

"Oh, my Lord!" ejaculated Gurney; "do you mean to say that women just accept these fashions without any sense or reason at all?"

"You're rather a blithering ass, at times, Gurney," remarked Thrale.

Gurney smiled. "You don't give me time to think," he said, "I feel like an accumulator being charged. I haven't had time yet to begin working on my own account. You're so mighty—so mighty dynamic—and positive, old chap."

"Well, it's so absurdly obvious that there must be a reason for women accepting the fashions, you idiot!" returned Thrale. "And the first and biggest reason is class distinction. The women with money want to brag of it by differentiating themselves from the ruck of their sisters, and the poor women try to imitate them to the best of their ability. Women dress for other women. There is sex rivalry as well as class rivalry at the bottom of it, but they dare not put sex rivalry first and dress to please men alone, because they are afraid of the opinions of other women."

"Sounds all right," said Gurney, and sighed.

"And we, damned fools of men, stand all this foolishness and *pay* for it. Pay, by Jove! I should think so! I should like to see the trade returns of all the stuff of this kind that is sold in England alone in one year. They would make the naval estimates look small, I'll warrant. We even imitate the women's foolishness in some degree. There are men's fashions too, but the madness is not so marked; fortunately the body of middle-class men can't afford to make fools of themselves as well as of their women—though they are asses enough to wear linen shirts and collars which are uncomfortable unsightly and expensive to wash."

Gurney regarded his lecturer's canvas shirt and collar, and then stood up and observed his own immaculate linen in the glass over the fireplace. "I must say I like stiff collars and shirts," he remarked; "gives one a kind of spruceness."

Thrale laughed. "It's only another sex instinct," he said. "Women like men to look 'smart.' When you are playing games with other men, or camping out, you don't care a hang for your 'spruceness.' Oh! and I'll admit the class distinction rot comes in too. You're afraid of public opinion, afraid of being thought common. If the *jeunesse dorée* started the soft shirt in real earnest, you would soon be able to persuade your women that that looked smart or spruce, or whatever you liked to call it."

"Look here, you know," said Gurney, "you're an anarchist, that's what you are."

"You're half a woman, Gurney," said Thrale. "You think in names. All people are 'anarchists' who think in ideas instead of following conventions."

## 5

Not until he had been staying with Gurney for more than a week did Thrale speak explicitly of his purpose in London. But one cold evening at the end of January, as the two men were sitting by a roaring fire that Gurney had built up, the younger man unknowingly opened the subject by saying, "Things are pretty slack at the present moment. The *Evening Chronicle* has even fallen back on the 'New Plague' for the sake of news."

"What do they say?" asked Thrale. He was lying back in his chair, nursing one knee, and staring up at the ceiling.

"Oh, the usual rot!" said Gurney "That the thing isn't understood, has never been 'described' by any medical or scientific authority; that it is apparently confined to one little corner of Asia at the present time, but that if it got hold in Europe it might be serious. And then a lot of yap about the unknown forces of Nature; special article by a chap who's been reading too much Wells, I should imagine."

"It seems so incredible to us in twentieth-century England that anything really serious could happen," remarked Thrale. "We are so well looked after and cared for. We sit down and wait for some authority to move, with a perfect confidence that when it does move, everything is bound to be all right."

"With such an organism as society has become," said Gurney, "things must be worked like that. A certain group to perform one function, other groups for other functions, and so on."

"Cell-specialization?" commented Thrale. "Some day to be perfected in socialism."

"I believe socialism must come in some form," said Gurney.

"Yes, it's an interesting speculation, in some ways," said Thrale, "but the higher forces are about to put a new spoke in the human wheel, and the machinery has to be stopped for a time."

"What have you got hold of now?" asked Gurney.

"The thoughtful man," went on Thrale, still staring up at the ceiling, "would have asked me to define my expression 'the higher forces.'"

"Well, old man, I knew that was beyond even your capacity," returned Gurney, "so I thought we might 'cut the cackle and come to the 'osses.'"

Thrale suddenly released his knee and sat upright; then he moved his chair so that he directly confronted his companion.

"Look here, Gurney," he said, and the pupils of his eyes contracted till they looked like black crystal glowing with dark red light. "Do you realize how some outside control has always diverted man's progress; how when nations have tended to crystallize into specialized government, some irruption from outside has always broken it up? You can trace the principle through all known history, but the most marked cases are those of the Egyptians and the Incas—two nations which had developed specialized government to a science. There is some power—whether we can credit it with an intelligence in any way comprehensible to us from the feeble basis of our own knowledge, I doubt—but there is some outside power which will not permit mankind to crystallize into an organism. From our, human, point of view, from the point of view of individual comfort and happiness, it would be of enormous benefit to us if we could develop a system of specialization and swamp the individual in the community. And in times of peace and prosperity that is always the direction in which civilization tends to evolve. But beyond a certain point—as the individualists have not failed to point out—that state of perfect government will lead to stagnation, degeneration, death. Now, in the little span of time that we know as the history of mankind, there has been no world-civilization. As soon as a nation tended to become over-civilized and degenerate, some other, younger, more barbarous people flowed over them and wiped them out. In the case of Peru the process had gone very far, owing to the advantages of the Incas' peculiar segregation. But then, you see, the development in the East, the new world (I ought to explain that I find the oldest civilization of the present epoch in America) reached a point in Spain and England which sent them out across a hemisphere to wreck and destroy the Incas.

"Well, we have now reached a condition when the nations are in touch with one another and progress becomes more general. We are in sight of a system of European, Colonial and Trans-Atlantic Socialism, more or less reciprocal and carrying the promise of universal peace. Whence, you ask, is any irruption to come that will break up this strong crystallizing system which is admittedly to work for the happiness and comfort of the individual? There has been much talk of an Asiatic invasion, a rebellious India or an invading China, but those civilizations are older than ours; if we can trust the precedents of history in this connexion, the conquerors have always been the younger race." He broke off abruptly.

Gurney had been sitting fascinated and hypnotized by the compulsion of Thrale's personality; he had been held by the keen, intent stare of those wonderful dark eyes. When Thrale stopped, however, the tension snapped.

"Well," remarked Gurney, "I think that's a jolly good argument to prove that we have, at last, reached a stage of universal progress towards the ideal."

"You can't conceive," asked Thrale, "of any cataclysm that would involve a return to the old segregation of nations, and bring about a new epoch beginning with separated peoples evolving on more or less racial lines?"

Gurney pondered for a moment or two and then shook his head.

"Little wonder," said Thrale, "I had often considered this problem, and I could think of no upheaval which would bring about the familiar effect of submersion. Years ago there was always the possibility of a European war, but even that would have only a temporary effect despite the forecast of Mr Wells in *The War in the Air*. No, I considered and wondered if my theory was faulty. I was willing to reject it if I could find a flaw...."

"And then?" questioned Gurney.

Thrale leaned forward again and once more compelled the other's fascinated attention.

"And then, when I was in Northern China, seven weeks ago, I saw a solution, so appalling, so inconceivably ghastly, that I rejected it with horror. For days I went about fighting my own conviction. I couldn't believe it! By God, I would not believe it!

"There, within a hundred and fifty miles of the border of Tibet, the outside forces have planted a seed which has been maturing in secret for more than a year. There that seed has taken root, and from that centre is spreading more and more rapidly, and it may spread over the whole world. It is like some filthily poisonous and incredibly prolific weed, and its seeds, now that it has once established itself, are borne by every wind, dropping here and there in an ever-widening circle, every seed becoming a fresh centre of distribution outwards."

"But what, in Heaven's name, is the weed?" whispered Gurney.

"A new disease—a new plague—unknown by man, against which, so far as we know, he has no weapon. In those scattered villages among the mountains there are no men left to work. Everything is done by women. They are prohibited more fiercely than any leper settlement. No one dares to approach within five miles of them. But every week or two another village is smitten, and the inhabitants fly in terror and carry the infection with them.

"Gurney, it's come to Europe! There are new centres of distribution in Russia at the present time. If it isn't stopped it will come to England. And it doesn't decimate the population. It wipes the men clean out of existence; not one man in ten thousand, the Chinese say, escapes.

"Is it possible that this can be the means of the 'higher forces' I spoke of, the means to segregate the nations once more?"

## CHAPTER 3

*London's Incredulity*

### 1

JASPER THRALE'S MISSION was no easy one. England, it appeared, was slightly preoccupied at the moment, and had no ear for warnings. Generally, he was either treated as a fanatic and laughed at, or he was told that he greatly exaggerated the danger and that these matters could safely be entrusted to the Local Government Board, which had brilliantly handled the recent outbreak of foot-and-mouth disease. But there were some exceptions to this rule.

His first definite statement had been made to his own editor, Watson Maxwell of the *Daily Post*.

"Yes," said Maxwell, when he had given Thrale a patient hearing, "it is certainly a matter that needs attention. Would you care to go out as our special commissioner and report at length? ..."

"There isn't time," replied Thrale. "The thing is urgent."

Maxwell brought his eyebrows together and looked keenly at his correspondent. "Do you really think it's so serious, Thrale?" he asked. "After all, what evidence have you, beyond the Chinese reports?"

"I know there are several cases in Russia," said Thrale.

"Yes, yes; I don't doubt that," returned Maxwell, with a touch of impatience. "But unless you can bring evidence to show that this new disease is as deadly as you say, it is not a matter that I could give space to at the present time. For one thing, the *Evening Chronicle* has been making rather a feature of it for the last three or four days, and I don't see that I could do much unless we had some special inside information. Then, the House will be sitting again next week, and it seems to me not altogether improbable that we shall have a stormy session, which will mean that a good deal of ordinary matter will have to give way...." He broke off, and then added, with a friendly smile: "But if you would go out as our commissioner, we should be glad to make you a proposal."

"There will be no need for a commissioner in a week's time," replied Thrale. "You don't seem to understand that I'm not looking out for a job. I don't want to write articles; I don't want to be paid for the information I can supply. I foresee a grave danger, which is growing more grave hourly by reason of the Russian Government's censorship of all reports referring to the plague. It is a danger which should be understood at once. If you send any commissioner, send the cleverest physician you can find, and a bacteriologist."

There could be no doubt of Thrale's earnestness, and Maxwell, who was not only a very capable editor, but also an able and intellectual man, was impressed. Unfortunately, the interests of his proprietors at that moment necessitated a great effort to prop up the very unstable Liberal Government, which had been in power for four years and was now on its last legs. It was so essential from the proprietors' point of view—three of them were on the Government front bench—that the dissolution should be postponed until such time as the Ministry could go to the country with a reasonable prospect of success. A tentative English Church Disestablishment Bill was to be introduced in the coming session, and it was hoped that if the Government had to go to the country they could make a platform on that one clear issue. It was a good Bill, designed to win the Nonconformist vote, without completely alienating the High Church party. In other words, the Government was eager at that moment to please the majority of the electors, which is, presumably, the highest object of a representative government.

"If it had been at any other time," said Maxwell, and pushed his chair back.

Thrale understood that the interview was at an end. He rose from his chair and picked up his hat.

"We shall be glad to print any articles you care to send us," said Maxwell, with his kind smile, "but I can't undertake a campaign, you understand, at the present moment."

It was nearly four o'clock, but Thrale just managed to catch Groves of the *Evening Chronicle*.

# 2

Groves had his hat on, and was just off to tea at his club when Thrale's name was sent in to him. He told the messenger that he would see Mr Thrale in the waiting-room downstairs.

Thrale had had some experience of newspaper methods, and he inferred that the reception was equivalent to a refusal to see him. He knew what those interviews in downstairs waiting-rooms implied. It was not the first time that he had been treated like an insurance agent or a tradesman and told, in effect, "Not to-day, thank you."

In this case he was mistaken in his inference. Groves had had an eye on Thrale's articles for some time past, and though he thought it a diplomatic essential to keep his man waiting for ten minutes, he had no intention of offending him.

Groves came into the waiting-room with a slightly abstracted air. "Sorry to keep you waiting Mr Thrale," he said. "The fact is, that I wanted to finish before I left. Did you want to see me about anything particular?"

"Yes," returned Thrale; "I have some facts about the new plague which ought to be given publicity at once."

Groves pursed his thick lips and shook his head. "Well, well," he said, "will you come and have tea with me at the club?"

He took Thrale's assent for granted, and went out abruptly, leaving his guest to follow.

In the taxicab Groves talked of nothing but the lack of originality in invention in reference to aeroplanes. He seemed to take it as a personal affront that no workable adaptation of the aeroplane had been made to short-distance passenger traffic.

Indeed, it was not till after "tea"—in Groves' case an euphemism for whisky and soda—that he would approach the subject of Thrale's visit.

"The fact is, my dear fellow," he said, "that our campaign hasn't caught on. I'm going to let it down gently and drop it after to-day's edition. You see, we've got to get the Government out this session, and I'm going to start a new campaign. Can't give you any particulars yet, but you'll see the beginning of it next Monday." Like Maxwell, Groves differentiated between the uses of the singular and plural pronouns in speaking of his work. There was a distinction to be inferred between the initiation and responsibilities of the editor and those of his proprietors.

Groves was not at all impressed by any earnestness or forebodings. He seemed to think that a touch of the plague in London might be rather a good thing in some ways. People wanted waking up—especially to the importance of getting rid of the present Government.

It appeared that Thrale's articles on other subjects would be acceptable to the readers of the *Evening Chronicle*, but there was no suggestion that he should go out to Russia as a special commissioner.

## 3

Grant Lacey, of *The Times*, listened seriously to Thrale's exposition, and then, in a finely delivered speech which lasted twenty minutes, proved to his own complete satisfaction that Thrale's premisses, deductions, and whole argument were thoroughly unsound. Lacey, however, was greatly interested in the condition of Russia, and promised Thrale magnificent terms if he would tour St Petersburg, Moscow, Kiev, Warsaw—and then return and contribute a special series of articles. References to the new plague would not be prohibited in the series if Thrale still found any cause for alarm.

In all, Thrale had interviews with the editors of nine important journals; the other six developed on the general lines already indicated—either he was not taken seriously or was told that the danger was greatly exaggerated. The real causes of his failure were two:—first, the critical position of the Government; second, the precocious campaign of the *Evening Chronicle*—the latter had taken the wind out of the sails of less enterprising journals.

Thrale's next step was to obtain introductions to Ministers and prominent members of the Opposition; but from them he received even less attention—he did not obtain interviews on many occasions—and, if possible, less encouragement. The President of the Local Government Board informed him that the matter was already engaging that department's energies; the others were all manifestly preoccupied with more immediate interests.

But little less than a fortnight after the initiation of his campaign Thrale received a special message from the editor of the *Daily Post*. It was nearly midnight, and the messenger was waiting with a taxicab.

The message ran: "Received through news agency report of three cases of plague in Berlin. Can you come down at once?—Maxwell."

# CHAPTER 4
## *Mr Barker's Flair*

### 1

Jasper Thrale, in the partial exposition of his philosophy (if that description is not too large for such vague imaginings), had included very definite reference to certain "higher forces" to which he had attributed peculiar powers of interference in humanity's management of its own concerns. Doubtless these powers had control of various instruments, and were able to exercise their influence in any direction and by any means. In the present case it would seem that they were working in devious and subtle ways—and in this at least they differed not at all from the methods attributable to that we have called Providence, or the Laws of Nature; any assumed guide or irrefragable, incomprehensible ordination. It is a common characteristic of these forces that they seem able to control the inconceivably great and the inconceivably small with equal certitude.

Not that George Gosling touched any limits. He was moderately large in body and small in intellect, but neither the physical excess nor the mental deficiency marked him out from his fellow men. In the office, indeed, he was regarded by the firm and his colleagues as a capable man of business whose *embonpoint* was quite consistent with his employment by a firm of wholesale provision merchants.

On the Thursday morning that saw the announcement in the morning papers that a case of the new plague was reported in Berlin, Gosling was called into the partners' private office on some matter of accountancy.

The senior partner of Barker and Prince was eager, grasping and imaginative; his name had originally been German, and ended in "stein," but he had changed it for the convenience of his English connexion. Prince was a large rubicund man, friendly and noisy in his manners, but accounted a shrewd buyer.

It was not until Gosling was about to depart that the higher forces turned their attention to Barbican and then they suddenly urged Gosling to say, without premeditation on his part, "I see there's a case of this 'ere new plague in Berlin."

Mr Prince laughed and winked at his subordinate. "Some of us'll have to start a hareem, soon; who knows?" he said, and laughed again, more loudly than ever.

"I suppose you haf not heard any other reports, eh?" asked Mr Barker.

"Well, curiously enough, I 'ave," said Gosling. "A young feller who used to lodge with us five years back, come 'ome from Russia about a fortnight since, and 'e tells me as the plague's spreadin' like wildfire in Russia."

Mr Prince laughed again, and Mr Barker seemed about to turn his attention to other matters, when the higher forces sent Gosling the one great inspiration of his life. It came to him with startling suddenness, but he gave utterance to it as simply and with as little verve as he spoke his "good morning" to the office-boy.

"I been thinkin', sir," he said (he had never once thought of it until this moment), "as it might be well to keep an eye on this plague, so to speak."

"Ah! Zo?" said Mr Barker; a phrase which Gosling correctly interpreted as the expression of a desire for the elucidation of his last remark.

"Well, I been thinkin', if you'll excuse me, sir," he went on, "as though the plague's only in the bud, so to speak, at the present time, it seems very likely to spread so far as we can judge; and that what with quarantine, p'raps, and p'raps shortage of labour and so on, it might mean 'igher prices for our stuff."

"Zo!" said Mr Barker, but this time the monosyllable was reflexive. The great inspiration had found fruitful soil.

"Brince," continued Barker after a minute's thought, "I haf a flair. We will buy heavily at once. But not through our London house, no; or others will follow us too quickly. *You* must not go, we will zend Ztewart from Dundee, it will zeem that we prepare for the zhipping strike in the north. We buy heavily; yes? I haf a flair."

"But, I say," said Mr Prince, who had the greatest confidence in his partner's insight, "I say, Barker, d'you think this plague's serious?"

"I am putting money on it, ain't I?" asked Barker.

Prince and Gosling exchanged a scared glance. Until that moment it had not come home to either of them that it was possible for English affairs to be affected by this strange and deadly disease.

The remainder of the conversation was complicated and exceedingly technical.

## 2

When he came back into the counting-house, Gosling looked unnaturally thoughtful.

"Anything gorne wrong?" asked his crony, Flack.

"There's nothing wrong with the 'ouse, if that's what you mean," replied Gosling mysteriously.

"What then?" asked Flack.

"It's this 'ere new plague," returned Gosling.

"Tchah! That's all my eye," said Flack. He was a narrow-chested, high-shouldered man of sixty, with a thin grey beard, and he had a consistently incredulous mind.

Out here in the counting-house, Gosling's thrill of fear was rapidly subsiding, and he had no intention of passing over his own important part in the house's decision to buy for a rise; so he bulged out his cheeks, shook his head and said:

"Not by a long chalk it ain't, Flack; not by a long chalk. There was that young feller, Thrale, as I was tellin' you about; 'e gave me a hidea or two, and now s'mornin' we 'ave this very serious news from Berlin."

"Papers 'ave to make the worst of everything," said Flack. "It's their livin'."

"Anyways," continued Gosling, "I put it quite straight to the 'ouse this mornin', as we might do worse under the circumstances than buy 'eavily...."

"You *did*?" asked Flack, and he cocked up his spectacles and looked at Gosling underneath them.

"I did," replied Gosling.

"What did Mr Barker say to that?" asked Flack.

"He took my advice."

"Lord's sakes, you don't tell me so?" said Flack, his spectacles on his forehead.

"I'm now about to dictate various letters to our 'ouse in Dundee," replied Gosling, dropping his voice to a whisper, and assuming an air of mysterious importance, "advising them to send our Mr Stewart to Vienna immediate, from where 'e is to proceed to Berlin. 'E is, also, to 'ave private instructions from the 'ouse as to the extent of 'is buyin' which I may tell you in confidence, Flack, will be enormous—e-*nor*mous." Gosling raised his head slowly on the first syllable, brought it down with a jerk on the second, and left the third largely to the imagination.

"But d'yer mean to tell me," expostulated Flack, "as all this is on account of this plague? They been usin' that as a blind, my boy."

Gosling laid a bunch of swollen fingers on his colleague's arm. "I tell you, Flack, old boy," he said, "that this is serious. When Mr Barker took up my advice, as 'e did very quick, Mr Prince said, 'You don't tell me as you really take this plague serious, Barker?' 'e said. And Mr Barker looked up and says, "I'm goin' to put all my money on it.'" Gosling paused and then repeated, "Mr Barker says as 'e's goin' to put all our money on it, Flack."

"Lord's sakes!" said Flack. Here, indeed, was an argument strong enough to break down even his consistent incredulity. "But d'yer mean to tell me," he persisted, "that Mr Barker thinks as it'll come to England?"

"We-el, you know," returned Gosling, "we need not, p'raps go quite so far as that. But it may go far enough to interfere with European markets, there may be trouble with quarantine, and such-like...."

"Ah, well, that," said Flack with an air of relief. "Jus' *so*, jus' *so*. Mr Barker can see as far through a brick wall as most people, and so I've always said." He dropped his spectacles on to his nose again, and returned to his interrupted accountancy.

Gosling went fussily into his own room and rang for his typist—a competent and presentable young woman, among whose duties that of turning her superior's letters into equivalent English was not the lightest.

## 3

Gosling was very full of importance that day, and during lunch he wore the air of a man who had secret and valuable information. He was too well versed in City methods and too loyal to his own house to give any hint of Barker and Prince's speculations in Austria and Germany; but when the subject of the new plague inevitably came into the conversation, he spoke with an authority that was heightened by the hint of reserve implicit in his every dictum.

When the latest joke on the subject, fresh from the Stock Exchange, had been retailed by one of the usual group of lunchers, and had been received with the guffaws it merited, Gosling suddenly screwed his face to an unaccustomed seriousness and said, "But it's serious, you know, extremely serious."

And by degrees, from this and many other better informed sources, the rumour ran through the City that the new plague was serious, extremely serious. That afternoon there was a slight drop of prices in certain industrial shares, and a slight rise in wheat and some other imported food stuffs; fluctuations which could not be attributed to ordinary causes. Mr Barker's foresight was justified once again in the eyes of Gosling and Flack. Before five o'clock another letter was posted to Dundee, enforcing haste.

In the bosom of his family that evening, Gosling was a little pompous, and talked of economy. But his wife and daughters, although they assumed an air of interest, were quite convinced that the head of the house in Wisteria Grove was making the most of a rumour for his own purposes.

As Blanche said to Millie, later, father was always finding some excuse for keeping them short of dress money. That five pounds had proved inadequate to supply even their immediate necessities, and they were already meditating another attack. "We simply must get another three pounds somehow," said Millie. And Blanche quite agreed with her.

# CHAPTER 5

*The Closed Door*

1

There was a lull for forty-eight hours after that announcement of the case of the new plague in Berlin, and Maxwell was beginning to regret his headlines when the news began to come in, this time in volume. The Russian censorship had broken down, and the news agencies were suddenly flooded with reports. There were several thousand cases of the plague in Eastern Russia; the north and south were affected, many men were dying in such towns as Kharkov and Rostov; there were a dozen cases in St Petersburg; there was a such a rush of reports that it was quite impossible to distinguish between those that were probably true and those that were certainly false.

The morning papers gave as much space as they could spare, and had even broken up some of the matter dealing with the arrangements for the opening of Parliament on that day. But the evening papers had news that put all previous reports in the shade. Eleven more cases were reported in Berlin, three in Hamburg, five in Prague, and one in Vienna. But more important, more thrilling still, was the news that H.I.H. the Grand Duke Kirylo, the Tsar's younger brother, had died of the plague in Moscow, and Professor Schlesinger in Berlin. Until that startling announcement came, the English public had incomprehensibly imagined that only peasants, Chinamen and people of the lower social grades were attacked by this strange new infection.

In the later editions it was reported on good authority that Professor Schlesinger had been observing a sample of the blood of the first case of plague that had been recognized in Berlin.

Nevertheless the majority of readers, after glancing through the obituary notices of H.I.H. the Grand Duke Kirylo and of the world-famed bacteriologist, turned to the account—only slightly abbreviated—

of the opening of Parliament. And in many households the subject of the new plague gave place to the fiercely controversial topic of the English Church Disestablishment Bill, which had been indicated in the King's Speech as a measure that was to be introduced in the forthcoming session. Many opponents of the Bill coupled the two chief items of news and said that the plague was a warning against infidelity. It may be assumed that they found sufficient warrant for the killing of a few thousand Russians, including a prince of the blood and a great German scientist, in the acknowledged importance of England among the nations. The death of half a million or so Chinamen in the first instance had been a delicate hint; now came the more urgent warning. Who knew but that if this sacrilegious Bill were passed, England herself might not be smitten. When warnings are disregarded, judgments follow. The Evangelicals found a weapon ready to their hands...

But what precisely was the nature of the new plague, none of the journals was as yet able to say. The symptoms had not as yet been "described" by any medical authority, for it appeared that, contrary to modern precedent, the doctor himself, despite all precautions, was peculiarly subject to infection. Out of the eleven new cases in Berlin, no less than four were medical men.

From the layman's point of view the symptoms were briefly as follows: Firstly, violent pains at the base of the skull, followed by a period of comparative relief which lasted from two to five hours. Then, a numbness in the extremities, followed by rapid paralysis. Death ensued in from twenty-four to forty-eight hours after the pains were first experienced. No case, as yet, was known to have recovered. A well-known physician in London gave it as his opinion that the disease was a hitherto unknown form of cerebro-spinal meningitis of unexampled virulence. He protested that the word "plague" was a false description, but that word had already been impressed on the public mind, and the disease was spoken of as the "new plague" until the end.

## 2

The next morning all London was reading a heavily-leaded article by Jasper Thrale. It appeared first in the *Daily Post*, with the announcement that it was not copyright, and all the evening papers took it up, and some of them reprinted it in its entirety. The article began by pointing out that in the recent history of civilization Europe had been subject to a long succession of pestilences. From the fourteenth to the seventeenth centuries, wrote Thrale, the Black Death, now commonly supposed to be a form of the bubonic plague, was practically endemic in England. In more recent times small-pox had been responsible for enormous mortality among all classes, and, in our own day, tuberculosis. In the two former examples, Thrale pointed out, and in many other diseases, infectious or contagious, or both, these pestilences had gradually lost virulence. By the elimination of those most susceptible to infection and incapable to resist the onslaught of the disease, and by the survival of those whose vitality was strong enough either to resist attack or to achieve recovery, mankind at last were gradually becoming immune against certain infections which had prevailed in the past. And in a greater or less degree this immunity was without doubt being obtained against a whole host of lesser ills. This comparative immunity, in fact, was one of the means of man's evolution towards a more perfect physical body.

"But let us consider for a moment," wrote Thrale, "the appalling danger which threatens us when we are attacked by a pestilence which is entirely new to humanity; new, so far as we know, to the world. In the middle of the fourteenth century the Black Death is recorded in some places to have killed two-thirds of the whole population, and, notwithstanding the modern improvement in sanitation and general hygiene, there is no inherent reason why another pestilence may not appear, which may be even more deadly. And we are faced at the present moment with the awful threat that such a pestilence has appeared, the pestilence commonly known as the 'new plague.' There is no reason why we should consider the appearance as without precedent in history; there is no reason why we should regard its coming as outside the laws of common probability; finally, and most decisively, there is no reason why England should not be smitten.

"According to report among the Chinese, this 'new plague' has been spasmodically epidemic in Tibet for more than a century. We have, as yet, no certain facts upon which to base any hypothesis, but is it not credible that during that time some bacterium or bacillus hitherto harmlessly parasitic, perhaps, in the blood of lower animals has changed its life habit? In the isolated and sparsely inhabited regions of Tibet, it is possible that for many thousand years the assumed bacterium was never bred in the blood of man; it is possible that when it first found a new host it was comparatively harmless to him, but within a hundred years it may have become so altered by new conditions that it has developed into what is practically a new species. If these theories are relatively true, it is not unlikely that this new bacterium is working out its own destruction by the destruction of its hosts. It may be that it is one of those blind alleys of evolution which reach a certain stage of development and then disappear. But meanwhile what of mankind? We know so little of the history of microscopic life. There is a whole world of evolution in process of which we have no conception, and at this stage, whether my hypothesis be a possible one or not, we are at least sure that an unknown organism—animal or vegetable—has become visible to us in its effects and may alter the whole history of mankind.

"I lay stress on these aspects, because we are so hide-bound, so restricted, so conventional in our ideas that we assume, without thought, that the process of life as we know of it from a few thousand years of history can never be interrupted. In our few years of individual existence we become accustomed to certain apparent laws of cause and effect, and will not believe that there can be any exception to those assumed laws. But, now, in the face of recent evidence, it is absolutely essential that we should realize instantly and practically that we are threatened with a new factor in life, which imperils the whole human race. It is no longer safe to comfort ourselves with the belief begotten of our vanity that the world was necessarily made for man. It behoves us to take measures for our protection without delay, to undertake our own cause and trust no longer in any beneficent Providence that works always for our ultimate benefit.

"These measures of protection are clearly indicated. We must close our doors against the invasion of the plague. Quarantine will not protect us; we must have no traffic with Europe until the danger is past. By the happy accident of our position we can become isolated from the rest of the world. We must close our doors before it is too late."

If the people had not been seriously scared by the sudden irruption of news on the day preceding that on which this article was published, they would have ignored Thrale's hyperboles or laughed. But, caught in a moment of agitation and fear, a certain section of the crowd took up Thrale's suggestion, talked about the "closed door," held meetings, and started propaganda. The Press, with its genius for appreciating and following public opinion, also took up the suggestion, and was automatically divided into two sections, recognizable as Liberal and Conservative.

*The Times* took command of the situation with a leader, in which Thrale's argument was pounded, rather than picked, to pieces; but the *Daily Mail* produced more effect with two special articles contributed, one by a bacteriologist, the other by a professor of economics. The first had little weight—all argument under that head was as yet founded on the most uncertain hypotheses. The second was so convincing that the less ardent supporters of the "closed door" policy were shaken in their convictions.

The writer of the economic article pointed out that an England with closed doors could not feed herself for a month. He was scrupulously fair in his argument, and was at great pains to show that even if preparation was instantly made to lay in large stores of grain from Canada, tinned meats from America, and food-stuffs generally from the many places which were as yet free from any taint of plague, it would still be impossible to provide for more than a three months' isolation. Then, leaving this aspect of the question, he went on to show in detail that even if the food could be supplied, the practical cessation of our enormous foreign trade would mean the destruction of England's commerce, and he wound up with an earnest exhortation to the country at large, warning the people to beware of scaremongers, pessimists, and opportunists who had their own ends to serve, and cared nothing for the general welfare. It was an excellent article in every way; quite one of the best that the *Daily Mail* had ever published. And as this, too, was declared free of any copyright restrictions, it was largely circulated.

The *Daily Post* replied next morning by pointing out that the celebrated professor of economics was nullifying all his own previous utterances on the case for Tariff Reform, but that retort carried little weight. No one cared if the professor contradicted himself; anyone, except the faddists, could see that the argument of the article was sound, in fact incontrovertible. What had to be done was to put pressure on the Local Government Board. It was true that the *Daily Post*, the semi-official organ of the Government, affirmed that the Board in question was alert and active, but that announcement was regarded as a cliché; what was wanted were particulars of the preventive measures that were being taken.

The members of the great Gosling family, in offices, warehouses and shops followed the line of least resistance, while making some assertion of their rights as citizens.

George Gosling's arguments with his crony Flack were excellently representative. "What yer think of this 'closed door' business?" asked Flack.

"Goin' a bit too far, in my opinion," returned Gosling judicially.

Flack's natural incredulity had inclined him in the same direction, but his colleague's certainty swung him round at once.

"I ain't so sure o' that," he said. "Looks to me as things is going pretty bad."

"Bad enough, I grant you," returned Gosling. "But there isn't no need for us to lose our 'eads over it. Take it all round, you know, it's pretty certain as things isn't as bad as is made out, whereas, on the other 'and, the 'closed door' policy'd mean ruin and starvation for 'undreds of thousands—there's no gettin' round that."

"Better a few 'undred thousands than the 'ole male population," said Flack.

"If it come to that, but it won't; no fear, not by a long chalk, it won't," replied Gosling. "What's got to be done is to get the Local Government Board to work. We've got to 'ave a regular system o' quarantine established, that's what we've got to 'ave."

It did, indeed, appear the most practical form of prevention at the moment; it is hard to see what other measures could have been adopted. The supporters of the "closed door" policy soon began to lose adherents. The scheme was obviously alarmist, far-fetched and utterly impracticable....

## 3

Through February and the early part of March the plague spread through Central Europe, but not with an alarming rapidity.

In the second week of March, Berlin was reporting a weekly roll of over five hundred deaths attributable to this cause, and Vienna was second with between four and five hundred. In St Petersburg and Moscow the figures were no higher, and there were as yet comparatively few cases in France, and none in Spain or Portugal.

Many authorities were of opinion that the mortality had reached the maximum, and that the plague would work itself out in the course of a few more weeks. Moreover it appeared that the early reports of the highly infectious character of the plague must have been grossly exaggerated, for as yet there had been not a single case in the British Isles despite the enormous traffic between England and the Continent. It is true that the strictest quarantine had been established—it had been ascertained that the period of gestation of the germ was about fifty hours—but not one single case had so far been detained in quarantine ships or hospitals. It was argued from this that the plague was not infectious at all in the ordinary sense, and only mildly contagious; that it flourished in certain centres and was not easily transferable from one centre to another.

The only aspect of the thing that was seriously alarming was the horrible mortality among doctors and the specialists who were endeavouring to recognize and isolate the characteristic germ of the disease. Nine English experts who had dared martyrdom in the cause of science had gone to Berlin to make investigations, and not one of them had returned. As a consequence of this strange susceptibility of the investigator, whether medical man or bacteriologist, there was still an extraordinary ignorance of the general nature and action of the disease.

Nevertheless, despite this one intimidating aspect of the plague, the general attitude in the middle of March was that the quarantine arrangements were enormously impeding trade and should be relaxed. The foreign governments were alive to the seriousness of the scourge, and were doing all in their power to prevent infection. There had been a scare, but people were calm again, now, and able to realize the extent of the earlier exaggerations.

The Government passed the second reading of the English Church Disestablishment Bill by a majority of nineteen, before the Easter recess, and the Goslings, who had grown used to the plague, whose chief attitude towards it was that it was an infernal nuisance which interfered with trade, turned their attention gladly to the new topic; they all thought that a general election at that moment would result in an overwhelming Conservative majority. And as the Liberals had been in power for more than ten years, that eventuality was regarded with complacency.

But at this critical moment—to the joy of the Evangelicals—the new plague set to work in earnest.

# CHAPTER 6

*Disaster*

## 1

Russia was smitten. Once more communication was cut off from Moscow, this time by a different agent. The work of the city was paralysed. Men were falling dead in the street, and there were only women to bury them. A wholesale emigration had begun. The roads were choked with people on foot and in carriages, for the trains had ceased to run.

The news filtered in by degrees: it was confirmed, contradicted and definitely confirmed again every few hours.

Then came final confirmation, with the news that something approaching war had broken out—a war of defence. Germany had sent troops to the frontier to stem the tide of emigrants from smitten Russia and Poland; and Austria-Hungary was following her example.

Parliament re-assembled before the Easter recess had expired. The time for more drastic measures had come, and the Premier explained to the House that it was proposed to bring in a Bill immediately to cut off communication with Europe.

There can be no doubt that England was now badly scared, but centuries of protection had established a belief in security which was not easily shaken.

The enthusiasts for the "closed door" policy found plenty of recruits, but on the other side there was a solid body of opinion which maintained that the danger was grossly exaggerated. And when the *Evening Chronicle* came out with a long leader and a backing of expert opinion, to prove that the "Closed Door" Bill—as it was commonly called—was a dodge of the Government's in order to retain office, a well-marked reaction followed against the last and terrible step of cutting off all communication with Europe; and the Conservative party was joined by some avowed Liberals who had personal interests to consider in this connexion.

In committee-rooms, members of the Opposition were inclined to be jubilant: "If we can throw out the Government on this Bill we shall simply sweep the country... all the manufacturers in the North will be with us... even Scotland, most likely... we should come back with a record majority...."

The prospects were so magnificent that there could be no hesitation in making a party question of the Bill.

No time was to be lost, for the Bill was to be rushed, it was an emergency measure, and it was proposed that it should become law within four days. Preparations were already in hand to carry out the provisions enacted.

An urgent rally of the Opposition was made, and when the Bill came up for the second reading the Premier addressed a well-filled House. The House was not crowded because a large number of people, including many members of Parliament, were on their way to America. All the big liners were packed on their outward voyage and were returning, contrary to all precedent, in ballast—this ballast was exclusively food-stuffs.

The Premier introduced the Bill in a speech which was remarkable for its sincerity and earnestness. He outlined the arrangements that were being made to feed the community, and showed clearly that while communication remained open with America, there was no fear of any serious shortage. Pausing for a moment on this question of intercourse with America, he made a point of the fact that American ports were already closed to emigrants from all European countries with the one exception of Great Britain, and that if a single case of plague were reported in these islands the difficulties of obtaining food-stuffs from America and the Colonies would be enormously increased. He wound up by almost imploring the House not to make a party question of so urgent and necessary a measure at a time when the safety of England was so terribly threatened. He pleaded that at this critical moment, unparalleled in the history of humanity, it was the duty of every man to sink his own personal interests, to be ready to make any sacrifice, for the sake of the community.

Mr Brampton, the leader of the Opposition, then completely destroyed the undoubted effect which had been made upon the House. He did not openly speak in a party spirit, but he hinted very plainly that the

Bill under consideration was a mere subterfuge to win votes. He poured contempt upon the fear of the plague, which he characterized throughout as the "Russian epidemic," and ended with the advice to keep a cool head, to preserve the British spirit of sturdy resistance instead of shutting our doors and bringing the country to commercial ruin. "Are we all cravens," he concluded, "scurrying like rabbits to our burrows at the first hint of alarm?"

The further debate, although lengthy, had comparatively little influence; the House divided, and the Government was defeated by a majority of nine.

## 2

The news was all over the country by ten o'clock that night, and it was noticeable that a large percentage of the younger generation still regarded the danger as "rather a lark." This threat of the plague held a promise of high adventure; youth can only realize the possibility of death in its relation to others.

"I say, if this bally old plague did come..." remarked a young man of twenty-two, who was sitting with a friend in the little private bar of the "Dun Taw" Hotel.

His friend drew his feet up on to the rungs of his tall stool and winked at the barmaid.

"Well, go on. What if it did?" remarked that young woman.

The young man considered for a moment and then said: "Those that got left would have a rare old time."

"It's the women as'd get left, seems to me," replied the barmaid, and scored a point.

"I say, surely you don't come from this part of the world?" was the compliment evoked by her wit.

"Not me!" was the answer, "I'm a Londoner, I am. Only started yesterday, and sha'n't stay long if today's a fair sample. There 'asn't been a dozen customers in all day, and they were in such a 'urry to get their tonic and go that I'm sure they couldn't 'ave told you whether me 'air was black or ches'nut."

Both men immediately looked at the crown of pretty fair hair which had been so churlishly slighted.

"First thing I noticed about you," said one.

The other, who had hardly spoken before, took the cigarette out of his mouth and remarked: "You can never get that colour with peroxide."

The barmaid looked a little suspicious.

"Oh, he means it all right, kid," put in the younger man quickly. "Dicky's one of the serious sort. Besides, he's in that line; travels for a firm of wholesale chemists."

Dicky nodded gravely. "I could see at once it was natural," he remarked with the air of an expert.

"Ah! you're one of them that keeps their eyes open," returned the barmaid approvingly, and Dicky modestly acknowledged the compliment by saying that his business necessitated close observation.

"Most men are as blind as bats," continued the barmaid, and the examples she gave from her own experience led to an absorbing conversation, which was presently interrupted by the shriek of the swing door.

The newcomer was a small, fair man with a neatly waxed moustache. He came up to the counter with the air of an habitué, and remarked, "Hallo! where's Cis? You're new here, aren't you?"

The barmaid, recognizing the marks of a regular customer, quietly admitted that this was only her second day at the "Dun Taw."

"I've been away for two months," explained the fair man, and ordered "Scotch." He was evidently in the mood for company, for he brought up a stool and, sitting a little way back from the bar, he began to address his three hearers at large.

"Only came back from Europe this evening," he said, "and glad to be home, I assure you." He raised his left hand with a gesture intended to convey horror, and drank half his whisky at a gulp.

Dicky turned to give his serious attention to the narrative which was plainly to follow, and somewhat ostentatiously observed the details of the newcomer's dress. Dicky had a new-found reputation to maintain.

His friend looked bored and a little sulky, and tried to continue his conversation with the barmaid, but that young woman, appreciating the difference in value between a casual and a regular customer, passed a broad hint by with a smile and said: "Europe? Just fancy!"

"It's a place to get out of, I assure you," said the fair man. "I've been over there for two months—Germany and Austria chiefly—but for the last fortnight I've been wasting my time. There's nothing doing."

"Isn't there?" commented Dicky with great seriousness.

"Oh, we're sick to death of this bally plague," put in the other young man quickly. "There's been simply nothing else in the papers for the last I don't know how long. I want to forget it."

The fair man reached forward and put down his empty glass on the bar counter. "Same again, Miss," he said, and then: "We'll all be more sick of the plague before we've finished with it. It's a terror. If I was to tell you a few of the things I've seen in the past fortnight, I don't suppose you'd believe me."

"That's all right; I'd believe you quick enough," returned the young man. "Point is, what's the good of getting yourself in a funk about it? Personally I don't believe it's coming to England. If it was it would have been here before this. What I say is..."

His pronouncement of opinion ceased abruptly. The fair man's behaviour riveted attention. He was gazing past the barmaid at the orderly rows of shining glasses and various shaped bottles behind her. His mouth was open. He gazed intensely, horribly.

The barmaid backed nervously and looked over her shoulder. The two young men hastily rose and pushed back their stools. The same thought was in all their minds. This neat, fair man was on the verge of delirium tremens.

In a moment the air of intercourse and joviality that had pervaded the little room was dissipated; in place of it had come shocked surprise and fear.

There was an interval of slow desolating silence, and then the convulsive grip of the fair man shattered the glass he held, and the fragments fell tinkling to the floor.

"I say, what's up?" stammered the barmaid's admirer, while the barmaid herself shrank back against the shelves and watched nervously. She had had experience.

The fair man's head was being pulled slowly backwards by some invisible force. His eyes, staring straight before him, appeared to watch with fierce intensity some point that moved steadily up the wall of shelves behind the counter; up till it reached the ceiling and began to move over the ceiling toward him.

Then, quite suddenly, the horrible tension was relaxed; his head fell loosely forward and he clapped both hands to the nape of his neck. He was breathing loudly in short quick gasps.

"I say, do you think he's ill?" asked the young man. At the suggestion Dicky made a step towards the sufferer; his knowledge of chemistry gave him a professional air.

"He's come from Europe.... Suppose it's the plague," whispered the barmaid.

And at that the two young men started back. As the words were spoken realization swept upon them.

Mumbling something about "get a doctor," they rushed for the door. One of them made a wide detour—he had to pass the man who sat doubled forward in his chair, frantically gripping the base of his skull.

Hardly had the clatter of the swing door subsided before he fell forward on to the floor. He was groaning now, groaning detestably. The barmaid whimpered and stared.

"Women don't get it," she said aloud. But she kept to her own side of the counter.

Later the owner of the "Dun Taw" identified the fair man from a distance as Mr Stewart, of the firm of Barker and Prince.

## 3

Thrale's "higher forces" had shown their hand.

The humble and rotund instrument of their choice had served his purpose, and he was probably the first man in London to receive the news—a delicate acknowledgment, perhaps, of his services.

The telegram was addressed to the firm, but as neither of the heads of the house had arrived, Gosling opened it according to precedent.

"Gosh!" was his sole exclamation, but the tone of it stirred the interest of Flack, who turned to see his colleague's rather protuberant blue eyes staring with a fishy glare at a flimsy sheet of paper which visibly trembled in the hold of two clusters of fat fingers.

Flack lifted his spectacles and holding them on a level with his eyebrows, said, "Bad news?"

Gosling sat down, and in the fever of the moment wiped his forehead with his snuff handkerchief, then discovered his mistake and laid the handkerchief carelessly on the desk. This infringement of his invariable practice produced even more effect upon Flack than the staring eyes and wavering fingers. Gosling might be guilty of mild histrionics, but not of such a touch as this. The utter neglect of decency exhibited by the display of that shameful bandanna could only portend calamity.

"Lord's sakes, man, what's the matter?" asked Flack, still taking an observation under his spectacles.

"It's come, Flack," said Gosling feebly. "It's in Scotland. Our Mr Stewart died of it in Dundee this mornin'."

Flack rose from his seat and grabbed the telegram, which was brief and pregnant. "Stewart died suddenly five a.m. Feared plague. Macfie."

"Tchah!" said Flack, still staring at the telegram. "'*Feared plague*.' Lost their 'eads, that's what they've done. Pull yourself together, man. I don't believe a word of it."

Gosling swallowed elaborately, discovered his bandanna on the desk and hastily pocketed it. "Might a been 'eart-disease, d'you think?" he said eagerly.

"We-el," remarked Flack, "I never 'eard as 'is 'eart was affected, did you?"

Gosling held out his hand for the telegram, and made a further elaborate study of it, without, however, discovering any hitherto unsuspected evidence relating to the unsoundness of Stewart's heart.

"It says 'feared,' of course," he remarked at last. "Macfie wouldn't have said feared if 'e'd been sure."

"They'd 'ardly have mentioned plague in a telegram if they 'adn't been pretty certain, though," argued Flack.

Gosling was so upset that he had to go out and get a nip of brandy, a thing he had not done since the morning after Blanche was born.

The partners looked grave when they heard the news from Dundee, and London generally looked very grave indeed, when they read the full details an hour later in the *Evening Chronicle.*

Stewart, it appeared, had come straight through from Berlin to London via Flushing and Port Victoria, and on landing in England he had managed to escape quarantine. His was not an isolated case. For some weeks it had been possible for British subjects to get past the officials. There was nothing in the regulations to allow such an evasion of the order, but it could be managed occasionally. Stewart had been told to spare no expense.

The *Evening Chronicle*, although it made the most of its opportunity in contents bill and headlines, said that there was no cause for alarm, that these things were managed better in Great Britain than on the Continent; that the case had been isolated from the first moment the plague was recognized (about five hours before death), that the body had been burned, and that the most extensive and elaborate process of disinfection was being carried out even the sleeping coach in which Stewart had travelled from London to Dundee twelve hours before, had been identified and burned also.

London still looked grave, but was nevertheless a little inclined to congratulate itself on the thoroughness of British methods. "We'll never get it in England, you see if we do," was the remark chiefly in vogue among the great Gosling family.

But twelve hours or so too late, England was beginning to regret that the Government had been defeated. It was rumoured that the Premier had broken down, had immediately resigned his office, and would not seek re-election as a private member.

This rumour was definitely confirmed in the later editions of the evening papers. Mr Brampton had been summoned to Buckingham Palace and was forming a temporary ministry which was to take office. In the circumstances it was deemed inadvisable to plunge the country into a general election at that moment.

## 4

Mr Stewart died in the small hours of Friday morning, and the next day, Saturday, the 14th of April, was the first day of panic.

The day began with comparative quiet. No further case had been notified in Great Britain, but telegraphic communication was interrupted between London and Russia, Prague, Vienna, Budapest, and other continental centres. In Germany matters were growing desperate. There had been riots and looting. Military law had been declared in several towns; in some cases the mob had been fired upon. Business was at a standstill, and the plague was spreading like a fire. Between two and three hundred cases were reported from Reims, and upwards of fifty from Paris…

Business houses were being closed in the City of London, and the banks noted a marked tendency among their depositors to withdraw gold; so marked, indeed, that many banks of high standing were glad to be able to close their doors at one o'clock.

It was on this Saturday morning, also, that the bottom suddenly fell out of the money market. For weeks past, prices had been falling steadily, but now they dropped to panic figures. Every one was selling, there were no buyers left. Consols were quoted at 53½.

The air of London was heavy with foreboding, and throughout the morning the gloom grew deeper. The depressed and worried faces to be met at every turn contrasted strangely with the brilliance of the weather.

For April had come with clear skies and soft, warm winds.

As the day advanced the atmosphere of depression became continually more marked, and how extraordinary was the effect upon all classes may be judged from the fact that less than 5,000 people paid to witness the third replay between Barnsley and Everton, in the semi-final of the English Cup....

In London, men and women hung aimlessly about the streets waiting for the news they dreaded to hear. The theatres were deserted. The feeling of gloom was so real that many women afterwards believed that the sky had been overcast, whereas Nature was in one of her most brilliant moods.

It was a few minutes past three when the pressure was exploded by the report of the final catastrophe. "Two more cases of plague in Dundee and one in Edinburgh," was the first announcement. That would have been enough to show that all the vaunted precautions had been useless, and within an hour came the notification of two further cases. Before six o'clock, eight more were notified in Dundee, three more in Edinburgh, and one in Newcastle.

The new plague had reached England. It was then that the panic began.

# CHAPTER 7

*Panic*

## 1

Gurney, when he left his office on that Saturday, was influenced by the general depression. He went to lunch at the "White Vine," in the Haymarket, quite determined to keep himself in hand, to argue himself out of his low spirits.

He made a beginning at once.

"Every one seems to have a fit of the blues, Ernst," he remarked to the waiter with a factitious cheerfulness.

Ernst, less polite than usual, shrugged his shoulders. "There is enough cause already," he said.

"Have you had bad news from Germany?" asked Gurney, feeling that he had probably been rather brutal.

"Ach Gott! 's'ist bald Keiner mehr da," blubbered Ernst, and he wept without restraint as he arranged the table, occasionally wiping his eyes with his napkin.

"I'm most awfully sorry," murmured the embarrassed Gurney, and retreated behind the horror of his evening paper. He found small cause for rejoicing there, however, and discarded it as soon as his lunch had been brought by the red-eyed Ernst.

"I wonder what Mark Tapley would have done," Gurney reflected moodily as he attacked his chop.

There were few other people in the restaurant, and they were all silent and engrossed. That dreadful cloud hung over England, the spirit of pestilence threatened to take substance, the air was full of horror that might at any moment become a visible shape of destruction.

Gurney did not finish his lunch, he lighted a cigarette, left four shillings on the table, and hurried out into the air.

He did not look up at the sky as he turned eastwards towards Fleet

Street; no one looked up at the sky that afternoon. Heads and shoulders were burdened by an invisible weight which kept all eyes on the ground.

Fleet Street was full of people who crowded round the windows of newspaper offices, not with the eagerness of a general election crowd, but with a subdued surliness which ever and again broke out in spurts of violent temper.

Gurney, still struggling to maintain his composure, found himself unreasonably irritated when a motorbus driver shouted at him to get out of the way. It seemed to Gurney that to be knocked down and run over was preferable to being shouted at. The noise of those infernal buses was unbearable, so, also, was that dreadful patter of feet upon the pavement and the dull murmur of mournful voices. Why, in the name of God, could not people keep quiet?

He bumped into someone on the pavement as he scrambled out of the way of the bus, and the man swore at him viciously. Gurney responded, and then discovered that the man was known to him.

"Hallo!" he said. "You?"

"Hallo," responded the other.

For a moment they stood awkwardly, staring; then Gurney said, "Any more news?"

The man, who was a sub-editor of the *Westminster Gazette*, shook his head. "I'm just going back now," he said. "There was nothing ten minutes ago."

"Pretty awful, isn't it?" remarked Gurney.

The sub-editor shrugged his shoulders and hurried away.

Presently Gurney found himself wedged among the crowd, watching the *Daily Chronicle* window.

A few minutes after three, a young man with a very white face fastened a type-written message to the glass.

There was a rapid constriction of the crowd. Those behind, Gurney among them, could not read the message, and pressed forward. There were cries of "What is it?... I can't see.... Read it out...." Then those in front gave way slightly, a wave of eagerness agitated the mass of watchers, and the news ran back from the front. "Two more cases of plague in Dundee; one in Edinburgh."

And with that the pressure of dread was suddenly dissipated, giving place to something kinetic, dynamic. Now it was fear that took the people by the throat: active, compelling fear. Men looked at each other with terror and something of hate in their eyes, the crowd broke and melted. Every man was going to his own home, possessed by an instinct to fly before it was too late.

Gurney shouldered his way out, and stopped a taxi that was crawling past.

"Jermyn Street," he said.

The driver leaned over and pointed to the *Daily Chronicle* window. "What's the news?" he asked.

"The plague's in Dundee and Edinburgh," said Gurney, and climbed into the cab and slammed the door.

"Gawd!" muttered the driver, as he drove recklessly westwards.

Sitting in the cab, finding some comfort in the feeling of headlong speed, Gurney was debating whether he would not charter the man to take him right out of London. But he must go home first for money.

At the door of the house in Jermyn Street he met Jasper Thrale.

## 2

"Have you heard?" asked Gurney excitedly.

"No. What?" said Thrale, without interest.

"There are two more cases in Dundee and one in Edinburgh," said Gurney. The driver of the cab got down from his seat, and looked from Gurney to Thrale with doubt and question.

Thrale nodded his head. "I knew it was sure to come," he remarked.

"Better get out of this," put in the driver.

"Yes, rather," agreed Gurney.

"Where to?" asked Thrale.

"Well, America."

Thrale laughed. "They'll have it in America before you get there," he said. "It'll go there via Japan and 'Frisco."

"You seem to know a lot about it," said the driver of the cab.

"Do you mean to tell me there's nowhere we can go to?" persisted Gurney.

Thrale smiled. "Nowhere in this world," he said. "This plague has come to destroy mankind." He spoke with a quiet assurance that carried conviction.

The driver of the cab scowled. "May as well 'ave a run for my money first, then," he said, and thus gave utterance to the thought that was fermenting in many other minds.

There was no hope of escape for the mass, only the rich could seek railway termini and take train for Liverpool, Southampton or any port where there was the least hope of finding some ship to take them out of Europe.

That night there was panic and riot. The wealthy classes were trying to escape, the mob was trying to "get a run for its money." Yet very little real mischief was done. Two or three companies of infantry were sufficient to clear the streets, and not more than forty people in all were seriously injured....

In Downing Street the new Premier sat alone with his head in his hands, and wondered what could be done to stop the approach of the pestilence. One of the evening papers had suggested that a great line of fire should be built across the north of England. The Premier wondered whether that scheme were feasible. He had never held high office before; he did not know how to deal with these great issues. All his political life he had learned only the art of party tactics. He had learned that art very well, he was a master of debate, and he had shown a wonderful ability to judge the bent of the public mind and to make use of his judgments for party ends. But now that any action of his was divorced from its accustomed object, he was as a man suddenly forced into some new occupation. Whenever he tried to think of some means to stay the progress of the plague his mind automatically began to consider what influence the adoption of such means would have upon the general election which must soon come....

"A line of fire across the north," he was thinking, "would shut off the whole of Scotland. They would never forgive us for that. We should lose the entire Scottish vote—it's bad enough as it is." He sat up late into the night considering what policy he should put before the Cabinet. He tried honestly to consider the position apart from politics, but his mind refused to work in that way....

## 3

In Jermyn Street Thrale was arguing with Gurney, trying to persuade him into a philosophic attitude.

"Yes, I suppose there's absolutely nothing to be done but sit down and wait," said Gurney.

"Personally," returned Thrale, "I have no intention of spending my time flying from country to country like a marked criminal. That way leads to insanity. I've seen men become animals before now under the influence of fear."

"Yes, of course, you're quite right," agreed Gurney. "One must exercise self-control. After all, it's only death, and not such a terrible death at that." He got up and began to pace the room restlessly, then went to the window and looked out. Jermyn Street was almost deserted, but distant sounds of shouting came from the direction of Piccadilly. He left the window open and turned back into the room.

"It's so infernally hard just to sit still and wait," he said. "If only one could do something."

"I doubt, now," said Thrale, quietly, "whether one could ever have done anything. The public and the Government took my warnings in the characteristic way, the only possible way in which you could expect twentieth-century humanity to take a warning a thrill of fear, perhaps, in some cases; frank incredulity in others; but no result either way that endured for an hour.... Belief in national and personal security, inertia outside the routine of necessary, stereotyped employment; these things are essential to the running of the machine."

"I suppose they are," agreed Gurney absently. He had sat down again and was sucking automatically at an extinguished pipe.

"In a complex civilization," went on Thrale "any initiative on the part of the individual outside his own tiny sphere of energy is just so much grit in the machine. There are recognized methods, they may not be the best, the most efficient, but they are accepted and understood. Every clerk who has to calculate twelve pence to the shilling knows how his work would be lightened if he had only to calculate ten, but he accepts that difficulty, because he can do nothing as an individual to introduce the decimal system. And that spirit of acceptance grows upon him until the individual has the characteristics of the class. Only when a man is stirred by too great discomfort does he open his eyes to the possibility of initiative; then come labour strikes. If labour had a sufficiency of ease and comfort, if its lot were not so violently contrasted with that of even the middle-classes, labour would settle down to complacency. But the contrast is too great, and to attain that complacency of uninitiative we must level down. That was coming; that would have come if this plague...."

"What was that?" asked Gurney excitedly, jumping to his feet. "Did you hear firing?" He went to the window again, and leaned out. From Piccadilly came the sound of an army of trampling feet, of confused cries and shouting. "By God, there's a riot," exclaimed Gurney. He spoke over his shoulder.

Thrale joined him at the window. "Panic," he said. "Senseless, hysterical panic. It won't last."

"I think I shall go out of London," said Gurney. "I'd sooner... I'd sooner die in the country, I think." He withdrew from the window and began to pace up and down the room again.

"Going to stampede with the rest of 'em?" asked Thrale. "Extraordinarily infectious thing, panic."

"I don't think it's that exactly..." hesitated Gurney.

"Animal fear," said Thrale. "The terror of the wild thing threatened with the unknown. The runaway horse terrified and rushing to its own destruction. Fly, fly, fly from the threat of peril as you did once on the prairies, when to fly meant safety."

"It's so infernally depressing in London," said Gurney.

"All right, go and brood on death in the country," replied Thrale. "That may cheer you up a bit. But, take my advice, don't run. Walk at a snail's pace and check the least tendency to hurry. Once you begin to quicken your pace, you will find yourself hurrying desperately and then stampede the hell of terror at your heels. After all, you know, you may survive. It isn't likely that every man will die."

Gurney caught eagerly at that. "No, no, of course it isn't," he said. "But wouldn't one be much more likely to survive if one were living in the country, or by the sea in some fairly isolated place, for example. I meant to go down to Cornwall for my holiday this year, to a little cottage on the coast about four miles from Padstow; don't you think in pure air and healthy surroundings like that, one would stand a better chance?"

"Very likely," said Thrale carelessly. "But don't run. In any case you'd better wait till the middle of the week. The first rush will be over then."

"Yes. Perhaps. I'll go on Wednesday, or Tuesday...."

Thrale smiled grimly. "Well, good night," he said. "I'm going to bed."

When he had gone, Gurney went to the window again. The sounds of riot from Piccadilly had died down to a low, confused murmur. A motor-car whizzed by along Jermyn Street, and two people passed on foot, a man and a woman; the woman was leaning heavily on the man's arm.

Gurney turned once more to his pacing of the room. He was trying to realize the unrealizable fact that the world offered no refuge. For a full hour he struggled with himself, with that new, strange instinct which rose up and urged him to fly for his life. At last weary and overborne he threw himself into a chair by the dying fire and began to cry like a lost child; even as Ernst, the waiter, had cried....

## 4

The panic emigration lasted until Monday evening, and then came news which checked and stayed the rush for the ports of Liverpool, Southampton and Queenstown. The plague was already in America. It had come, as Thrale had prophesied from the West. At the docks many of those favoured emigrants who had secured berths, hesitated; if it was to be a choice between death in America and death in England, they preferred to die at home.

Yet, even on Tuesday morning, when doubt as to the coming of the plague was no longer possible, when Dundee could only give approximate figures of the seizures in that town, reporting them as not less than a thousand, when it was evident that the whole of Scotland was becoming infected with incredible rapidity, and two cases were notified as far south as Durham, there remained still an enormous body of people who stoutly maintained that, bad as things were, the danger was grossly exaggerated, who believed that the danger would soon pass, and who, steadfast to the habits of a lifetime, continued their routine wherever it was possible so to do, determined to resist to the last.

To this body, possibly some two-fifths of the whole urban population, was due the comparative maintenance of law and order. In face of the growing destitution due to the wholesale closing of factories, warehouses and offices, necessitated by the now complete cessation of foreign trade and to the hoarding of food stores and gold which was already so marked as to have seriously affected the commerce not dependent on foreign sellers and buyers, a semblance of ordinary life was still maintained. Newspapers were issued, trains and 'buses were running, theatres and music-halls were open, and many normal occupations were carried on.

Yet everything was infected. It was as if the cloak of civilization was worn more loosely. Crime was increasing and justice was relaxed. Robberies of food were so common that there was no place for the confinement of those who were convicted. Shopkeepers were becoming at once more reliant upon their own defences, and less scrupulous in their dealings with bona-fide customers. No longer could the protection of the State be exclusively relied upon, the citizen was becoming lost in the individual. Public opinion was being resolved into individual opinion; and with the failing of the great restraint every man was developing an unsuspected side of his character. Thrown upon his own resources, he became continually less civilized, more conscious of possibilities to fulfill long-thwarted tendencies and desires; he began to understand that when it is a case of *sauve qui peut*, the weakest are trampled under foot.

So the cloak of civilization gaped and showed the form of the naked man, with all its blemishes and deformities. And women blenched and shuddered. For woman, as yet, was little, if at all, altered in character by the fear that was brutalizing man. Her faith in the intrinsic rectitude of the beloved conventions was more deeply rooted. Moreover woman fears the strictures of woman, more than man fears the judgments of man.

# CHAPTER 8

*Gurney In Cornwall*

## 1

Gurney's alternative to flying from the plague was to run away from himself. He shirked the issue in his conversations with Thrale, shuffled, sophisticated, and in a futile endeavour to convince his companion, convinced himself that his reasoning was sound and his motive unprejudiced.

It was not until the following Thursday, however, that he took train to Cornwall. He had succeeded in realizing between two and three hundred pounds in gold, and this he took with him. He intended to lay in stores of flour, sugar and other primary necessities; to buy and keep two or three cows, to rear chickens, to grow as much garden produce as possible, especially potatoes; and generally to provide against the coming scarcity of food and the cessation of transport.

The bungalow on the shores of Constantine Bay, to which he departed, was a place well suited to the carrying out of these prudent arrangements. It belonged to a friend of his, who was rich enough to indulge his whims, and who had spent a considerable sum of money in building the place and enclosing ground, but who rarely occupied the bungalow himself, and was too careless to bother about letting it. Gurney had the keys in his possession. When he had asked his friend for permission to spend his summer holiday there, he had been told to use the place as if it were his own. "Jolly good thing for me, you know," his friend had said. "Keep it dry and all that."

Gurney was not an idle man. Arrived at his bungalow, he lost no time in carrying out the arrangements he had schemed, and for nearly three weeks he was so absorbed in this work, in learning new occupations and perfecting his plan, that he did, indeed, achieve his purpose of running away from himself.

He became imbued with a new feeling of security; he received neither letters nor papers from the outside, and the old labourer who assisted him in setting potatoes, who taught him to milk a cow and instructed him generally in the primitive arts of self-supporting toil, seemed to regard all rumours of the new plague which filtered through to the village of St Merryn as some foreign nonsense which had little bearing on life in the county of Cornwall, as represented by the twenty-five or thirty square miles which were to him all the essential world.

Gurney began to believe that the plague would never cross the Tamar, and one day in early May, when his provisions against a seige were practically completed, he was stirred to attempt a journey across the peninsula in order to visit an acquaintance in East Looe. Gurney had become conscious of a longing for some companionship. Old Hawken was very good at cows and potatoes, but he was rather deaf and his range of ideas was severely restricted.

## 2

From Padstow to Looe is not an ideal journey by rail at the best of times, involving as it does, a change of train at Wadebridge, Bodmin Road and Liskeard; but Gurney was in no hurry, and the conversations he overheard in his compartment were not destructive of his new-found complacency. There was, indeed, some mention of the plague, but only in relation to the scarcity of food supply and its effect on trade. One passenger, very obviously a farmer, was congratulating himself that he was getting higher prices for stock than he had ever known, and that as luck would have it he had sown an unusual number of acres with wheat that year. “I’ll be gettun sixty or seventy a quarter, sure ’nough,” he boasted.

Dickenson—Gurney’s friend in Looe—regarded the matter more seriously, but he, too, seemed untouched by any fear of personal infection. He was an ardent Liberal, and his chief cause for concern seemed to be that the plague should have come at a time when so much progress was being made with legislation. He was, also, very distressed at the reports of poverty and starvation which abounded, and at the terrible blow to trade generally. But he seemed hopeful that the trouble would pass and be followed by a new era of enlightened government, founded on sound Liberal principles.

Gurney stayed the night and the greater part of the next day at Looe.

## 3

On his return journey he had to wait at Liskeard to pick up the main line train for London, which would take him to Bodmin Road.

It was a glorious May evening. The day had been hot, but now there was a cool breeze from the sea, and the long shadow from the high bank of the cutting enwrapped the whole station in a pleasant twilight.

Gurney, deliberately pacing the length of the platform, was conscious of physical vigour and a great enjoyment of life. He had an imaginative temperament, and in his moments of exaltation he found the world both interesting and beautiful, an entirely desirable setting for the essential Gurney.

So he strolled up and down the platform, regarded any female figure with interest, and was in no way concerned that the train was already an hour late. He had expected it to be late. His own train from Looe, for no particular reason, had been half an hour late. If he missed his connexion at Wadebridge he would only have some seven or eight miles to walk.

Fifteen or twenty other people were waiting on the down platform, and presently Gurney became conscious that his fellow-passengers were no longer detached into parties of two and three, but were collected in groups, discussing, apparently, some matter of peculiar interest.

Gurney had been lost in his dreams and had hardly noticed the passage of time. He looked at his watch and found that the train was now two hours overdue. The sun had set, but there was still light in the sky. A man detached himself from one of the groups and Gurney approached him.

"Two hours late," he remarked by way of introducing himself, and looked at his watch again.

The man nodded emphatically. "Funny thing is," he said, "that they've had no information at the office. The stationmaster generally gets advice when the train leaves Plymouth."

"Good lord," said Gurney. "Do you mean to say that the train hasn't got to Plymouth yet?"

"Looks like it," said the stranger. "They say it's the plague. It's dreadfully bad in London, they tell me."

"D'you mean it's possible the train won't come in at all?" asked Gurney.

"Oh! I should hardly think that," replied the other. "Oh, no, I should hardly think that, but goodness knows when it will come. Very awkward for me. I want to get to St Ives. It's a long way from here. Have you far to go?"

"Well, Padstow," said Gurney.

"Padstow!" echoed the stranger. "That's a good step."

"Further than I want to walk."

"I should say. Thirty miles or so, anyway?"

"About that," agreed Gurney. "I wonder where one could get any information."

"It's very awkward," was all the help the stranger had to offer.

Gurney crossed the line and invaded the stationmaster's office. "Sorry to trouble you," he said, "but do you think this train's been taken off, for any reason?"

"Oh, it 'asn't been taken off," said the stationmaster with a wounded air. "It may be a bit late."

Gurney smiled. "It's something over two hours behind now, isn't it?" he said.

"Well, I can't 'elp it, can I?" asked the stationmaster. "You'll 'ave to 'ave patience."

"You've had no advice yet from Plymouth?" persisted Gurney, facing the other's ill-temper.

"No, I 'aven't; something's gone wrong with the wire. We can't get no answer," returned the stationmaster. "Now, if you please, I 'ave my work to do."

Gurney returned to the down platform and joined a group of men, among whom he recognized the man he had spoken to a few minutes before.

The afterglow was dying out of the sky, in the south-west a faint young moon was setting behind the high bank of the cutting. A porter had lighted the station lamps, but they were not turned full on.

"The stationmaster tells me that something has gone wrong with the telegraphic communication," said Gurney, addressing the little knot of passengers collectively. "He can't get any answer it seems."

"Been an accident likely," suggested some one.

"Or the engine-driver's got the plague," said another.

"They'd have put another man on."

"If they could find one."

"If we ain't careful we shall be gettin' the plague down 'ere."

After all why not? The horrible suggestion sprang up in Gurney's mind with new force. That remote city seemed suddenly near. He saw in imagination the train leaving Paddington, and only a journey of six or seven hours divided that departure from its arrival at Liskeard. It might come in at any moment, bearing the awful infection. Why should he wait? There was an inn near the station. He might find a conveyance there.

"Constantine Bay?" questioned the landlord.

"It's near St Merryn," said Gurney, but still the landlord shook his head.

"Not far from Padstow," explained Gurney.

"Pard-stow!" exclaimed the landlord on a rising note. "Drive over to Pard-stow at this time o' night?" He appeared to think that Gurney was joking.

"Well, Bodmin, then," suggested Gurney.

"Aw, why not take the train?" asked the landlord.

Gurney shrugged his shoulders. "The train doesn't seem to be coming," he said.

"Bad job, that," answered the landlord. "Been an accident, sure 'nough; this new plague or something." He was evidently prepared to accept the matter philosophically.

"You can't drive me then?" asked Gurney.

The landlord shook his head with a grin. He was inclined to look upon this foreigner as rather more foolish than the majority of his kind.

Gurney came out of the little inn, and looked down into the station. The number of waiting passengers seemed to be decreasing, but the light was so dim that he could not see into the shadows.

"I must keep hold of myself," he was saying. "I mustn't run."

A man was coming up the steep incline towards him, and Gurney moved slowly to meet him. He found that it was the stranger he had spoken to on the platform.

"Any news?" asked Gurney.

"Yes, they've got a message through from Saltash," replied the stranger. "It's the plague right enough. They say they don't know when there'll be another train…."

## 4

Days grew into weeks, and still there were no trains. Trade was at a standstill, and the prices of home produce mounted steadily. Fish there was, but not in great abundance, and the towns inland, such as Truro and Bodmin, organized a motor service with coast fishing villages, a service which only lasted for a week, by reason of the failure of the petrol supply. After that there was a less effective horse service.

Within three weeks after that last train arrived from outside, a new system of exchange was coming into vogue. In this little congeries of communities in Cornwall, men were beginning to learn the uselessness of gold, silver and bronze coins as tokens. Credit had collapsed, and a system of barter was being introduced, mainly between farmer and fisherman. In time it was possible that Cornwall might have become a self-supporting community, for its proportionately few inhabitants were rapidly being depleted by want and starvation; but, although it was the last place in the British Isles to become infected, the plague came there, too, in the end.

A steamer sent out from Cardiff on a plundering expedition carried the plague to the Scillies, and a fishing vessel from St Ives carried it on to Newlyn….

# CHAPTER 9

## *The Devolution of George Gosling*

### 1

THE PROGRESS OF the plague through London and the world in general was marked, in the earlier stages, by much the same developments as are reported of the plague of 1665. The closed houses, the burial pits, the deserted streets, the outbreaks of every kind of excess, the various symptoms of fear, cowardice, fortitude and courage, evidenced little change in the average of humanity between the seventeenth and the twentieth centuries. The most notable difference during these earlier stages was in the enormously increased rapidity with which the population of London was reduced to starvation point. Even before the plague had reached England, want had become general, so general, indeed, as to have demonstrated very clearly the truth of the great economist's contention that England could not exist for three months with closed doors.

The coming of the plague threw London on to its own very limited resources. That vast city, which produced nothing but the tokens of wealth, and added nothing to the essentials that support life, was instantly reduced to the state of Paris in the winter of 1870–71; with the difference, however, that London's population could be decreased rapidly by emigration, and was, also, even more rapidly decreased by pestilence. Yet there was a large section of the population which clung with blind obstinacy to the only life it knew how to live.

There was, for instance, George Gosling, more fortunate in many respects than the average citizen, who clung desperately to his house in Wisteria Grove until forced out of it by the lack of water.

On the ninth day after the first coming of the plague to London—it appeared simultaneously in a dozen places and spread with fearful rapidity—Gosling broke one of the great laws he had hitherto observed with such admirable prudence. The offices and warehouse in Barbican had been shut up (temporarily, it was supposed), and the partners had disappeared from London. But Gosling had a duplicate set of keys, and, inspired by the urgency of his family's need, he determined to dare a journey into the City in order to *borrow* (he laid great stress on the word) a few necessaries of life from the well-stored warehouse of his firm.

In this scheme, planned with some shrewdness, he co-operated with a friend, a fellow-sidesman at the Church of St John the Evangelist. This friend was a coal merchant, and thus fortunately circumstanced in the possession of wagons and horses.

These two arranged the details of their borrowing expedition between them. Economically, it was a deal on the lines of the revived methods of exchange and barter. Gosling was willing to exchange certain advantages of knowledge and possession for the hire of wagons and horses. It was decided, for obvious reasons, to admit no other conspirator into the plot, and Boost, the coal merchant, drove one cart and Gosling drove the other. Perhaps it should rather be said that he led the other, for, after a preliminary trial, he decided that he was safer at the horses' heads than behind their tails.

The raid was conducted with perfect success. Boost had a head for essentials. The invaluable loads of tinned meats, fruits and vegetables were screened by tarpaulins from the possibly too envious eyes of hungry passers-by—quite a number of vagrants were to be seen in the streets on that day—and Boost and Gosling, disguised in coal-begrimed garments, made the return journey lugubriously calling, "Plague, plague," the cry of the drivers of the funeral carts which had even then become necessary. Their only checks were the various applications they received for the cartage of corpses; applications easily put on one side by pointing to the piled-up carts—they had spent six laborious hours in packing them. "No room; no room," they cried, and on that day the applicants who accosted Boost and Gosling were not the only ones who had to wait for the disposal of their dead.

Gosling arrived at Wisteria Grove, hot and outwardly jubilant, albeit with a horrible fear lurking in his mind that he had been in dangerous proximity to those tendered additions to his load. His booty was stored in one of the downstairs rooms with the assistance of Mrs Gosling and the two girls; they managed the unpacking without interruption in two hours and a half and then, with boarded windows and locked doors, the Goslings sat down to await the passing of horror.

Boost died of the plague forty-eight hours after the great adventure, but as he had a wife and four daughters his plunder was not wasted.

## 2

For nearly a fortnight after the raid the Goslings lay snug in their little house in Wisteria Grove, for they, in company with the majority of English people at this time, had not yet fully appreciated the fact that women were almost immune from infection. In all, not more than eight per cent of the whole female population was attacked, and of this proportion the mortality was almost exclusively among women over fifty years of age. When the first faint rumours of the plague had come to Europe, this curious, almost unprecedented, immunity of women had been given considerable prominence. It had made good copy, theories on the subject had appeared, and the point had aroused more interest than that of the mortality among males—infectious diseases were commonplace enough; this new phase had a certain novelty and piquancy. But the threat of European infection had overwhelmed the interest in the odd predilection of the unknown bacterium, and the more vital question had thrown this peculiarity into the background. Thus the Goslings and most other women feared attack no less than their husbands, brothers and sons, and found justification for their fears in the undoubted fact that women had died of the plague.

The Goslings had always jogged along amiably enough; their home life would have passed muster as a tolerably happy one. The head of the family was out of the house from 8.15 a.m. to 7.15 p.m. five days of the week, and it was only occasionally in the evening of some long wet Sunday that there was any open bickering.

Now, confinement in that little house, aggravated by fear and by the absence of any interest or diversion coming from outside, showed the family to one another in new aspects. Before two days had passed the air was tense with the suppressed irritation of these four people, held together by scarcely any tie other than that of a conventional affection.

By the third day the air was so heavily charged that some explosion was inevitable. It came early in the morning.

Gosling had run out of tobacco, and he thought in the circumstances that it would be wiser to send Blanche or Millie than to go himself. So, with an air of exaggerated carelessness, he said:

"Look here, Millie, my gel, I wish you'd just run out and see if you can get me any terbaccer."

"Not me," replied Millie, with decision.

"And why not?' asked Gosling.

Millie shrugged her shoulders, and called her sister, who was in the passage. "I say, B., father wants us to go out shopping for him. Are you on?"

Blanche, duster in hand, appeared at the doorway.

"Why doesn't he go himself?" she asked.

"Because," replied her father, getting very red, and speaking with elaborate care, "men's subject to the infection and women is not."

"That's all my eye," returned Millie. "Lots of women have got it."

"It's well known," said Gosling, still keeping himself in hand, "a matter of common knowledge, that women is comparatively immune."

"Oh, that's a man's yarn, that is," said Blanche, "just to save themselves. We all know what men are—selfish brutes!"

"Are you going to fetch me that terbaccer or are you not?" shouted Mr Gosling suddenly.

"No, we aren't," said Millie, defiantly. "It isn't safe for girls to go about the streets, let alone the risk of infection." She had heard her father shout before, and she was not, as yet, at all intimidated.

"Well, then, I say you are!" shouted her father. "Lazy, good-for-nothing creatures, the pair of you! 'Oose paid for everything you've eat or drunk or wore ever since you was born? An' now you won't even go an errand."

Then, seeing the ready retort rising to his daughters' lips, he grew desperate, and, advancing a step towards them, he said savagely: "If you don't go, I'll find a way to make yer!"

This was a new aspect, and the two girls were a little frightened. Natural instinct prompted them to scream for their mother.

She had been listening at the top of the stairs, and she answered the call for help with great promptitude.

"You ought to be ashamed of yourself, Gosling," she said, on a high note. "The streets isn't safe for gels, as you know well enough; and why should my gels risk their lives for the sake of your nasty, dirty, wasteful 'abit of smoking, I should like to know?"

Gosling's new-found courage was evaporating at the attack of this third enemy. He had been incensed against his daughters, but he had not yet overcome the habit of giving in to his wife, for the sake of peace. She had managed him very capably for a quarter of a century, but on the occasions when she had found it necessary to use what she called the "rough side of her tongue" she had demonstrated very clearly which of the two was master.

"I should have thought I might 'a been allowed a little terbaccer," he said, resentfully. "'Oo risked his life to lay in provisions, I should like to know? An' it's a matter o' common knowledge as women is immune from this plague."

"And Mrs Carter, three doors off, carried out dead of it the day before yesterday!" remarked Mrs Gosling, triumphantly.

"Oh, 'ere and there, a case or two," replied her husband. "But not one woman to a thousand men gets it, as every one knows."

"And how do you know I mightn't be the one?" asked Millie, bold now under her mother's protection.

For that morning, the matter remained in abeyance; but Gosling, muttering and grumbling, nursed his injury and meditated on the fact that his daughters had been afraid of him. Things were altered now. There was no convention to tie his hands. He would work himself into a protective passion and defy the three of them. Also, there was an unopened bottle of whisky in the sideboard.

Nevertheless, he would have put off the trial of his strength if he had had to seek an opportunity. He was, as yet, too civilized to take the initiative in cold blood.

The opportunity, however, soon presented itself in that house. The air had been little cleared by the morning's outbreak, and before evening the real explosion came. A mere trifle originated it a warning from Gosling that their store of provisions would not last for ever, and a sharp retort from Millie to the effect that her father did not stint himself, followed by a reminder from Mrs Gosling that the raid might be repeated.

"Oh! yes, you'd be willing enough for *me* to die of the plague, I've no doubt!" broke out Gosling. "*I* can walk six mile to get you pervisions, but you can't go to the corner of the street for my terbaccer."

"Pervisions is necessary, terbaccer ain't," said Mrs Gosling. She was not a clever woman. She judged this to be the right opportunity to keep her husband in his place, and relied implicitly on the quelling power of her tongue. Her intuitions were those of the woman who had lived all her life in a London suburb; they did not warn her that she was now dealing with a specimen of half-decivilized humanity.

"Oh! ain't it?" shouted Gosling, getting to his feet. His face was purple, and his pale blue eyes were starting from his head. "I'll soon show you what's necessary and what ain't, and 'oose master in this 'ouse. And *I* say terbaccer is necessary, an' what's more, one o' you three's goin' to fetch it quick! D'ye 'ear—one—o'—you—three!"

This inclusion of Mrs Gosling was, indeed, to declare war.

Millie and Blanche screamed and backed, but their mother rose to the occasion. She did not reserve herself; she began on her top note; but Gosling did not allow her to finish. He strode over to her and shook her by the shoulders, shouting to drown her strident recriminations. "'Old your tongue! 'old your tongue!" he bawled, and shook her with increasing violence. He was feeling his power, and when his wife crumpled up and fell to the floor in shrieking hysterics, he still strode on to victory. Taking the cowed and terrified Millie by the arm, he dragged her along the passage, unlocked and opened the front door and pushed her out into the street. "And don't you come back without my terbaccer!" he shouted.

"How much?" quavered the shrinking Millie.

"'Alf-a-crown's worth," replied Gosling fiercely, and tossed the coin down on the little tiled walk that led up to the front door.

After Millie had gone he stood at the door for a moment, thankful for the coolness of the air on his heated face. "I got to keep this up," he murmured to himself, with his first thought of wavering. Behind him he heard the sound of uncontrolled weeping and little cries of the "first time in twenty-four years" and "what the neighbours'll think, I don't know."

"Neighbours," muttered Gosling, contemptuously, "there aren't any neighbours—not to count."

A distant sound of slow wheels caught his ear. He listened attentively, and there came to him the remote monotonous chant of a dull voice crying: "Plague! Plague!"

He stepped in quickly and closed the door.

## 3

Millie found the Kilburn High Road deserted. No traffic of any kind was to be seen in the street, and the rare foot-passengers, chiefly women, had all a furtive air. Starvation had driven them out to raid. No easy matter, as Millie soon found, for all shutters were down, and in many cases shop-fronts were additionally protected by great sheets of strong hoarding.

Millie, recovering from her fright, was growing resentful. Her little conventional mind was greatly occupied by the fact that she was out in the High Road wearing house-shoes without heels, in an old print dress, and with no hat to hide the carelessness of her hair-dressing. At the corner of Wisteria Grove she stopped and tried to remedy this last defect; she had red hair, abundant and difficult to control.

The sight of the deserted High Road did not inspire her with self-confidence; she still feared the possibility of meeting some one who might recognize her. How could one account for one's presence in a London thoroughfare at seven o'clock on a bright May evening in such attire? Certainly not by telling the truth.

The air was wonderfully clear. Coal was becoming very scarce, and few fires had been lighted that day to belch forth their burden of greasy filth into the atmosphere. The sun was sinking, and Millie instinctively clung to the shadow of the pavement on the west side of the road. She, too, slunk along with the evasive air that was common to the few other pedestrians, the majority of them on this same shadowed pavement. That warm, radiant light on the houses opposite seemed to hold some horror for them.

So preoccupied was Millie with her resentment that she wandered for two or three hundred yards up the road without any distinct idea of what she was seeking. When realization of the futility of her search came to her, she stopped in the shadow of a doorway. "What *is* the good of going on?' she argued. "All the shops are shut up." But the thought of her father in his new aspect of muscular tyrant intimidated her. She dared not return without accomplishing her errand. "I'll have another look, anyway," she said; and then: "Who'd have thought he was such a brute?" She rubbed the bruise on her arm; her mouth was twisted into an ugly expression of spiteful resentment. Her thoughts were busy with plans of revenge even as she turned to prosecute her search for the tyrant's tobacco.

Here and there shops had been forcibly, burglariously entered, plate-glass windows smashed, and interiors cleared of everything eatable; the debris showed plainly enough that these rifled shops had all belonged to grocers or provision merchants. Into each of these ruins Millie stared curiously, hoping foolishly that she might find what she sought. She ventured into one and carried away a box of soap—they were running short of soap at home. A sense of moving among accessible riches stirred within her, a desire for further pillage.

She came at last to a shop where the shutters were still intact, but the door hung drunkenly on one hinge. A little fearfully she peered in and discovered that fortune had been kind to her. The shop had belonged to a tobacconist, and the contents were almost untouched—there had been more crying needs to satisfy in the households of raiders than the desire for tobacco.

It was very dark inside, and for some seconds Millie stared into what seemed absolute blackness, but as her eyes became accustomed to the gloom, she saw the interior begin to take outline, and when she moved a couple of steps into the place and allowed more light to come in through the doorway, various tins, boxes and packets in the shelves behind the counter were faintly distinguishable.

Once inside, the spirit of plunder took hold of her, and she began to take down boxes of cigars and cigarettes and packets of tobacco, piling them up in a heap on the counter. But she had no basket in which to carry the accumulation she was making, and she was feeling under the counter for some box into which to put her haul, when the shadows round her deepened again into almost absolute darkness. Cautiously she peered up over the counter and saw the silhouette of a woman standing in the doorway.

For ten breathless seconds Millie hung motionless, her eyes fixed on the apparition. She was very civilized still, and she was suddenly conscious of committing a crime. She feared horribly lest the figure in the doorway might discover Millicent Gosling stealing tobacco. But the intruder, after recognizing the nature of the shop's contents, moved away with a sigh. Millie heard her dragging footsteps shuffle past the window.

That scare decided her movements. She hastily looped up the front of her skirt, bundled into it as much plunder as she could conveniently carry, and made her way out into the street again.

She was nearly at the corner of Wisteria Grove before she was molested, and then an elderly woman came suddenly out of a doorway and laid a hand on Millie's arm.

"Whacher got?" asked the woman savagely.

Millie, shrinking and terrified, displayed her plunder.

"Cigars," muttered the woman. "Whacher want with cigars?" She opened the boxes and stirred up the contents of Millie's improvised bundle in an eager search for something to eat. "Gawd's truth! yer must be crazy, yer thievin' little slut!" she grumbled, and pushed the girl fiercely from her.

Millie made good her escape, dropping a box of cigars in her flight. Her one thought now was the fear of meeting a policeman. In three minutes she was beating fiercely on the door of the little house in Wisteria Grove, and, disregarding her father's exclamations of pleased surprise when he let her in, she tumbled in a heap on to the mat in the passage.

Gosling's first declaration of male superiority had been splendidly successful.

## 4

A few minutes after Millie's return, Mrs Gosling, red-eyed and timidly vicious, interrupted her husband's perfect enjoyment of the long-desired cigar by the announcement: "The gas is off!"

Gosling got up, struck a match, and held it to the sitting-room burner. The match burned steadily. There was no pressure even of air in the pipes.

"Turned off at the meter!" snapped Gosling. "'Ere, lemme go an' see!" He spoke with the air of the superior male, strong in his comprehension of the mechanical artifices which so perplex the feminine mind. Mrs Gosling sniffed, and stood aside to let him pass. She had already examined the meter.

"Well, we got lamps!" snarled Gosling when he returned. He had always preferred a lamp to read by in the evening.

"No oil," returned Mrs Gosling, gloomily. She'd teach him to shake her!

Gosling meditated. His parochial mind was full of indignation. Vague thoughts of "getting some one into trouble for this"—even of that last, desperate act of coercion, writing to the papers about it—flitted through his mind. Plainly something must be done. "'Aven't you got any candles?" he asked.

"One or two. They won't last long," replied his studiously patient partner.

"Well, we'll 'ave to use them to-night and go to bed early," was Gosling's final judgment. His wife left the room with a shrug of forbearing contempt.

When she had gone, the head of the house went upstairs and peered out into the street. The sun had set, and an unprecedented mystery of darkness was falling over London. The globes of the tall electric standards, catching a last reflection from the fading sky, glimmered faintly, but were not illuminated from within by any fierce glare of violet light. Darkness and silence enfolded the great dim organism that sprawled its vast being over the earth. The spirit of mystery caught Gosling in its spell. "All dark," he murmured, "and quiet! Lord! how still it is!" Even in his own house there was silence. Downstairs, three injured, resentful women were talking in whispers.

Gosling, still sucking his cigar, stood entranced, peering into the darkness; he had ventured so far as to throw up the sash. "It's the stillness of death!" he muttered. Then he cocked his head on one side, for he caught the sound of distant shouting. Somewhere in the Kilburn Road another raid was in progress.

"No light," murmured Gosling, "and no fire!"

An immediate association suggested itself. "By gosh! and no *water!*" he added. For some seconds he contemplated with fearful awe the failure of the great essential of life. In the cistern room he was reassured by the sound of a delicious trickle from the ball-cock. "Still going," he said to himself; "but we'll 'ave to be careful. Surely they'll keep the water goin', though; whatever 'appens, they'd surely keep the water on?"

## 5

Nothing but the failure of the water could have driven them from Wisteria Grove. Half-a-dozen times every day Gosling would climb up to the top of the house to reassure himself. And at last came the day when a dreadful silence reigned under the slates, when no delicious tinkle of water gave promise of maintained security from water famine.

"It'll come on again at night," said Gosling to himself. "We'll 'ave to be careful, that's all."

He went downstairs and issued orders that no more water was to be drawn that day.

"Well, we must wash up the breakfast things," was his wife's reply.

"You mustn't wash up nothing," said Gosling, "not one blessed thing. It's better to go dirty than die o' thirst. Hevery drop o' the water in that cistern must be saved for drinkin'."

Mrs Gosling noisily put down the kettle she was holding. "Oh! very well, my lord!" she remarked, sarcastically. She looked at her two daughters with a twist of her mouth. There were only two sides in that house; the women were as yet united against the common foe.

When Gosling, fatuously convinced of his authority, had gone, his wife quietly filled the kettle and proceeded with her washing up.

"Your father thinks 'e knows everything these days," remarked the mother to her allies.

There was much whispering for some time.

Gosling spent most of the day in the roof, but not until the afternoon did he realize that the cistern was slowly being emptied. His first thought was that one of the pipes leaked, his second that it was time to make a demonstration of force. He found a walking-stick in the hall....

But even when that precious half-cistern of water was only called upon to supply the needs of thirst, and the Goslings, sinking further into the degradation of savagedom, slunk furtive and filthy about the gloomy house, it became evident that a move must be made sooner or later. Two alternatives were presented: they might go north and east to the Lea, or south to the Thames.

Gosling chose the South. He knew Putney; he had been born there. He knew nothing of Clapton and its neighbourhood.

So one bright, clear day at the end of May, the Goslings set out on their great trek. The head of the house, driven desperate by fear of thirst, raided his late partner's coal sheds and found one living horse and several dead ones. The living horse was partly revived by water from an adjacent butt, and the next day it was harnessed to a coal cart and commandeered to convey the Goslings' provisions to Putney. It died half-a-mile short of their destination, but they were able, by the exercise of their united strength, to get the cart and its burden down to the river.

They found an empty house without difficulty, but they had an unpleasant half-hour in removing what remained of one of the previous occupants. Gosling hoped it was not a case of plague. As the body was that of a woman, and terribly emaciated, there were some grounds for his optimism.

Gosling was in a state of some bewilderment. When water had been fetched in buckets from the river, and the three women had explored, criticized and sniffed over their new home somewhat in the manner of strange cats, the head of the house settled down to a cigar and a careful consideration of his perplexities.

In the first place, he wondered why those horses of Boost's had not been used for food; in the second, he wondered why he had not seen a single man during the whole of the long trek from Brondesbury to Putney. By degrees an unbelievable explanation presented itself: no men were left. He remembered that the few needy-looking women he had seen had looked at him curiously; in retrospect he fancied their regard had had some quality of amazement. Gosling scratched the bristles of his ten-days'-old beard and smoked thoughtfully. He almost regretted that he had stared so fiercely and threateningly at every chance woman they had seen; he might have got some news. But the whole journey had been conducted in a spirit of fear; they had been defending their food, their lives; they had been primitive creatures ready to fight desperately at the smallest provocation.

"No man left," said Gosling to himself, and was not convinced. If that indeed were the solution of his perplexity, he was faced with an awful corollary; his own time would come. He thought of Barbican, E.C., of Flack, of Messrs Barker and Prince, of the office staff, and the office itself. He had not been able to rid his mind of the idea that in a few weeks he would be back in the City again. He had several times rehearsed his surprise when he should be told of the depredations in the warehouse; he had wondered only yesterday if he dared go to the office in his beard.

But to-night the change of circumstance, the breaking up of old associations, was opening his eyes to new horizons. There might never be an office again for him to go to. If he survived—and he was distinctly hopeful on that score he might be almost the only man left in London; there might not be more than a few thousand in the whole of England, in Europe....

For a time he dwelt on this fantastic vision. Who would do the work? What work would there be to do?

"Got to get food," murmured Gosling, and wondered vaguely how food was "got" when there were no shops, no warehouses, no foreign agents. His mind turned chiefly to meat, since that had been his trade. "'Ave to rear sheep and cattle, I suppose," said Gosling. As an afterthought he added: "An' grow wheat."

He sighed heavily. He realized that he had no knowledge on the subject of rearing cattle and growing wheat; he also realized that he was craving for ordinary food again milk, eggs, and fresh vegetables. He had a nasty-looking place on his leg which he rightly attributed to unwholesome diet.

## 6

After forty-eight hours' residence in the new house, Gosling began to pluck up his courage and to dare the perils of the streets. He was beginning to have faith in his luck, to believe that the plague had passed away and left him untouched.

And as day succeeded day he ventured further afield; he went in search of milk, eggs and vegetables, but he only found young nettles, which he brought home and helped to eat when they had been boiled over a wood fire. They were all glad to eat nettles, and were the better for them. Occasionally he met women on these excursions, and stayed to talk to them. Always they had the same tale to tell—their men were dead, and themselves dying of starvation.

One day at the beginning of June he went as far as Petersham, and there at the door of a farmhouse he saw a fine, tall young woman. She was such a contrast to the women he usually met on his expeditions that he paused and regarded her with curiosity.

"What do *you* want?" asked the young woman, suspiciously.

"I suppose you 'aven't any milk or butter or eggs to sell?" asked Gosling.

"Sell?" echoed the girl, contemptuously. "What 'ave you got to give us as is worth food?"

"Well, money," replied Gosling.

"Money!" came the echo again. "What's the good of money when there's nothing to buy with it? I wouldn't sell you eggs at a pound apiece."

Gosling scratched his beard it looked quite like a beard by this time. "Rum go, ain't it?" he asked, and smiled.

His new acquaintance looked him up and down, and then smiled in return, "You're right," she said. "You're the first man I've seen since father died, a month back."

" 'Oo's livin' with you?" asked Gosling, pointing to the house.

"Mother and sister, that's all."

" 'Ard work for you to get a livin', I suppose?"

"So, so. We're used to farm-work. The trouble's to keep the other women off."

"Ah!" replied Gosling reflectively, and the two looked at one another again.

"You 'ungry?" asked the girl.

"Not to speak of," replied Gosling. "But I'm fair pinin' for a change o' diet. Been livin' on tinned things for five weeks or more."

"Come in and have an egg," said the girl.

"Thank you," said Gosling, "I will, with pleasure."

They grew friendly over that meal two eggs and a glass of milk. He ate the eggs with butter, but there was no bread. It seemed that the young woman's mother and sister were at work on the farm, but that one of them had always to stay at home and keep guard.

They discussed the great change that had come over England, and wondered what would be the end of it; and after a little time, Gosling began to look at the girl with a new expression in his pale blue eyes.

"Ah! Hevrything's changed," he said. "Nothin' won't be the same any more, as far as we can see. There's no neighbours now, f'rinstance, and no talk of what's going on—or anythin'."

The girl looked at him thoughtfully. "What we miss is some man to look after the place," she said. "We're robbed terrible."

Gosling had not meant to go as far as that. He was not unprepared for a pleasant flirtation, now that there were no neighbours to report him at home, but the idea that he could ever separate himself permanently from his family had not occurred to him.

"Yes," he said, "you want a man about these days."

"Ever done any farm work?" asked the girl.

Gosling shook his head.

"Well, you'd soon learn," she went on.

"I must think it over," said Gosling suddenly. "Shall you be 'ere to-morrow?"

"One of us will," said the girl.

"Ah! but shall *you*?"

"Why me?"

"Well, I've took a fancy to you."

"Very kind of you, I'm sure," said the girl, and laughed.

Gosling kissed her before he left.

He returned the next afternoon and helped to cut and stack sainfoin, and afterwards he watched the young woman milk the cows. It was so late by the time everything was finished that he was persuaded to stay the night.

In the new Putney house three women wondered what had happened to "father." They grew increasingly anxious for some days, and even tried in a feeble way to search for him. By the end of the week they accepted the theory that he too had died of the plague.

They never saw him again.

## CHAPTER 10
*Exodus*

### 1

IN WEST HAMPSTEAD a Jewess, who had once been fat, looked out of the windows of her gaudy house. She was partly dressed in a garish silk neglige. Her face was exceedingly dirty, but the limp, pallid flesh was revealed in those places where she had wiped away her abundant tears. Her body was bruised and stiff, for in a recent raid on a house suspected of containing provisions she had been hardly used by her sister women. She had made the mistake of going out too well dressed; she had imagined that expensive clothes would command respect....

As she looked out she wept again, bewailing her misery. From her earliest youth she had been pampered and spoilt. She had learnt that marriage was her sole object in life, and she had sold herself at a very respectable price. She had received the applause and favour of her family for marrying the man she had chosen as most likely to provide her with the luxury which she regarded as her birthright.

Two days ago she had cooked and eaten the absurdly expensive but diminutive dog upon which she had lavished the only love of which she had been capable. She had wept continuously as she ate her idol, but for the first time she had regretted his littleness.

Hunger and thirst were driving her out of the house of which she had been so vain; the primitive pains were awakening in her primitive instincts that had never stirred before. From her window she could see naught but endless streets of brick, stone and asphalt, but beyond that dry, hot, wilderness she knew there were fields—she had seen them out of the corner of her eye when she had motored to Brighton. Fields had never been associated in her mind with food until the strange new stirring of that unsuspected instinct. Food for her meant shops. One went to shops and bought food and bought the best at the lowest price possible. With all her pride of position, she had never hesitated to haggle with shopkeepers. And when the first pinch had come, when her husband had selfishly died of the plague, and her household had deserted her, it was to the shops she had gone, autocratically demanding her rights. She had learned by experience now that she had no longer any rights.

She dressed herself in her least-conspicuous clothes, dabbed her face with powder to cover some of the dirt—there was no water, and in any case she did not feel inclined to wash—carefully stowed away all her money and the best of her jewels in a small leather bag, and set out to find the country where food grew out of the ground. Instinct set her face to the north. She took the road towards Hendon....

## 2

In every quarter of London, in every great town and city throughout Europe, women were setting their faces towards the country.

By the autumn London was empty. The fallen leaves in park squares and suburban streets were swept into corners by the wind, and when the rain came the leaves clung together and rotted, and so continued the long routine of decay and birth.

When spring came again, Nature returned with delicate, strong hands to claim her own. For hundreds of years she had been defied in the heart of this great, hard, stone place. Her little tentative efforts had been rudely repulsed, no tender thread of grass had been allowed to flourish for an hour under the feet of the crushing multitude. Yet she had fought with a steady persistence that never relaxed a moment's effort. Whenever men had given her a moment's opportunity, even in the very heart of that city of burning struggle, she had covered the loathed sterility with grass and flowers, dandelions, charlock, grounsel and other life that men call weeds.

Now, when her full opportunity came, she set to work in her slow, patient way to wreck and cover the defilement of earth. Her winds swept dust into every corner, and her rain turned it into a shallow bed of soil, ready to receive and nurture the tiny seeds that sailed on little feathered wings, or were carried by bird and insect to some quiet refuge in which they might renew life, and, dying, add fertility to the mother who had brought them forth.

Nature came, also, with her hurricanes, her lightnings and her frosts, to rend and destroy. She stripped slates from roofs, thrust out gables and overturned solid walls. She came with fungi to undermine and with the seeds of trees to split asunder.

She asked for but a few hundred years of patient, continuous work in order to make of London once more a garden; where the nightingale might sing in Oxford Street and the children of a new race pluck sweet wild flowers over the site of the Bank of England....

## 3

The spirit of London had gone out of her, and her body was crumbling and rotting. There was no life in all that vast sprawl of bricks and mortar; the very dogs and cats, deserted by humanity, left her to seek their only food, to seek those other living things which were their natural quarry.

In her prime, London had been the chief city of the world. Men and women spoke of her as an entity, wrote of her as of a personality, loved her as a friend. This aggregate of streets and parks, this strange confusion of wealth and squalor, had stood to men and women for something definitely lovable. It was not her population they loved, not the polyglot crowd that swarmed in her streets, but she herself and all the beauty and intoxication of life she had gathered into her embrace.

Now she was dead. Whatever fine qualities she had possessed, whatever vices, had gone from her. She sprawled in all her naked ugliness, a huge corpse rotting among the hills, awaiting the slow burial which Nature was tediously preparing.

All those wonderful buildings, the great emporiums in the West End, the magnificent banks and insurance offices, museums and picture galleries, regarded as the storehouses of incalculable wealth, vast hotels, palatial private residences, the thundering railway termini, Government offices, Houses of Parliament, theatres, churches and cathedrals, all had become meaningless symbols. All had represented some activity, some ambition of man, and man had fled to the country for food, leaving behind the worthless tokens of wealth that had intrigued him for so many centuries.

Gold and silver grew tarnished in huge safes that none wished to rifle, banknotes became mildewed, damp and fungus crept into the museums and picture galleries, and in the whole of Great Britain there was none to grieve. Every living man and woman was back at the work of their ancestors, praying once more to Ceres or Demeter, working with bent back to produce the first essentials of life.

Each individual must produce until such time as there was once more a superfluity, until barns were filled and wealth re-created, until the strong had seized from the weak and demanded labour in return for the use of the stolen instrument, until civilization had sprung anew from the soil.

Meanwhile London was not a city of the dead, but a dead city.

# BOOK II

## THE MARCH OF THE GOSLINGS

# CHAPTER 11

*The Silent City*

1

JULY CAME IN with temperate heat and occasional showers, ideal weather for the crops; for all the precious growths which must ripen before the famine could be stayed. The sudden stoppage of all imports, and the flight of the great urban population into the country, had demonstrated beyond all question the poverty of England's resources of food supply, and the demonstration was to prove of value although there was no economist left to theorize. England was once again an independent unit, and no longer a member of a great world-body. Indeed England was being subdivided. The unit of organization was shrinking with amazing rapidity. The necessity for concentration grew with every week that passed, the fluidity of the superfluous labour was being resolved by death from starvation. The women who wandered from one farm to the next died by the way.

In the Putney house, Mrs Gosling and her daughters were faced by the failure of their food supply. The older woman had little initiative. She was a true Londoner. Her training and all the circumstances of her life had narrowed her imaginative grasp till she was only able to comprehend one issue. And as yet her daughters, and more particularly Millie, were so influenced by their mother's thought that they, also, had shown little evidence of adaptability to the changed conditions.

"We shall 'ave to be careful," was Mrs Gosling's first expression of the necessity for looking to the future. She had arranged the bulk of her stores neatly in one room on the second floor, and although a goodly array of tins still faced her she experienced a miserly shrinking from any diminishment of their numbers. Moreover, she had long been without such necessities as flour. Barker and Prince had not dealt in flour.

Returning from her daily inspection one morning in the second week of July, Mrs Gosling decided that something must be done at once. Fear of the plague was almost dead, but fear of invasion by starving women had kept them all close prisoners. That house was a fortress.

"Look 'ere, gels," said Mrs Gosling when she came downstairs. "Somethin' 'll 'ave to be done."

Blanche looked thoughtful. Her own mind had already begun to work on that great problem of their future. Millie, lazy and indifferent, shrugged her shoulders and replied: "All very well, mother, but what can we do?"

"Well, I been thinking as it's very likely as things ain't so bad in some places as they are just about 'ere," said Mrs Gosling. "We got plenty o' money left, and it seems to me as two of us 'ad better go out and 'ave a look about, London way. One of us could look after the 'ouse easy enough, now. We 'aven't 'ardly seen a soul about the past fortnight."

The suggestion brought a gleam of hope to Blanche. She visualized the London she had known. It might be that in the heart of the town, business had begun again, that shops were open and people at work. It might be that she could find work there. She was longing for the sight and movement of life, after these two awful months of isolation.

"I'm on," she said briskly. "Me and Millie had better go, mother, we can walk farther. You can lock up after us and you needn't open the door to anyone. Are you on, Mill?"

"We must make ourselves look a bit more decent first," said Millie, glancing at the mirror over the mantelpiece.

"Well, of course," returned Blanche, "we brought one box of clothes with us."

They spent some minutes in discussing the resources of their wardrobe.

"Come to the worst we could fetch some more things from Wisteria. I don't suppose anyone has touched 'em," suggested Blanche.

At the mention of the house in Wisteria Grove, Mrs Gosling sighed noticeably. She was by no means satisfied with the place at Putney, and she could not rid herself of the idea that there must be accessible gas and water in Kilburn, as there had always been.

"Well, you might go up there one day and 'ave a look at the place," she put in. "It's quite likely they've got things goin' again up there."

In less than an hour Blanche and Millie had made themselves presentable. Life had begun to stir again in humanity. The atmosphere of horror which the plague had brought was being lifted. It was as if the dead germs had filled the air with an invisible, impalpable dust, that had exercised a strange power of depression. The spirit of death had hung over the whole world and paralyzed all activity. Now the dust was dispersing. The spirit was withdrawing to the unknown deeps from which it had come.

"It is nice to feel decent again," said Blanche. She lifted her head and threw back her shoulders.

Millie was preening herself before the glass.

"Well, I'm sure you *'ave* made yourselves look smart," said their mother with a touch of pride. "They were good girls," she reflected, "if there had been more than a bit of temper shown lately. But, then, who could have helped themselves? It had been a terrible time."

The July sun was shining brilliantly as the two young women, presentable enough to attend morning service at the Church of St John the Evangelist, Kilburn, set out to exhibit their charms and to buy food in the dead city.

## 2

They crossed Putney Bridge and made their way towards Hammersmith.

The air was miraculously clear. The detail of the streets was so sharp and bright that it was as if they saw with wonderfully renewed and sensitive eyes. The phenomenon produced a sense of exhilaration. They were conscious of quickened emotion, of a sensation of physical well-being.

"Isn't it *clean*?" said Blanche.

"H'm! Funny!" returned Millie. "Like those photographs of foreign places."

Under their feet was an accumulation of sharp, dry dust, detritus of stone, asphalt and steel. In corners where the fugitive rubbish had found refuge from the driving wind, the dust had accumulated in flat mounds, broken by scraps of paper or the torn flag of some rain-soaked poster that gave an untidy air of human refuse. Across the open way of certain roads the dust lay in a waved pattern of nearly parallel lines, like the ridged sand of the foreshore.

For some time they kept to the pavements from force of habit.

"I say, Mill, don't you feel adventurous?" asked Blanche.

Millie looked dissatisfied. "It's so lonely, B.," was her expression of feeling.

"Never had London all to myself before," said Blanche.

Near Hammersmith Broadway they saw a tram standing on the rails. Its thin tentacle still clung to the overhead wire that had once given it life, as if it waited there patiently hoping for a renewal of the exhilarating current.

Almost unconsciously Blanche and Millie quickened their pace. Perhaps this was the outermost dying ripple of life, the furthest outpost of the new activity that was springing up in central London.

But the tram was guarded by something that in the hot, still air seemed to surround it with an almost visible mist.

"Eugh!" ejaculated Millie and shrank back. "Don't go, Blanche. It's awful!"

Blanche's hand also had leapt to her face, but she took a few steps forward and peered into the sunlit case of steel and glass. She saw a heap of clothes about the framework of a grotesquely jointed scarecrow, and the gleam of something round, smooth and white.

She screamed faintly, and a filthy dog crept, with a thin yelp, from under the seat and came to the door of the tram. For a moment it stood there with an air that was half placatory, wrinkling its nose and feebly raising a stump of propitiatory tail, then, with another protesting yelp, it crept back, furtive and ashamed, to its unlawful meat.

The two girls, handkerchief to nose, hurried by breathless, with bent heads. A little past Hammersmith Broadway they had their first sight of human life. Two gaunt faces looked out at them from an upper window. Blanche waved her hand, but the women in the house, half-wondering, half-fearful, at the strange sight of these two fancifully dressed girls, shook their heads and drew back. Doubtless there was some secret hoard of food in that house and the inmates feared the demands of charity.

"Well, we aren't quite the last, anyway," commented Blanche.

"What were they afraid of?" asked Millie.

"Thought we wanted to cadge, I expect," suggested Blanche.

"Mean things," was her sister's comment.

"Well! *We* weren't so over-anxious to have visitors," Blanche reminded her.

"*We* didn't want their beastly food," complained the affronted Millie.

The shops in Hammersmith did not offer much inducement to exploration. Some were still closely shuttered, others presented goods that offered no temptation, such as hardware; but the majority had already been pillaged and devastated. Most of that work had been done in the early days of the plague when panic had reigned, and many men were left to lead the raids on the preserves of food.

Only one great line of shuttered fronts induced the two girls to pause.

"No need to go to Wisteria for clothes," suggested Blanche.

"How could we get in?" asked Millie.

"Oh! get in some way easy enough."

"It's stealing," said Millie, and thought of her raid on the Kilburn tobacconist's.

"You can't steal from dead people," explained Blanche; "besides, who'll have the things if we don't?"

"I suppose it'd be all right," hesitated Millie, obviously tempted.

"Well, of course," returned Blanche and paused. "I say, Mill," she burst out suddenly. "There's all the West-end to choose from. Come on!"

For a time they walked more quickly.

In Kensington High Street they had an adventure.

They saw a woman decked in gorgeous silks, strung and studded with jewels from head to foot. She walked with a slow and flaunting step, gesticulating, and talking. Every now and again she would pause and draw herself up with an affectation of immense dignity, finger the ropes of jewels at her breast, and make a slow gesture with her hands.

"She's mad," whispered Blanche, and the two girls, terrified and trembling, hastily took refuge in a great square cave full of litter and refuse that had once been a grocer's shop.

The woman passed their hiding-place in her stately progress westward without giving any sign that she was conscious of their presence. When she was nearly opposite to them she made one of her stately pauses. "Queen of all the Earth," they heard her say, "Queen and Empress. Queen of the Earth." Her hand went up to her head and touched a strange collection of jewels pinned in her hair, of tiaras and brooches that flashed brighter than the high lights of the brilliant sun. One carelessly fastened brooch fell and she pushed it aside with her foot. "You understand," she said in her high, wavering voice, "you understand, Queen and Empress, Queen of the Earth."

They heard the refrain of her gratified ambition repeated as she moved slowly away.

A long submerged memory rose to the threshold of Millie's mind. "Thieving slut," she murmured.

## 3

As they came nearer to representative London the signs of deserted traffic were more numerous. By the Albert Memorial they saw an overturned motor-bus which had smashed into the park railings, and a little further on were two more buses, one standing decently at the curb, the other sprawling across the middle of the road. The wheels of both were axle deep in the dust which had blown against them, and out of the dust a few weak threads of grass were sprouting. There were other vehicles, too, cabs, lorries and carts: not a great number altogether, but even the fifty or so which the girls saw between Kensington and Knightsbridge offered sufficient testimony to the awful rapidity with which the plague had spread. For it seems probable that in the majority of cases the drivers of these deserted vehicles must have been attacked by the first agonizing pains at the base of the skull while they were actually employed in driving their machines. There were few skeletons to be seen. The lull which intervened between the first unmistakable symptoms of the plague and the oncoming of the paralysis had given men time to obey their instinct to die in seclusion, the old instinct so little altered by civilization. Those vestiges of humanity which remained had, for the most part, been cleansed by the processes of Nature, but twice the girls disturbed a horrible cloud of blue flies which rose with an angry buzzing so loud that the girls screamed and ran, leaving the scavengers to swoop eagerly back upon their carrion. Doubtless the thing in the Hammersmith tram had been the body of a woman, recently dead from starvation. Even from the houses there was now little exhalation.

In Knightsbridge, a little past the top of Sloane Street, Blanche and Millie came to a shop which diverted them from their exploration for a time. Most of the huge rolling shutters had been pulled down and secured, but one had stopped half way, and, beyond, the great plate-glass windows were uncovered. One of ten million tragedies had descended swiftly to interrupt the closing of that immense place, and some combination of circumstances had followed to prevent the completion of the work. The imaginative might stop to speculate on the mystery of that half-closed shutter; the two Goslings stopped to admire the wonders behind the glass.

For a time the desolation and silence of London were forgotten. In imagination Blanche and Millie were once again units in the vast crowd of antagonists striving valiantly to win some prize in the great competition between the boast of wealth and the pathetic endeavour of make-believe.

They stayed to gaze at the "creations" behind the windows, at dummies draped in costly fabrics such as they had only dreamed of wearing. The silks, satins and velvets were whitened now with the thin snow of dust that had fallen upon them, but to Blanche and Millie they appeared still as wonders of beauty.

For a minute or two they criticized the models. They spoke at first in low voices, for the deep stillness of London held them in unconscious awe, but as they became lost in the fascination of their subject they forgot their fear. And then they looked at one another a little guiltily.

"No harm in seeing if the door's locked, anyway," said Blanche.

Millie looked over her shoulder and saw no movement in the frozen streets, save the sweep of one exploring swallow. Even the sparrows had deserted the streets. She did not reply in words, but signified her agreement of thought by a movement towards the entrance.

The swing doors were not fastened, and they entered stealthily.

They began with the touch of appraising fingers, wandering from room to room. But most of the rooms on the ground floor were darkened by the drawn shutters, and no glow of light came in response to the clicking of the electric switches that they experimented with with persistent futility. So they adventured into the clearly lit rooms upstairs and experienced a fallacious sense of security in the knowledge that they were on the floor above the street.

Fingering gave place to still closer inspection. They lifted the models from the stands and shook them out. They held up gorgeous robes in front of their own suburban dresses and admired each other and themselves in the numerous cheval glasses.

"Oh! bother!" exclaimed Blanche at last, "I'm going to try on."

"Oh! B.," expostulated the more timid Millie.

"Well! why to goodness not?" asked her elder sister. "Who's to be any the wiser?"

"Seems wrong, somehow," replied Millie, unable to shake off the conventions which had so long served her as conscience.

"Well, I am," said Blanche, and retired into a little side room to divest herself of her own dress. She had always shared a bedroom with her sister, and they observed few modesties before each other, but Blanche was mentally incapable of changing her dress in the broad avenues of that extensive show-room. It is true that the tall casement windows were wide open and the place was completely overlooked by the massive buildings opposite, but even if the windows had been screened she would not have changed her skirt in the publicity of that open place, though every human being in the world were dead.

When she emerged from her dressing-room she was transformed indeed. She went over to her still hesitating sister.

"Do me up, Mill," she said.

Blanche had chosen well; the fine cloth walking dress admirably fitted her well-developed young figure. When she had discarded her hat and touched up her hair before the glass, only her boots and her hands remained to spoil the disguise. Well gloved and well shod, she might have passed down the Bond Street of the old London, and few women and no man would have known that she had not sprung from the ruling classes.

She posed. She stepped back from the mirror and half-unconsciously fell to imitating the manners of the revered aristocracy she had respectfully studied from a distance.

In a few minutes she was joined by Millie, also arrayed in peacock's feathers and anxious to be "fastened."

Their excitement increased. Walking dresses gave place to evening gowns. They lost their sense of fear and ran into other departments searching for long white gloves to hide the disfigurements of household work. They paraded and bowed to each other. The climax came when they discovered a Court dress, immensely trained, and embroidered with gold thread, laid by with evidences of tenderest care in endless wrappings of tissue paper. Surely the dress of some elegant young duchess!

For a moment they wrangled, but Blanche triumphed. "You shall have it afterwards," she said, as she ran to her dressing-room.

Millie followed in an elaborate gown of Indian silk; a somewhat sulky Millie, inclined to resent her duty of lady's maid. She dragged disrespectfully at the innumerable fastenings.

"My!" ejaculated Blanche when she could indulge herself in the glory of full examination before a cheval glass in the open show-room. She struggled with her train and when she had arranged it to her satisfaction, threw back her shoulders and lifted her chin haughtily.

"I ought to have some diamonds," she reflected.

"It drags round the hips," was Millie's criticism.

"You should say 'Your Majesty,'" corrected Blanche.

"Oh! a Queen, are you?" asked Millie.

"Rather—"

"Queen of all the Earth," sneered Millie.

Blanche's face suddenly fell. "I wonder if she began like this," she said, and a note of fear had come into her voice.

Millie's eyes reflected her sister's alarm.

"Oh! let's get out of this, B.," she said, and began to tear at the neck of her Indian silk gown.

"I wanted diamonds, too," persisted Blanche.

"Oh! B., it *isn't* right," said Millie. "I said it wasn't right and you *would* come."

Silence descended upon them for a moment, and then both sisters suddenly screamed and ducked, putting up their hands to their heads.

"Goodness! What was that?" cried Blanche.

A swallow had swept in through the open window, had curved round in one swift movement, and shot out again into the sunlight. "Only a bird of some sort," said Millie, but she was trembling and on the verge of hysterics. "Do let's get out, B."

After they had put on their own clothes once more they became aware that they were hungry.

"We have wasted a lot of time here," said Blanche as they made their way out.

She did not pause to wonder how many women had spent the best part of their lives in a precisely similar manner.

"And we ought to have been looking for food," she added.

"Come on," replied Millie. "That place has given me the creeps."

## 4

Growing rather tired and footsore they made their way to Piccadilly Circus, and so on to the Strand. Everywhere they found the same conditions: a few skeletons, a few deserted vehicles, young vegetation taking hold wherever a pinch of soil had found an abiding place, and over all a great silence. But food there was none that they were able to find, though it is probable that a careful investigation of cellars and underground places might have furnished some results. The more salient resources of London had been effectively pillaged so far as the West-end was concerned. They were too late.

In Trafalgar Square, Millie sat down and cried. Blanche made no attempt to comfort her, but sat wide eyed and wondering. Her mind was opening to new ideas. She was beginning to understand that London was incapable of supporting even the lives of three women; she was wrestling with the problem of existence. Everyone had gone. Many had died; but many more, surely, must have fled into the country. She began to understand that she and her family must also fly into the country.

Millie still sobbed convulsively now and again.

"Oh! Chuck it, Mill," said Blanche at last. "We'd better be getting home."

Millie dabbed her eyes. "I'm starving," she blubbered.

"Well, so am I," returned Blanche. "That's why I said we'd better get home. There's nothing to eat here."

"Is—is every one dead?"

"No, they've gone off into the country, and that's what we've got to do."

The younger girl sat up, put her hat straight, and blew her nose. "Isn't it awful, B.?" she said.

Blanche pinched her lips together. "What are you putting your hat straight for?" she asked. "There's no one to see you."

"Well, you needn't make it any worse," retorted Millie on the verge of a fresh outburst of tears.

"Oh! come on!" said Blanche, getting to her feet.

"I don't believe I can walk home," complained Millie; "my feet ache so."

"You'll have to wait a long time if you're going to find a bus," returned Blanche.

Three empty taxicabs stood in the rank a few feet away from them, but it never occurred to either of the two young women to attempt any experiment with these mechanisms. If the thought had crossed their minds they would have deemed it absurd.

"Let's go down by Victoria," suggested Blanche. "I believe it's nearer."

In Parliament Square they disturbed a flock of rooks, birds which had partly changed their natural habits during the past few months and, owing to the superabundance of one kind of food, were preying on carrion.

"Crows," commented Blanche. "Beastly things."

"I wonder if we could get some water to drink," was Millie's reply. "Well, there's the river," suggested Blanche, and they turned up towards Westminster Bridge.

In one of the tall buildings facing the river Blanche's attention was caught by an open door.

"Look here, Mill," she said, "we've only been looking for shops. Let's try one of these houses. We might find something to eat in there."

"I'm afraid," said Millie.

"What of?" sneered Blanche. "At the worst it's skeletons, and we can come out again."

Millie shuddered. "You go," she suggested.

"Not by myself, I won't," returned Blanche.

"There you are, you see," said Millie.

"Well, it's different by yourself."

"I hate it," returned Millie with emphasis.

"So do I, in a way, only I'm fair starving," said Blanche. "Come on."

The building was solidly furnished, and the ground floor, although somewhat disordered, still suggested a complacent luxury. On the floor lay a copy of the *Evening Chronicle*, dated May 10; possibly one of the last issues of a London journal. Two of the pages were quite blank, and almost the only advertisement was one hastily-set announcement of a patent medicine guaranteed as a sure protection against the plague. The remainder of the paper was filled with reports of the devastation that was being wrought, reports which were nevertheless marked by a faint spirit of simulated confidence. Between the lines could be read the story of desperate men clinging to hope with splendid courage. There were no signs of panic here. Groves had come out well at the last.

The two girls hovered over this piece of ancient history for a few minutes.

"You see," said Blanche triumphantly, "even then, more'n two months ago, every one was making for the country. We shall have to go, too. I told you we should."

"I never said we shouldn't," returned Millie. "Anyhow there's nothing to eat here."

"Not in this room, there isn't," said Blanche, "but there might be in the kitchens. Do you know what this place has been?"

Millie shook her head.

"It's been a man's club," announced Blanche. "First time you've been in one, old dear."

"Come on, let's have a look downstairs, then," returned Millie, careless of her achievement.

In the first kitchen they found havoc: broken china and glass, empty bottles, empty tins, cooking utensils on the floor, one table upset, everywhere devastation and the marks of struggle; but in none of the empty tins was there the least particle of food. Everything had been completely cleaned out. The rats had been there, and had gone.

Exploring deeper, however, they were at last rewarded. On a table stood a whole array of unopened tins and in one of them was plunged a tin-opener, a single stab had been given, and then, possibly, another of these common tragedies had begun. Had he been alone, that plunderer, or had his companions fled from him in terror?

Here the two girls made a sufficient meal, and discovered, moreover, a large store of unopened beer-bottles. They shared the contents of one between them, and then, feeling greatly reinvigorated, they sought for and found two baskets, which they filled with tinned foods. They only took away one bottle of beer—a special treat for their mother—on account of the weight. They remembered that they had a long walk before them; and they were not over-elated by their discovery; they were sick to death of tinned meats.

In looking for the baskets they came across a single potato that the rats had left. From it had sprung a long, thin, etiolated shoot which had crept under the door of the cupboard and was making its way across the floor to the light of the window. Already that shoot was several feet in length.

"Funny how they grow," commented Millie.

"Making for the country, I expect," replied Blanche, "same as we shall have to do."

It was a relief to them to find their way into the sunlight once more. Those cold, forsaken houses held some suggestion of horror, of old activities so abruptly ended by tragedy. From these interiors Nature was still shut off. That ghostly tendril aching towards the light had no chance for life and reproduction....

## 5

The two Gosling girls had yet one more adventure before they toiled home with their load.

They were growing bolder, despite the gloom and oppression of those human habitations, and some freakish spirit prompted Blanche to suggest that they should visit the Houses of Parliament. After a brief demur, Millie acceded.

That great stronghold was open to them now. They might walk the floor of the House, sit in the Speaker's chair, penetrate into the sacred places of the Upper Chamber.

Gone were all the rules and formulas, the intricacies and precedents of an unwritten constitution, the whole cumbrous machinery for the making of new laws. The air was no longer disturbed by the wranglings, evasions and cunning shifts of those who had found here a stage for their personal ambitions. The high talk of progress had died into silence along with the struggle of parties which had played the supreme game, side against side, for the prize of power. Progress had been defined in this place, in terms of human activity, human comfort. The end in sight had been some vague conception of general welfare through accumulated riches. And from the sky had fallen a pestilence to change the meaning of human terms. In three months the old conception of wealth was gone. Money, precious stones, a thousand accepted forms of value had become suddenly worthless, of no more account than the symbol of power which lay coated with dust on the table of the House of law-makers. Even law itself, that slow growth of the centuries, had become meaningless. Who cared if some mad woman plundered every jeweller's shop in the whole City? Who was to forbid theft or avenge murder? The place of traffic was empty. Only one law was left and only one value; the law of self-preservation, the value of food.

The sunlight fell in broad coloured shafts upon two half-educated girls come on a plundering expedition, and they might sit in the high places if they would, and make new laws for themselves.

Blanche sat for a few moments in the Speaker's chair.

"It's a fine big place," she remarked.

"Oh! come on, B., do," replied Millie. "I want to get home."

As they crossed the Square, Millie looked up at Big Ben. "Quarter-past nine," she said. "It must have stopped."

"Well, of course, silly," replied Blanche. "All the clocks have stopped. Who's to wind 'em?"

# CHAPTER 12

*Emigrant*

## 1

For some time Mrs Gosling was quite unable to grasp the significance of her daughters' report on the condition of London. During the past two months she had persuaded herself that the traffic of the town was being resumed and that only Putney was still desolate. She had always disapproved of Putney; it was damp and she had never known anyone who had lived there. It is true that the late lamented George Gosling had been born in Putney, but that was more than half a century ago, the place was no doubt quite different then; and he had left Putney and gone to live in the healthy North before he was sixteen. Mrs Gosling was half inclined to blame Putney for all their misfortunes—it was sure to breed infection, being so near the river and all—and she had become hopeful during the past month that all would be well with them if they could once get back to Kilburn.

"D'you mean to say you didn't see no one at all?" she repeated in great perplexity.

"Those three we've told you about, that's all," said Blanche.

"Well, o' course, they're all shut up in the 'ouses, still; afraid o' the plague and 'anging on to what provisions they've got put by, same as us," was the hopeful explanation Mrs Gosling put forward.

"They ain't," said Millie, and Blanche agreed.

"Well, but 'ow d'you know?" persisted the mother. "Did you go in to the 'ouses?"

"One or two," returned Blanche evasively, "but there wasn't no need to go in. You could see."

"Are you quite sure there was no shops open? Not in the Strand?" Mrs Gosling laid emphasis on the last sentence. She could not doubt the good faith of the Strand. If that failed her, all was lost.

"Oh! can't you understand, mother," broke out Blanche petulantly, "that the whole of London is absolutely deserted? There isn't a soul in the streets. There's no cabs or buses or trams or anything, and grass growing in the middle of the road. And all the shops have been broken into, all those that had food in 'em, and—" words failed her. "Isn't it, Millie?" she concluded lamely.

"Awful," agreed Millie.

"Well, I can't understand it," said Mrs Gosling, not yet fully convinced. She considered earnestly for a few moments and then asked: "Did you go into Charing Cross Post Office? They'd sure to be open."

"Yes!" lied Blanche, "and we could have taken all the money in the place if we'd wanted, and no one any the wiser."

Mrs Gosling looked shocked. "I 'ope my gels'll never come to that," she said. Her girls, with a wonderful understanding of their mother's opinions, had omitted to mention their raid on the Knightsbridge emporium.

"No one'd ever know," said Millie.

"There's One who would," replied Mrs Gosling gravely, and strangely enough, perhaps, the two girls looked uneasy, but they were thinking less of the commandments miraculously given to Moses than of the probable displeasure of the Vicar of St John the Evangelist's Church in Kilburn.

"Well, we've got to do something, anyhow," said Blanche, after a pause. "I mean we'll have to get out of this and go into the country."

"We might go to your uncle's in Liverpool," suggested Mrs Gosling, tentatively.

"It's a long walk," remarked Blanche.

Mrs Gosling did not grasp the meaning of this objection. "Well, I think we could afford third-class, she said. "Besides, though we 'aven't corresponded much of late years, I've always been under the impression that your uncle is doin' well in Liverpool; and at such a time as this I'm sure 'e'll do the right thing, though whether it would be better to let 'im know we're comin' or not I'm not quite sure."

"Oh! dear!" sighed Blanche, "I do wish you'd try to understand, mother. There aren't any trains. There aren't any posts or telegraphs. Wherever we go we've just got to walk. Haven't we, Millie?"

Millie began to snivel. "It's 'orrible," she said.

"Well, I can't understand it," repeated Mrs Gosling.

By degrees, however, the controversy took a new shape. Granting for the moment the main contention that London was uninhabitated, Mrs Gosling urged that it would be a dangerous, even a foolhardy, thing to venture into the country. If there was no Government there would be no law and order, was the substance of her argument; government in her mind being represented by its concrete presentation in the form of the utterly reliable policeman. Furthermore, she pointed out, that they did not know anyone in the country, with the exception of a too-distant uncle in Liverpool, and that there would be nowhere for them to go.

"We shall have to work," said Blanche, who was surely inspired by her glimpse of the silent city.

"Well, we've got nearly a 'undred pounds left of what your poor father drew out o' the bank before we shut ourselves up," said her mother.

"I suppose we *could* buy things in the country," speculated Blanche.

"You seem set on the country for some reason," said Mrs Gosling with a touch of temper.

"Well, we've got to get food," returned Blanche, raising her voice. "We can't live on air."

"And if food's to be got cheaper in the country than in London," snapped Mrs Gosling, "my experience goes for nothing, but, of course, you know best, if I *am* your mother."

"There isn't any food in London, cheap or dear, I keep telling you," said Blanche, and left the room angrily, slamming the door behind her.

Millie sat moodily biting her nails.

"Blanche lets 'er temper get the better of 'er," remarked Mrs Gosling addressing the spaces of the kitchen in which they were sitting.

"It's right, worse luck," said Millie. "We shall have to go. I 'ate it nearly as much as you do."

The argument thus begun was continued with few intermissions for a whole week. A thunderstorm, followed by two days of overcast weather, came to the support of the older woman. One thing was certain among all these terrible perplexities, namely, that you couldn't start off for a trip to the country on a wet day.

Meanwhile their stores continued to diminish, and one afternoon Mrs Gosling consented to take a walk with Blanche as far as Hammersmith Broadway.

The sight of that blank desert impressed her. Blanche pointed out the house in which she had seen the two women five days before, but no one was looking out of the window on that afternoon. Perhaps they had fled to the country, or were occupied elsewhere in the house, or perhaps they had left London by the easier way which had become so general in the past few months.

When she returned to the Putney house, Mrs Gosling wept and wished she, too, was dead, but she consented at last to Blanche's continually urged proposition, in so far as she expressed herself willing to make a move of some sort. She thought they might, at least, go back and have a look at Wisteria Grove. And if Kilburn had, indeed, fallen as low as Hammersmith, then there was apparently no help for it and they must try their luck in the waste and desolation of the country. Perhaps some farmer's wife might take them in for a time, until they had a chance to look about them. They had nearly a hundred pounds in gold.

The girls found a builder's trolley in a yard near by, a truck of sturdy build on two wheels with a long handle. It bore marks of having held cement, and there were weeds growing in one end of it, but after it had been brought home and thoroughly scrubbed, it looked quite a presentable means for the transport of the "necessaries" they proposed to take with them.

They made too generous an estimate of essentials at first, piling their truck too high for safety and overtaxing their strength; but that problem, like many others, was finally solved for them by the clear-sighted guidance of necessity.

They started one morning—a Monday if their calculations were not at fault—about two hours after breakfast. Mrs Gosling and Millie pushed behind, and Blanche, the inspired one, went before, pulled by the handle of the pole and gave the others their direction.

It is possible that they were the last women to leave London.

By chance they discovered the Queen of all the Earth on a doorstep near Addison Road. She was quite dead, but they did not despoil her of the jewels with which she was still covered.

## 2

Mrs Gosling was a source of trouble from the outset. She had lived her life indoors. In the Wisteria Grove days, she never spent two hours of the twenty-four out of the house. Some times for a whole week she had not gone out at all. It was a mark of their rise in the world that all the tradesmen called for orders. She had found little necessity to buy in shops during recent years. And so, very surely, she had grown more and more limited in her outlook. Her attention had become concentrated on the duties of the housewife. She had not kept any servant, a charwoman who came for a few hours three times a week had done all that the mistress of the house had not dared, in face of neighbourly criticism in her position she could not be seen washing down the little tiled path to the gate nor whitening the steps.

The effect of this cramped existence on Mrs Gosling would not have been noticeable under the old conditions. She had become a specialized creature, admirably adapted to her place in the old scheme of civilization. No demand was ever made upon her resources other than those familiar demands which she was so perfectly educated to supply. Even when the plague had come, she had not been compelled to alter her mode of life. She had made trouble enough about the lack of many things she had once believed to be necessary—familiar foods, soap and the thousand little conveniences that the twentieth century inventor had patented to assist the domestic economy of the small householder; but the trouble was not too great to be overcome. The adaptability required from her was within the scope of her specialized vision. She could learn to do without flour, butter, lard, milk, sugar and the other things, but she could not learn to think on unfamiliar lines.

That was the essence of her trouble. She was divorced from a permanent home. She was asked to walk long miles in the open air. Worst of all, she was called upon for initiative, ingenuity; she was required to exercise her imagination in order to solve a problem with which she was quite unfamiliar. She was expected to develop the potentialities of the wild thing, and to extort food from Nature. The whole problem was beyond her comprehension.

The sight of Kilburn was a great blow to her. She had hoped against hope that here, at least, she would find some semblance of the life she had known. It had seemed so impossible to her that Aiken, the butcher's, or Hobb's, the grocer's, would not be open as usual, and the vision of those two desolated and ransacked shops the latter with but a few murderous spears of plate-glass left in its once magnificent windows depressed her to tears.

So shaken was she by the sight of these horrors that Blanche and Millie raised no objection to sleeping that night in the house in Wisteria Grove. Indeed, the two girls were almost tired out, although it was yet early in the afternoon. The truck had become very heavy in the course of the last two miles; and they had had considerable difficulty in negotiating the hill by Westbourne Park Station.

Mrs Gosling was still weeping as she let herself in to her old home, and she wept as she prowled about the familiar rooms and noted the dust which had fallen like snow on every surface which would support it. And for the first time the loss of her husband came home to her. She had been almost glad when he had vanished from the Putney house in that place she had only seen him in his new character of tyrant. Here, among familiar associations, she recalled the fact that he had been a respectable, complacent, hard-working, successful man who had never given her cause for trouble, a man who did not drink nor run after other women, who held a position in the Church and was looked up to by the neighbourhood. According to her definition he had certainly been an ideal husband. It is true that they had dropped any pretence of being in love with one another after Blanche was born, but that was only natural.

Mrs Gosling sat on the bed she had shared with him so long and hoped he was happy. He was; but if she could have seen the nature of his happiness the sight would have given her no comfort. Vaguely she pictured him in some strange Paradise, built upon those conceptions of the mediaeval artists, mainly Italians, which have supplied the ideals of the orthodox. She saw an imperfectly transfigured and still fleshly George Gosling, who did unaccustomed things with a harp, was dressed in exotic garments and was on terms with certain hybrids, largely woman but partly bird, who were clearly recognizable as the angelic host. If she had been a Mohammedan, her vision would have accorded far more nearly with the fact.

## 3

The successful animal is that which is adapted to its circumstances. Herbert Spencer would appear foolish and incapable in the society of the young wits who frequent the private bar; he might be described by them as an old Johnny who knew nothing about life. Mrs Gosling in her own home had been a ruler; she had had authority over her daughters, and, despite the usual evidences of girlish precocity, she had always been mistress of the situation. In the affairs of household management she was *facile princeps*, and she commanded the respect accorded to the eminent in any form of specialized activity. But even on this second morning of their emigration it became clear to Blanche that her mother had ceased to rule, and must become a subordinate. A certain respect was due to her in her parental relation, but if she could not be coaxed she must be coerced.

"She'll be better when we get her right away from here," was Blanche's diagnosis, and Millie, who had also achieved some partial realization of the necessities imposed by the new conditions, nodded in agreement.

"She wants to stop here altogether, and, of course, we can't," she said.

"We shall starve if we do," said Blanche.

From that time Mrs Gosling dropped into the humiliating position of a kind of mental incapable who must be humoured into obedience.

The first, and in many ways the most difficult, task was to persuade her away from Kilburn. She clung desperately to that stronghold of her old life.

"I'm too old to change at my age," she protested, and when the alternative was clearly put before her, she accepted it with a flaccidity that was as aggravating as it was unfightable.

"I'd sooner die 'ere," said Mrs Gosling, "than go trapesing about the fields lookin' for somethin' to eat. I simply couldn't do it. It's different for you two gels, no doubt. You go and leave me 'ere."

Millie might have been tempted to take her mother at her word, but Blanche never for a moment entertained the idea of leaving her mother behind.

"Very well, mother," she said, desperately, "if you won't come we must all stop here and starve, I suppose. We've got enough food to last a fortnight or so."

As she spoke she looked out of the window of that little suburban house, and for the first time in her life a thought came to her of the strangeness of preferring such an inconvenient little box to the adventure of the wider spaces of open country. Outside, the sun was shining brilliantly, but the windows were dim with dust and cobwebs.

Yet her mother was comparatively happy in this hovel; she would find delight in cleaning it, although there was no one to appraise the result of her effort. She was a specialized animal with habits precisely analogous to the instincts of other animals and insects. There were insects who could only live in filth and would die miserably if removed from their natural surroundings. Mrs Gosling was a suburban-house insect who would perish in the open air. After all, the chief difference between insects and men is that the insect is born perfectly adapted to its specialized existence, man finds, or is forced into, a place in the scheme after he has come to maturity....

"I can't see why you shouldn't leave me behind," pleaded Mrs Gosling.

"Well, we won't," replied Blanche, still looking out of the window.

"It's wicked of you to make us stop here and starve," put in Millie. "And even you must see that we *shall* starve."

Mrs Gosling wept feebly. She had wept much during the past twenty-four hours. "Where can we go?" she wailed.

"There's country on the other side of Harrow," said Blanche.

The thought of Harrow or Timbuctoo was equally repugnant to Mrs Gosling.

Then Millie had an idea. "Well, we only brought four bottles of water with us," she said, "where are we going to get any more in Kilburn?"

Mrs Gosling racked her brain in the effort to remember some convenient stream in the neighbourhood. "It may rain," she said feebly at last.

Blanche turned from the window and pointed to the blurred prospect of sunlit street. "We might be dead before the rain came," she said.

They wore her out in the end.

## 4

With Harrow as an immediate objective, they toiled up Willesden Lane with their hand-cart early the next morning. Blanche took that route because it was familiar to her, and after passing Willesden Green, she followed the tram lines.

As they got away from London they came upon evidences of the exodus which had preceded them. Bodies of women, for the most part no longer maladorous, were not infrequent, and pieces of household furniture, parcels of clothing, boxes, trunks and smaller impedimenta lay by the roadside, the superfluities of earlier loads that had been lightened, however reluctantly.

Mrs Gosling blenched at the sight of every body—only a few of them could be described as skeletons—and protested that they were all going to their death, but Blanche kept on resolutely with a white, set face, and as Millie followed her example, if with rather less show of temerity, there was no choice but to follow. When the gradients were favourable the girls helped their mother on to the truck and gave her a lift. She was a feeble walker.

Not till they reached Sudbury did they see another living being of their own species, or any sign of human habitation in the long rows of dirty houses.

The great surge of migration had spread out from the centre and become absorbed in circles of ever-widening amplitude. The great entity of London had eaten its way so far outwards into arable and pasturage that within a ten-mile radius from Charing Cross not a thousand women could be found who had been able to obtain any promise of security from the products of the soil. And although there were great open spaces of land, such as Wembley Park, which had to be crossed in the journey outwards, the exiles had been unable to wait until such time as seed could be transformed into food by the alchemy of Nature. So the pressure had been continually outwards, forcing the emigrants toward the more distant farms where some fraction of them, at least, might find work and food until the coming of the harvest. In Kent, vegetables were comparatively plentiful. In Northern Middlesex and Buckinghamshire the majority had to depend upon animal food. But in all the Home Counties and in the neighbourhood of every large town, famine was following hard upon the heels of the plague, and 70 per cent of the town-dwelling women and children who had escaped the latter visitation died of starvation and exposure before the middle of August.

In the first inner ring, still sparsely populated, were to be found those who had had vegetable gardens and had been vigorous enough to protect themselves against the flood of migration which had swept up against them.

It was the first signs of this inner ring that the Goslings discovered at Sudbury.

## 5

They came upon a little row of cottages, standing back a few yards from the road. All three women had been engaged in pushing their trolly up an ascent, and with heads down, and all their physical energies concentrated upon their task, they did not notice the startling difference between these cottages and other houses they had passed, until they stopped to take breath at the summit of the hill.

Mrs Gosling had immediately seated herself upon the sloping pole of the trolly handle. She was breathing heavily and had her hands pressed to her sides. Millie leaned against the side of the trolly, her eyes still on the ground. But Blanche had thrown back her shoulders and opened her lungs, and she saw the banner of smoke that flew from the middle of the three chimney-stacks smoke, in this wilderness, smoke the sign of human life! To Blanche it seemed the fulfilment of a great hope. She had begun to wonder if all the world were dead.

"Oh!" she gasped. "Look!"

They looked without eagerness, anticipating some familiar horror.

"Ooh!" echoed Millie, when she, too, had recognized the harbinger. But Mrs Gosling did not raise her eyes high enough.

"What?" she asked stupidly.

"There's some one living in that cottage," said Blanche, and pointed upwards to the soaring pennant.

Mrs Gosling's face brightened. "Well, to be sure," she said, "I wonder if they'd let me sit down and rest for a few minutes? And perhaps they might be willing to sell me a glass of milk. I'm sure I'd pay a good price for it."

"We can see, anyway," replied Millie, and they roused themselves and pushed on eagerly. The cottage was not more than thirty yards away.

Before they reached it, a woman came to the doorway, stared at them for a moment and then came down to the little wooden gate.

She was a thick-set woman of fifty or so, with iron grey hair cut close to her head. She wore a tweed skirt which did not reach the tops of her heavily soled, high boots. She looked capable, energetic and muscular. And in her hand she carried about three feet of stout broomstick.

She did not speak until the little procession halted before her gate, and then she pointed meaningly up the road with her broomstick and said: "Go on. You can't stop here." She spoke with the voice and inflection of an educated woman.

Blanche paused in the act of setting down the trolly handle. Mrs

Gosling and Millie stared in amazement; they had been prepared to weep on the neck of this human friend, found at last in the awful desert of Middlesex.

"We only wanted to buy a little milk," stammered Blanche, no less astonished than her mother and sister.

The big woman looked them over with something of pity and contempt. "I can see you're not dangerous," she sneered and crossed her great bare forearms over the top of the gate. "Only three poor feckless idiots going begging."

"We're *not* begging," retorted Blanche. "We've got money and we're willing to pay."

"Money!" repeated the woman. She looked up at the sky and nodded her head, as though beseeching pity for these feeble creatures. "My dear girl," she went on, "what do you suppose is the good of money in this world? You can't eat money, nor wear it, nor use it to light a fire. Now, if you'd offered me a box of matches, you should have had all the milk I can spare."

"Well, I never," put in Mrs Gosling, who had feebly come to rest again on the handle of the trolly.

"No, my good woman, you never did," said the stranger. "You never could and I should say the chances are that you never will."

Millie was intimidated and shrinking, even Blanche looked a little nervous, but Mrs Gosling was incapable of feeling fear of a fellow-woman. "You can't mean as you won't sell us a glass of milk?" she said.

"Have you got a box of matches you'll exchange for it?" asked the stranger. "I've got a burning glass I stole in Harrow, but you can't depend on the sun."

"No, nor 'aven't 'ad, the last three weeks," said Mrs Gosling. "But if you've more money a'ready than you know what to do with, I should 'ave thought as you'd 'a been willing to spare a glass o' milk for charity's sake."

The stranger regarded her petitioner with a hard smile. "Charity's sake?" she said. "Do you realize that I've had to defend this place like a fort against thousands of your sort? I've killed three mad women who fought me for possession and buried 'em in the orchard like cats. I held out through the first rush and I can hold out now easily enough. You three are the first I've seen for a month, and before that they'd begun to get weak and poor. These are your daughters, I suppose, and the three of you had always depended upon some fool of a man to keep you. Yes? Well, you deserve all you've got. Now you can start and do a little healthy, useful work for yourselves. I've no pity for you. I've got a damned fool of a sister and an old fool of a mother to keep in there," she pointed to the cottage with her broomstick. "Parasitic like you, both of 'em, and pretty well all the use they are is to keep the fire alight. No, my good woman, you get no charity from me."

When she had finished her speech, which she delivered with a fluency and point that suggested familiarity with the platform, the stranger crossed her arms again over the gate and stared Mrs Gosling out of countenance.

"Come along, my dears," said that outraged lady, getting wearily to her feet. "I wouldn't wish your ears soiled by such language from a woman as 'as forgotten the manners of a lady. But, there, poor thing, I've no doubt 'er 'ead's been turned with all this trouble."

The stranger smiled grimly and made no reply, but as the Goslings were moving away, she called out to them suddenly: "Hi! You! There's a witless creature along the road who'll probably help you. The house is up a side road. Bear round to the right."

"What a beast," muttered Blanche when they had gone on a few yards.

"One o' them 'new' women, my dear," panted Mrs Gosling, who remembered the beginning of the movement and still clung to the old terminology. 'Orrible unsexed creatures! I remember how your poor father used to 'ate 'em."

"I'd like to get even with her," said Millie.

They bore to the right, and so avoided two turnings which led up repulsive-looking hills, but they missed the side road.

"I'm sure we must have passed it," complained Mrs Gosling at last. Her sighs had been increasing in volume and poignancy for the past half-mile, and the prospect of uninhabited country which lay immediately around her she found infinitely dispiriting.

"There isn't an 'ouse in sight," she added, "and I really don't believe I *can* walk much farther."

Blanche stopped and looked over the fields on her right towards London. In the distance, blurred by an oily wriggle of heat haze, she could see the last wave of suburban villas which had broken upon this shore of open country. They had left the town behind them at last, but they had not found what they sought. This little arm of land which cut off Harrow and Wealdstone from the mother lake of London had not offered sufficient temptation to delay their forerunners in the search for food. Most of them, with a true instinct for what they sought, had followed the main road into the Chiltern Hills, and those who for some cause or another had wandered into this side track had pushed on, even as Blanche and Millie would have done had they not been dragged back by their mother's complaints.

The sun was falling a little towards the west, and bird and animal life, which had seemed to rest during the intenser heat of mid-day, was stirring and calling all about them. A rabbit lolloped into the road, a few yards away, pricked up its ears, stared for an instant, and then scuttled to cover. A blackbird flew out of the hedge and fled chattering up the ditch. The air was murmurous with the hum of innumerable insects, and above Mrs Gosling's head hovered a group of flies which ever and again bobbed down as if following some concerted plan of action, and tried to settle on the poor woman's heated face.

"Oh! get away, do!" she panted, and flapped a futile handkerchief.

"How quiet it is!" said Blanche; and although the air was full of sound it did indeed appear that a great hush had fallen over the earth. No motor-horn threateningly bellowed its automatic demand for right of way; there was no echo of hoofs nor grind of wheels; no call of children's voices, nor even the bark of a dog. The wild things had the place to themselves again, and the sound of their movements called for no response from civilized minds. The ears of the Goslings heard, but did not note these, to them, useless evidences of life. They were straining and alert for the voice of humanity.

"I don't know when I've felt the 'eat so much," said Mrs Gosling suddenly, and Blanche and Millie both started.

"Hush!" said Blanche, and held up a warning finger.

In the distance they heard a sound like the closing of a gate, and then, very clear and small, a feminine voice. "*Chuck!* chuck! chuck!" it said. "Chuck! chuck! *chuck!!!*"

"I told you we'd passed it," said Mrs Gosling triumphantly. They turned the trolly and began to retrace their footsteps. Their eager eyes tried to peer through the spinney of trees which shut them off from the south. Once or twice they stopped to listen. The voice was fainter now, but they could hear the squawk of greedily competitive fowls.

# CHAPTER 13

*Differences*

1

THE ONLY SIDE road they could find proved to be no more than a track through the little wood. They almost passed it a second time, and hesitated at the gate—a sturdy five-barred gate bearing "Private" on a conspicuous label—debating whether this "could be right." They still suffered a spasm of fear at the thought of trespass, and to open this gate and march up an unknown private road pushing a handcart seemed to them an act of terrible aggression.

"We might leave the cart just inside," suggested Blanche.

"And get our food stole," said Mrs Gosling.

"There's no one about," urged Blanche.

"There's that broomstick woman," said Millie. "She may have followed us."

"I'm sure I dunno if it's safe to go foragin' in among them trees, neither," continued Mrs Gosling. "Are you sure this is right, Blanche?"

"Well, of course, I'm not sure," replied Blanche, with a touch of temper.

They peered through the trees and listened, but no sign of a house was to be seen, and all was now silent save for the long drone of innumerable bees about their afternoon business.

"Oh! come on!" said Blanche at last. She was rapidly learning to solve all their problems by this simple formula....

In the wood they found refuge from those attendant flies which had hung over them so persistently.

Mrs Gosling gave a final flick with her handkerchief and declared her relief. "It's quite pleasant in 'ere," she said, "after the 'eat."

The two girls also seemed to find new vigour in the shade of the trees.

"We *have* got a cheek!" said Millie, with a giggle.

"Well! needs must when the devil drives," returned Mrs Gosling, "and our circumstances is quite out of the ordinary. Besides which, there can't be any 'arm in offerin' to buy a glass of milk."

Blanche tugged at the trolley handle with a flicker of impatience. Why would her mother be so foolish? Surely she must see that everything was different now? Blanche was beginning to wonder at and admire the marvel of her own intelligence. How much cleverer she was than the others! How much more ready to appreciate and adapt herself to change! They could not understand this new state of things, but she could, and she prided herself on her powers of discrimination.

"Everything's different now," she said to herself. "We can go anywhere and do anything, almost. It's like as if we were all starting off level again, in a way." She felt uplifted: she took extraordinary pleasure in her own realization of facts. A strange, new power had come to her, a power to enjoy life, through mastery. "Everything's different now," she repeated. She was conscious of a sense of pity for her mother and sister.

## 2

The road through the wood curved sharply round to the right, and they came suddenly upon a clearing, and saw the house in front of them. It was a long, low house, smothered in roses and creepers, and it stood in a wild garden surrounded by a breast-high wall of red brick. At the edge of the clearing several cows were lying under the shade of the trees, reflectively chewing the cud with slow, deliberate enjoyment, while one, solitary, stood with its head over the garden gate, motionless, save for an occasional petulant whisp of its ropey tail.

"Now, then, what are we going to do?" asked Mrs Gosling.

The procession halted, and the three women regarded the guardian cow with every sign of dismay.

"Shoo!" said Millie feebly, flapping her hands; and Blanche repeated the intimidation with greater force; but the cow merely acknowledged the salutation by an irritable sweep of its tail.

" 'Orrid brute!" muttered Mrs Gosling, and flicked her handkerchief in the direction of the brute's quarters.

"I know," said Blanche, conceiving a subtle strategy. "We'll drive it away with the cart." She turned the trolly round, and the three of them grasping the pole, they advanced slowly and warily to the charge, pushing their siege ram before them. They made a slight detour to achieve a flank attack and allow the enemy a clear way of retreat.

"Oh, dear! what *are* you doing?" said a voice suddenly, and the three startled Goslings nearly dropped the pole in their alarm they had been so utterly absorbed in their campaign.

A young woman of sixteen or seventeen, very brown, hot and dishevelled, was regarding them from the other side of the garden wall with a stare of amazement that even as they turned was flickering into laughter.

"It's that great brute by the gate, my dear," said Mrs Gosling, "and we've just—"

"You don't mean Alice?" interrupted the young woman. "Oh! you couldn't go charging poor dear Alice with a great cart like that! Three of you, too!"

"Is its name Alice?" asked Blanche stupidly. She did not feel equal to this curious occasion.

"*Its* name!" replied the young woman, with scorn. "*Her* name's Alice, if that's what you mean." She shook back the hair from her eyes and moved down to the gate. The cow acknowledged her presence by an indolent toss of the head.

"Oh! but my sweet Alice!" protested the young woman; "you must move and let these funny people come in. It really isn't good for you, dear, to stand about in the sun like this, and you'd much better go and lie down in the shade for a bit!" She gently pulled the gate from under the cow's chin, and then, laying her hands flat on its side, made as if to push it out of the way.

"Well, I never!" declared Mrs Gosling, regarding the performance with much the same awe as she might have vouchsafed to a lion-tamer in a circus. "'Ood 'ave thought it'd 'a been that tame?"

The cow, after a moment's resistance, moved off with a leisurely walk in the direction of the wood.

"Now, you funny people, what do you want?" asked the young woman.

Mrs Gosling began to explain, but Blanche quickly interposed. "Oh! do be quiet, mother; you don't understand," she said, and continued, before her mother could remonstrate, "We've come from London."

"Goodness!" commented the young woman.

"And we want—" Blanche hesitated. She was surprised to find that in the light of her wonderful discovery it was not so easy to define precisely what they ought to want. As the broomstick woman had said, they were "beggars." Fairly confronted with the problem, Blanche saw no alternative but a candid acknowledgment of the fact.

"You want feeding, of course," put in the young woman. "They all do. You needn't think you're the first. We've had dozens!"

A solution presented itself to Blanche. "We don't really want food," she said. "We've got a lot of tinned things left still, only we're ill with eating tinned things. I thought, perhaps, you might be willing to let us have some milk and eggs and vegetables in exchange?"

"That's sensible enough," commented the young woman. "If you only knew the things we have been offered! Money chiefly, of course"—Mrs Gosling opened her mouth, but Blanche frowned and shook her head—"and it does seem as if money's about as useless as buttons. In fact, I'd sooner have buttons you can use them. But the other funny things—bits of old furniture, warming-pans, jewellery! You should have heard Mrs Isaacson! She was a Jewess who came from Hampstead a couple of months ago, and she had a lot of jewels she kept in a bag tied round her waist under her skirt; and when Aunt May and I simply had to tell her to go she tried to bribe us with an old brooch and rubbish. She was a terror. But, I say"—she looked at the sun—"I've got lots of things to do before sunset." She paused, and looked at the three Goslings. "Look here," she went on, "are you all right? You seem all right."

Again Mrs Gosling began to reply, but Blanche was too quick for her. "Tell me what you mean by 'all right'?" she asked, raising her voice to drown her mother's "Well, I never did 'ear such."

"Well, of course, mother'll give you any mortal thing you want," replied the young woman at the gate. "Dear old mater! She simply won't think of what we're going to do in the winter; and I mean, if you come in for to-night, say, and we let you have a few odd things, you won't go and plant yourselves on us like that Mrs Isaacson and one or two others, because if you do, Aunt May and I will have to turn you out, you know."

"What we 'ave we'll pay for," said Mrs Gosling with dignity.

The young woman smiled. "Oh, I dare say!" she said; "pay us with those pretty little yellow counters that aren't the least good to anyone. You wait here half a jiff. I'll find Aunt May."

She ran up the path and entered the house. A moment later they heard her calling "Aunt May! Auntie—*Aun-tee!*" somewhere out at the back.

"Let's 'ope 'er Aunt May'll 'ave more common sense," remarked Mrs Gosling.

Blanche turned on her almost fiercely. "For goodness sake, mother," she said, "do try and get it out of your head, if you can, that we can buy things with money. Can't you see that everything's different? Can't you see that money's no good, that you can't eat it, or wear it, or light a fire with it, like that other woman said? Can't you understand, or won't you?"

Mrs Gosling gaped in amazement. It was incredible that the mind of Blanche should also have been distorted by this terrible heresy. She turned in sympathy to Millie, who had taken her mother's seat on the pole of the trolly, but Millie frowned and said:

"B.'s right. You can't buy things with money; not here, anyway. What'd they do with money if they got it?"

Mrs Gosling looked at the trees, at the cows lying at the edge of the wood, at the sunlit fields beyond the house, but she saw nothing which suggested an immediate use for gold coin.

"Lemme sit down, my dear," she said. "What with the 'eat and all this walkin'—O! what wouldn't I give for a cup o' tea!"

Millie got up sulkily and leaned against the wall. "I suppose they'll let us stop here to-night, B.?" she asked.

"If we don't make fools of ourselves," replied Blanche, spitefully.

Mrs Gosling drooped. No inspiration had come to her as it had come to her daughter. The older woman had become too specialized. She swayed her head, searching like some great larva dug up from its refuse heap confused and feeble in this new strange place of light and air.

And as Blanche had repeated to herself "Everything's different," so Mrs Gosling seized a phrase and clung to it as to some explanation of this horrible perplexity. "I can't understand it," she said; "I *can't* understand it!"

## 3

Aunt May appeared after a long interval—a thin, brown-faced woman of forty or so. She wore a very short skirt, a man's jacket and an old deerstalker hat, and she carried a pitchfork. She must have brought the pitchfork as an emblem of authority, but she did not handle it as the other woman had handled her broomstick. The murderous pitchfork appeared little more deadly in her keeping than does the mace in the House of Commons, but as an emblem the pitchfork was infinitely more effective.

Aunt May's questions were pertinent and searching, and after a few brief explanations had been offered to her she drove off the young woman, her niece, whom she addressed as "Allie," to perform the many duties which were her share of the day's work.

Allie went, laughing.

"You can sleep here to-night," announced Aunt May. "We shall have a meal all together soon after sunset. Till then you can talk to my sister, who's an invalid. She's always eager for news."

She took charge of them as if she were the matron of a workhouse receiving new inmates.

"You'd better bring your truck into the garden," she said, "or Alice will be turning everything over. Inquisitive brute!" she added, snapping her fingers at the cow, who had returned, and stood within a few feet of them, eyeing the Goslings with a slow, dull wonder—a mournfully sleepy beast whose furiously wakeful tail seemed anxious to rouse its owner out of her torpor.

The invalid sister sat by the window of a small room that faced west and overlooked the luxuriance of what was still recognizably a flower-garden.

"My sister, Mrs Pollard," said Aunt May sharply, and then addressing the woman who sat huddled in shawls by the window, she added: "Three more strays, Fanny—from London, Allie tells me." She went out quickly, closing the door with a vigour which indicated little tolerance for invalid nerves.

Mrs Pollard stretched out a delicate white hand. "Please come and sit near me," she said, "and tell me about London. It is so long since I have had any news from there. Perhaps you might be able—" she broke off, and looked at the three strangers with a certain pathetic eagerness.

"I'll take me bonnet off, ma'am, if you'll excuse me," remarked Mrs Gosling. She felt at home once more within the delightful shelter of a house, although slightly overawed by the aspect of the room and its occupant. About both there was an air of that class dignity to which Mrs Gosling knew she could never attain. "I don't know when I've felt the 'eat as I 'ave to-day," she remarked politely.

"Has it been hot?" asked Mrs Pollard. "To me the days all seem so much alike. I want you to tell me, were there any young men in London when you left? You haven't seen any young man who at all resembles this photograph, have you?"

Mrs Gosling stared at the silver-framed photograph which Mrs Pollard took from the table at her side, stared and shook her head.

"We haven't seen a single man of any kind for two months," said Blanche, "not a single one. Have we, Millie?"

Millie, sitting rather stiffly on her chair, shook her head. "It's terrible," she said. "I'm sure I don't know where they can have all gone to."

Mrs Pollard did not reply for a moment. She looked steadfastly out of the window, and tears, which she made no attempt to restrain, chased each other in little jerks down her smooth pale cheeks.

Mrs Gosling pinched her mouth into an expression of suffering sympathy, and shook her head at her daughters to enforce silence. Was she not, also, a widow?

After a short pause, Mrs Pollard fumbled in her lap and discovered a black-bordered pocket-handkerchief—a reminiscence, doubtless, of some earlier bereavement. Her expression had been in no way distorted as she wept, and after the tears had been wiped away no trace of them disfigured her delicate face. Her voice was still calm and sweet as she said:

"I am very foolish to go on hoping. I loved too much, and this trial has been sent to teach me that all love but One is vain, that I must not set my heart upon things of the earth. And yet I go on hoping that my poor boy was not cut off in Sin."

"Dear, dear!" murmured Mrs Gosling. "You musn't take it to 'eart too much, ma'am. Boys will be a little wild and no doubt our 'eavenly Father will make excuses."

Mrs Pollard shook her head. "If it had only been a little wildness," she said, "I should have hope. He is, indeed, just and merciful, slow to anger and of great kindness, but my poor Alfred became tainted with the terrible doctrines of Rome. It has been the greatest grief of my life, and I have known much pain...." And again the tears slowly welled up and fell silently down that smooth, unchanging face.

Mrs Gosling sniffed sympathetically. The two girls glanced at one another with slightly raised eyebrows and Blanche almost invisibly shrugged her shoulders.

The warm evening light threw the waxen-faced, white-shawled figure of the woman in the window into high relief. Her look of ecstatic resignation was that of some wonderful mediaeval saint returned from the age of vision and miracle to a recently purified earth in which the old ideas of saintship had again become possible. Her influence was upon the room in which she sat. The sounds of the world outside, the evening chorus of wild life, the familiar noise of the farm, seemed to blend into a remote music of prayer—"Kyrie Eleison! Christe Eleison!" Within was a great stillness, as of a thin and bloodless purity; the long continuance of a single thought found some echo in every material object. While the silence lasted everything in that room was responsive to this single keynote of anaemic virtue.

Mrs Gosling tried desperately to weep without noise, and even the two girls, falling under the spell, ceased to glance covertly at one another with that hint of criticism, but sat subdued and weakened as if some element of life had been taken from them.

The lips of the woman in the window moved noiselessly; her hands were clasped in her lap. She was praying.

## 4

Firm and somewhat clumsy steps were heard in the passage, the door was pushed roughly open, banging back against the black oak chair which was set behind it, and Aunt May entered carrying a large tray.

"Here's your dinner, Fanny," she said. "We've done earlier to-night, in spite of interruptions." She bustled over to the little table in the window, pushed back the Bible and photograph with the edge of the tray until she could release one hand, and then, having driven the tray into a position of safety, moved Bible and photograph to the centre table.

There was something protestingly vigorous about her movements, as though she endeavoured to combat by noise and energy the impoverished vitality of that emasculate room.

"Now, you three!" she went on. "You had better come out into the kitchen and take your things off and wash."

As the Goslings rose, Mrs Pollard turned to them and stretched out to each in turn her delicate white hand. "There is only one Comforter," she said. "Put your trust in Him."

Mrs Gosling gulped, and Blanche and Millie looked as they used to look when they attended the Bible-classes held by the vicar's wife.

Blanche gave a shiver of relief as they came out into the passage. Her mind was suddenly filled by the astounding thought that everything was not different....

Supper was laid on the kitchen table cold chicken, potatoes and cabbage, stewed plums and cream, and warm, new milk in a jug; no bread, no salt, and no pepper.

As the three Goslings washed at the scullery sink they chattered freely. They felt pleasure at release from some cold, draining influence; they felt as if they had come out of church after some long, dull service, into the air and sunlight.

"I'm sure she's a very 'oly lady," was Mrs Gosling's final summary.

Blanche shivered again. "Oh! freezing!" was her enigmatic reply.

Millie said it gave her "the creeps."

They were a party of seven at supper—the meal was referred to as "supper," although to Mrs Pollard it had been dignified by the name of "dinner"—including two young women whom the Goslings had not hitherto seen; strong, brown-faced girls, who spoke with a country accent. They had something still of the manner of servants, but they were treated as equals both by Allie and Aunt May.

There was little conversation during the meal, however, for all of them were too intent on the business in hand. To the Goslings that meal was, indeed, a banquet.

When they had all finished, Aunt May rose at once. "Thank Heaven for daylight," she remarked; "but we must set our brains to work to invent some light for the winter. We haven't a candle or a drop of oil left," she went on, addressing the Goslings, "and for the past five weeks we have had to bustle to get everything done before sunset, I can tell you. Last night we couldn't wash up after supper."

"We know," replied Blanche.

Aunt May nodded. "We all know," she said. "Now, you three girls, get busy!" And Allie and the two brown-faced young women rose a little wearily.

"I'm getting an old woman," remarked Aunt May, "and I'm allowed certain privileges, chief of them that I don't work after supper." She paused and looked keenly at the three Goslings. "Which of you three is in command?" she asked.

"Well, it seems as if my eldest, Blanche, that is, 'as sort o' taken the lead the past few days," began Mrs Gosling.

"Ah! I thought so," said Aunt May. "Well, now, Blanche, you'd better come out into the garden and have a talk with me, and we'll decide what you had better do. If your mother and sister would like to go to bed, Allie will show them where they can sleep."

She moved away in the direction of the garden and Blanche followed her.

# CHAPTER 14

*Aunt May*

## 1

The sun had set, but as yet the daylight was scarcely faded. Under the trees the fowls muttered in subdued duckings, and occasionally one of them would flutter up into the lower branches with a squawk of effort and then settle herself with a great fluttering and swelling of feathers, and all the suggestion of a fussy matron preparing for the night—preparing only, for these early roosters sat open-eyed and watchful, as if they knew that there was no chance of sleep for them until every member of that careless crowd below had found its appointed place in the dormitory.

"We put 'em inside in the winter," remarked Aunt May, as she and Blanche paused, "but they prefer the trees. We haven't any foxes here, but I've noticed that the wild things seem to be coming back."

Blanche nodded. She was thinking how much there was to learn concerning those matters which appertained to the production of food.

"They're rather a poor lot," Aunt May continued, "but they have to forage for themselves, except for the few bits of vegetable and such things we can spare them. We've no corn or flour or meal of any kind for ourselves yet. But a farmer's wife about a mile from here has got a few acres of wheat and barley coming on, and we shall help her to harvest and take our share later. We shall be rich then," she added, with a smile.

"I'm town-bred, you know," said Blanche. "We've got an awful lot to learn, Millie and me."

"You'll learn quickly enough," was the answer. "You'll have to."

"I suppose," returned Blanche.

At the end of the orchard through which they had been passing they came to a knoll, crowned by a great elm. Round the trunk of the elm a rough seat had been fixed, and here Aunt May sat down with a sigh of relief.

"It's a blessed thing to earn your own bread day by day," she said. "It's a beautiful thing to live near the earth and feel physically tired at night. It's delightful to be primitive and agricultural, and I love it. But I have a civilized vice, Blanche. I have a store of cigarettes I stole from a shop in Harrow, and every night when it's fine I come out here after supper and smoke three; and when it's wet I smoke 'em in my own bedroom, and I dream. But tonight I'm going to talk to you, because you want help."

She produced a cigarette case and matches from a side pocket of her jacket, lit a cigarette, inhaled the smoke with a long gasp of intensest enjoyment, and then said: "Men weren't fools, my dear; they had pockets in their coats."

"Yes?" said Blanche. She felt puzzled and a little awkward. She knew that this woman was a friend, but the girl's town-bred, objective mind was critical and embarrassed.

"Do you smoke?" asked Aunt May. "I can spare you a cigarette, though I know the time must come when there won't be any more. Still, it's a long way off yet. Bless the clever man who invented air-tight tins!"

"No, I don't smoke, thanks," replied Blanche, conventionally; and, try as she would, she could not keep some hint of stiffness out of her voice. Modern manners take a long time to influence suburban homes of the Wisteria Grove type.

"Ah! well, you miss a lot!" said Aunt May; "but you're better without it, especially now, when tobacco isn't easy to get, and will soon be impossible."

"But do you think," asked Blanche, drawing her eyebrows together, "that this sort of thing is going on always?"

"I dare say. Don't ask me, my dear; the problem's beyond me. What we poor women have got to do is to keep ourselves alive in the meantime. And that's what we've come out here to talk about. What about your mother and you two girls? Where are you going? And what are you proposing to do?"

"*I* don't know," said Blanche. "I—I've been trying to think."

"Good!" remarked Aunt May. "I believe you'll do. I'm doubtful about your sister."

"We'll have to work on a farm, I suppose."

"It's the only way to live."

"Only where?"

"That's what I've been trying to worry out," said Aunt May. "We do get news here, of a sort. Our girls work in Mrs Jordan's fields, and meet girls and women who come from Pinner, and the Pinner people hear news from Northwood, and the Northwood people from somewhere else; and so we get into touch with half a county. But, coming to your affairs; you see, we here are just the innermost circle. Most of the women who came from London missed this place and passed us by, thanks be!... Now, that poor unfortunate Miss Grant, down the road, had to defend herself with weapons. Fortunately she's strong."

"Is Miss Grant the awful woman with the broomstick?" asked Blanche.

"She's not really awful, my dear," said Aunt May, smiling; "she's a very good sort. A little rough in her manners, perhaps, and quite mad about the uselessness of the creatures we used to know as men, but a fine, generous, unselfish woman, if she does boast of her three murders. Did she tell you that, by the way?"

Blanche nodded.

"She would, of course; and I believe it's true; but her theory was to defend her own people. She said they'd *all* have died if she hadn't. I'm not sure about the ethic, but I know dear old Sally Grant meant well. However, I'm wandering—I often do when I talk like this. The point was that just this little circle here, close to London, is very thickly populated, and there's precious little food ready to be got any way; but you'll have to pass through the country beyond Pinner before you'll find a place where they'll give you work and keep you. There's a surplus in the next ring, I gather, too much labour and too little to grow. You'll have to push out into the Chilterns, out to Amersham at the nearest. It's all on the main road, of course, which is bad in a general way, because that's the road they all took. But I think if you'll cut across towards Wycombe you might, perhaps, find a place of some sort, though whether they'll feed your mother free gratis I can't say. Women are of all sorts, but this plague hasn't made 'em more friendly to one another, or perhaps it is we notice it more, and the worst of the lot are the farmers' wives and daughters who've got the land. They get turned out, though, sometimes. We hear about it. The London women have made raids; only, you see, the poor dears don't know what to do with the land when they get it, so they have to keep the few who do know to teach 'em—when they're sensible enough—the raiders, I mean. They aren't always."

"It'll be an adventure," remarked Blanche.

Aunt May threw away the very short end of her second cigarette and lighted her third. "Adventure will do you good," she said.

It was nearly dark under the elm. The things of the night were coming out. Occasionally a cockchafer would go humming past them, the bats were flitting swiftly and silently about the orchard, and presently an owl swept by in one great stride of soundless flight.

"How they are all coming back!" murmured Aunt May. "All the wild things. I never saw an owl here before this year."

"I should be frightened if you weren't here," said Blanche.

"Nothing to be frightened of, yet."

"Yet?"

"In a few years' time, perhaps. I don't know. We killed a wild cat who came after the chickens a few days ago. The cats have gone back already, and the dogs aren't so respectful as they used to be. The dogs'll interbreed, I suppose, and evolve a common form—strike some kind of average in a beast which will be somewhere near the ancestral type, smaller, probably, I don't know. It's a wonderful world, and very interesting. I could almost wish man wouldn't return for twenty years or so—just to see how much of his handiwork Nature could undo in the interval. I often think about it out here in the evenings."

"I wish I knew more about it," said Blanche timidly. "Are there any books, do you know, that—"

"You won't want books, my dear. Keep your eyes open and think."

They lapsed into silence again. The third cigarette was finished, but Aunt May gave no indication of a desire to get back to the house, and Blanche's mind was so excited with all the new ideas which were pouring in upon her that she had forgotten her tiredness.

"It's awfully interesting," she said at last. "It's all so different. Mother and Millie hate it, and they'd like all the old things back; but I don't think I would."

"You're all right. You'll do," replied her companion. "You're one of the new sort, though you might never have found it out if it hadn't been for the plague. Now, your sister will do one of two things, in my opinion; either she'll stop in some place where there's a man—there's one at Wycombe, by the way—and have children, or she'll turn religious."

Blanche was about to ask a question, but Aunt May stopped her. "Never mind about the man, my dear," she said. "You'll learn quickly enough. It's like Heaven now, you see—no marrying or giving in marriage. With one man to every thousand women or so, what can you expect? It's no good kicking against it. It's got to be. That's where Fanny—" She broke off suddenly, with a little snort of impatience. "I think tonight's an exception," she went on. "I like talking to you, and one simply can't talk to Allie yet, so just tonight I'll have one more." She took out her cigarette case with a touch of impatience.

It was dark under the elm now, and she had to hold up her cigarette case close to her face in order to see the contents. "Two more," she announced. "It's a festival, and for once I can speak my mind to some one. An imprudence, perhaps, like this habit of smoking, but I shall probably never see you again, and I'm sure you won't tell."

"Oh, no!" interposed Blanche eagerly.

"You're not tired? You don't want to go to bed?"

"Not a bit. I love being out here."

"I can't see you, but I know you're speaking the truth," said Aunt May, after a pause. "In the darkness and silence of the night I will make a confession. I look weather-worn and fifty, I know, but I feel absurdly romantic, only there's no man in this case. I used to write novels, my dear—an absurd thing for any spinster to do, but they paid, and I've got the itch for self-expression. That's the one outlet I miss in this new world of ours. Sally Grant and I can't agree, and, in any case, she wants to do all the talking. And sometimes I'm idiot enough to go on writing little bits even now when I have become a capable, practical woman with at least four lives dependent upon me. Well, it shows, anyhow, that we writing women weren't all fools...." She hung on that for a moment or two, and then continued.

"Are you religious?"

"I don't know I suppose so. We always went to Church at home," said Blanche. "I thought every one was, almost. Not quite like Mrs Pollard, of course."

"Oh, well!" said Aunt May. "There's no harm and a lot of good in being religious, if you go about it in the right way. I don't want to change your opinions, my dear. It's just a question to me of the right way. And I *can't* see that Fanny's way is right. Here we are, and we've got to make the best of it; and to my mind that means facing life, and not shutting yourself into one room with a Bible and spending half your time on your knees. Fanny never was good for much. She brought up Alfred—my nephew, you know—with only one idea, and she stuffed him so full of holiness that the English Church couldn't hold him, and he had to work some of it off by going over to Rome. He thought he'd have better chances of saintship there. He was a poor, pale thing, anyway. Of course, that was anathema to Fanny. She might have forgiven him for committing a murder, but to become a Roman Catholic—! Oh, Lord! She's been praying for him ever since. And, my dear, what difference can it make? Alfred's apostasy, I mean. Do you think it matters what particular form of worship or pettifogging details of belief you adopt? Why can't the Churches take each other for granted, and be generous enough to suppose that all roads lead to Heaven, which is, according to all accounts, a much better place than Rome? But, oh! above all, if you have a religion, do be practical! Come out and do your work, instead of sighing and psalm-singing, and wearying dumb Heaven with fulsome praise and lamentations of your unworthiness, as if you were trying to propitiate a rich customer!

"There, my dear, I won't say any more. My last cigarette's done, and wasted, because I was too excited to enjoy it. I know I've been disloyal; but it's my temperament. I could slap Fanny sometimes. And she shan't have Allie.... It's the night that has affected me. To-morrow I shall be just as practical as ever, and you'll forget that you've seen this side of me. Come along. We must go to bed."

"This is the greatest night of my life," thought Blanche as they walked back in silence to the house.

Even when she was in bed, she did not go to sleep at once. She lay and listened to the heavy breathing of her mother and Millie, and she wondered. Everything, indeed, was different, but everybody was just the same, only, in some curious way, individualities seemed more pronounced.

Could it be that everybody was more natural, that there was less restraint?

Blanche was not introspective. She did not test the theory on herself. She thought of the women she had met that day, and of her mother and Millie.

She fell asleep, determined to be more like Aunt May.

## CHAPTER 15

*From Sudbury To Wycombe*

### 1

ALLIE KNOCKED ON the Goslings' door at sunrise the next morning, and Blanche, who had come to bed two hours after her mother and sister, was the only one to respond. She woke with the feeling that she had something important to do, and that the affair was in some way pleasant and inspiring.

Millie was not easily roused. She had slept heavily, and did not approve the suggestion that she should get up and dress herself.

"All right, B., all right!" she mumbled, and cuddled down under the bedclothes like a dormouse into its straw.

"Oh! do get up!" urged Blanche, impatiently, and at last resorted to physical force.

"What *is* the matter?" snapped Millie, struggling to maintain her hold of the blankets. "Why *can't* you leave me alone?"

"Because it's time to get up, lazy!" said Blanche, continuing the struggle.

"Well, I said I'd get up in a minute."

"Well, get up then."

"In a minute."

"No—now!"

"Oh, bother!" said Millie.

Blanche succeeded at last in obtaining possession of the blankets.

"You'll wake mother!" was Millie's last, desperate shaft.

"I'm going to try," replied Blanche.

Millie sat up in the bed and wondered vaguely where she was. These scenes had often been enacted at Wisteria Grove, and her mind had gone back to those delightful days of peace and security. When full consciousness returned to her, she was half inclined to cry, and more than half inclined to go to sleep again.

Mrs Gosling was quite as difficult.

"What's the time?" was her first question.

"I don't know," said Blanche.

"I'm sure it's not seven," murmured Mrs Gosling.

Millie, still sitting on the bed, wondered whether Blanche would let her get to the blankets which were tumbled on the floor a few feet away.

"No, you don't!" exclaimed Blanche, anticipating the attempt.

Finally she lost her temper and shook her mother vigorously.

At that, Mrs Gosling sat up suddenly and stared at her. "What in 'eaven's name's wrong, gel?" she asked. Her instinct told her with absolute certainty that it was still the middle of the night by Wisteria Grove standards.

"Oh! my goodness! I'm going to have my hands full with you two!" broke out Blanche impatiently. Her imagination pictured for her in that instant how great the trouble would be. She would never be able to wake them up....

They took the road before eight o'clock. Aunt May was generous in the matter of eggs and fruit, and she left her many urgent duties to point the way for the inexperienced explorers.

"Get right out as far as you can," was her parting word of advice.

They did not see Mrs Pollard again. She was still in bed when they set out.

## 2

Despite the promise of another cloudless day, none of the three travellers set out in high spirits. To all of them, even to Blanche, it seemed a return to weariness and pain to start out once more pushing that abominable truck. That truck represented all their troubles. It had become associated with all the discomforts they had endured since they left the Putney house. It indicated the paucity of their possessions, and yet it was intolerably heavy to push. After their brief return to the comfort and stability of a home and natural food, this adventuring out into the inhospitable country appeared more hopeless than ever. If they could have gone without the truck, they might, at least, have avoided that feeling of horrible certainty. They might have cheated themselves into the belief that they would return. The truck was the brand of their vagabondage.

Mrs Gosling did not spare her lamentations concerning the hopelessness of their endeavour, and gave it as her opinion that they had been most heartlessly treated by Aunt May.

"Turning out a woman of my age into the roads," she grumbled. "She might 'ave kept us a day or two, I should 'ave thought. It ain't as if we were beggars. We could 'ave paid for what we 'ad."

She had, indeed, made the suggestion and been repulsed. Aunt May had firmly put the offer on one side without explanation. She understood that explanations would be wasted on Mrs Gosling.

Millie was inclined to agree with her mother.

Blanche, at the handle, did not interrupt the statement of their grievances. She was occupied with the problem of the future, trying to think out some plan in her own confused inconsecutive way.

Their progress was tediously slow. Against the combined brake of the truck and Mrs Gosling, they did not average two miles an hour; and even before they came to Pinner it was becoming obvious to the two girls that they might as well let their mother ride on the trolly as allow her to lean her weight upon it as she walked.

They took the road through Wealdstone to avoid the hill and found that they were still in the track of one wing of the foraging army which had preceded them. That first rush of emigrants had ravaged the stores and houses as locusts will ravage a stretch of country. The suburb of regular villas and prim shops had been completely looted. Doors stood open and windows were smashed; the spread of ugly houses lay among the fields like an unwholesome eruption, awaiting the healing process of Nature. Wealdstone also was deserted by humanity. The flood had swept on towards the open country.

But as they approached Pinner the signs of devastation and desertion began to give way. Here and there women could be seen working in the fields; one or two children scuttled away before the approach of the Goslings and hid in the hedges, children who had evidently grown furtive and suspicious, intimidated by the experiences of the past two months; and when the outlying houses were reached—detached suburban villas, once occupied by relatively wealthy middle-class employers—it was evident that efforts were being made to restore the wreckage of kitchen gardens.

The Goslings had reached the point at which the wave had broken after its great initial energy was spent. Somewhere about this fifteen-mile limit, varying somewhat according to local conditions, the real disintegration of the crowd had begun. As the numerous tokens of the road had shown, a great number of women and children—possibly one-fifth of the whole crowd—had died of starvation and disease before any harbour was reached. From this fifteen-mile circle outwards, an increasing number had been stayed in their flight by the opportunities of obtaining food. Work was urgently demanded for the future, but the determining factor was the present supply of food, and the constriction of immediate supply had decided the question of how great a proportion of the women and children should remain. Here, about Pinner, was more land than the limited number of workers could till, but little of it was arable, and this year there would be almost no harvest of grain.

Vaguely, Blanche realized this. She remembered Aunt May's advice to keep her eyes open, and looking about her as she walked she found little promise of security in the grass fields and the rare signs of human activity.

Mrs Gosling, eager to find some home at any price, expressed her usual optimistic opinion with regard to the value of money. She saw signs of life again, at last, conditions familiar to her. She thought that they were returning once more to some kind of recognizable civilization, and began, with some renewal of her old vigour, to advise that they should find an hotel or inn and take "a good look round" before going any further.

Millie, heartened by her mother's belief, was of much the same opinion, and Blanche was summoned from the pole to listen to the proposition.

She shook her head stubbornly.

"I'm not going to argue it out all over again," she said. "You can just look round and see for yourselves that there's no food to be got here. We must get further out."

Mrs Gosling refused to be convinced, and advanced her superior knowledge of the world to support her judgment of the case.

"Oh! very well," said Blanche, at last. "Come on to the inn and see for yourselves."

The inn, however, was deserted. All its available supply of food, solid and liquid, had long been exhausted, and the gardenless house had offered no particular attractions as a residence. Houses were cheap in that place, the whole population of Pinner, including children, did not exceed three hundred persons.

They found a woman working in a garden near by, and she, with perhaps unnecessary harshness, warned them that they could not stay in the village. "There's not enough food for us as it is," she said, and made some reference to "silly Londoners."

That was an expression with which the Goslings were to become very familiar in the near future.

The appeal for pity fell on deaf ears. Mrs Gosling learned that she was only one of many thousands who had made the same appeal.

The sun was high in the sky as they trudged out of Pinner on the road towards Northwood. It was then Blanche suggested that her mother should always ride on the trolly, except when they were facing a hill; and after a few weak protestations the suggestion was accepted. The trolly was lightened of various useless articles of furniture—a grudging sacrifice on the part of Mrs Gosling—and the party pushed on at a slightly improved pace.

After her disappointment in Pinner, Mrs Gosling's interest in life began rapidly to decline. Seated in her truck, she fell into long fits of brooding on the past. She was too old and too stereotyped to change, the future held no hope for her, and as the meaning and purpose of her existence faded, the life forces within her surely and ever more rapidly ebbed. Reality to her became the discomfort of the sun's heat, the dust of the road, the creak and scream of the trolly wheels. She was incapable of relating herself to the great scheme of life, her consciousness was limited, as it had always been limited, to her immediate surroundings. She saw herself as a woman outrageously used by fate, but to fate she gave no name; the very idea, indeed, was too abstract to be appreciated by her. Blanche, Millie and that horrible truck were all that was left of her world, and in spirit she still moved in the beloved, familiar places of her suburban home.

## 3

As the Goslings trudged out into the Chilterns they came into new conditions. Soon they found overcrowding in place of desolation. The harvest was ripening and in a month's time the demand for labour would almost equal the supply, for the labour offered was quite absurdly unskilled and ten women would be required to perform the work of one man equipped with machines. But at the end of July the surplus of women, almost exclusively Londoners, had no employment and little food, and many were living on grass, nettles, leaves, any green stuff they could boil and eat, together with such scraps of meat and vegetables as they could steal or beg. Their experiments with wild green stuffs often resulted in some form of poisoning, and dysentery and starvation were rapidly increasing the mortality among them. Nevertheless, in Rickmansworth houses were still at a premium, and many of those who camped perforce in fields or by the roadside were too enfeebled by town-life to stand the exposure of the occasional cold, wet nights. The majority of the women in this ring were those who had been too weak to struggle on. They represented the class least fitted to adapt themselves to the new conditions. The stronger and more capable had persisted, and left these congested areas behind them; and it was evident that in a very few months a balance between labour and supply would be struck by the relentless extermination of the weakest by starvation and disease.

Blanche, if she was unable to grasp the problem which was being so inevitably solved by the forces of natural law, was at least able to recognize clearly enough that she and her two dependents must not linger in the district to which they had now come. Aunt May had warned her that she must push out as far as Amersham at the nearest, but Millie was too tired and footsore to go much further than Rickmansworth that night, and after a fruitless search for shelter they camped out half a mile from the town in the direction of Chorley Wood.

They made some kind of a shield from the weather by emptying and tilting the trolly, and they hid their supply of food behind them at the lowest point of this species of lean-to roof. The two girls had realized that that supply would soon be raided if the fact of its existence were to become known. They had been the object of much scrutiny as they passed, and their appearance of well-being had prompted endless demands for food, from that pitiful crowd of emaciated women and children. It had been a demand quickly put on one side by lying. Their applicants found it only too easy to believe that the Goslings had no food hidden in the truck.

"I hated to refuse some of 'em," Blanche said as they carefully hid what food was left to them, before turning in for the night, "but what good would our little bit have done among all that lot? It would have been gone in half a jiff."

"Well, of course," agreed Millie.

Mrs Gosling had taken little notice of the starving crowd. "We've got nothin' to give you," was her one form of reply. She might have been dealing with hawkers in Wisteria Grove.

She was curiously apathetic all that afternoon and evening, and raised only the feeblest protestation against the necessity for sleeping in the open air. But she was very restless during the night, her limbs twitched and she moved continually, muttering and sometimes crying out. And as the three women were all huddled together, partly to make the most of their somewhat insufficient lean-to, and partly because they were afraid of the terrors of the open air, both Blanche and Millie were constantly aroused by their mother's movements. Once they heard her calling urgently for "George."

"Mother's odd, isn't she?" whispered Blanche after one such disturbance. "Do you think she's going to be ill?"

"Shouldn't wonder," muttered Millie. "Who wouldn't be?"

In the morning Blanche was very careful with their food. For breakfast they ate only part of a tin of condensed beef between them—Mrs Gosling indeed ate hardly anything. The eggs which they had brought from Sudbury they reserved, chiefly because they had neither water nor fire.

They drank from a stream, later, and at midday Blanche and Millie each ate one of the eggs raw. Mrs Gosling refused all food on this occasion. She had been very quiet all the morning, and had made little complaint when she had been forced to walk the many hills which they were now encountering.

Blanche was uneasy and tried to induce her mother to talk. "Do you feel bad, mother?" she asked continually.

"I wish I could get 'ome," was all the reply she received.

"She'll be all right when we can get settled somewhere," grumbled Millie. "If such a time ever comes."

## 4

They came to Amersham in the afternoon. The signs of misery and starvation were here less marked. They were approaching the outer edge of this ring of compression, having passed through the node at Rickmansworth. The faint relief of pressure was evidenced to some extent in the attitude of the people they addressed. It is true that no immediate hope of food and employment were held out to them, but on the one hand Blanche's inquiries were answered with less acerbity and on the other they were less besieged by importunate demands for charity. Blanche gave an egg to one precocious girl of thirteen or so, who insisted on helping them to push the truck uphill, and she and Millie watched the deft way in which the child broke the shell at one end and sucked out the contents. Their own methods had been both unclean and wasteful.

They turned off the Aylesbury Road, towards High Wycombe late in the afternoon and about a mile from Amersham came to a farm where they made their last inquiry that day.

Blanche saw signs of life in the outbuildings and went to investigate, leaving Millie and her mother to guard the truck. She found three women and a girl of fourteen or so milking. For some minutes she stood watching them, the women, after one glance at her, proceeding with their work without paying her any further attention. But, at last, the eldest of the three rose from her stool with a sigh of relief, picked up her wooden bucket of milk, gave the cow a resounding slap on the side, and then, turning to Blanche, said, "Well, my gal, what's for you?"

"Will you change two pints of milk for a small tin of tongue?" asked Blanche. It was the first time she had offered any of their precious tinned meats in exchange for other food, but she wanted milk for her mother, who had hardly eaten anything that day.

The two other women and the girl looked round and regarded Blanche with the first signs of interest they had shown.

"Tongue, eh?" said the older woman. "Where from did you get tongue, my gal?"

"London," replied Blanche tersely.

"When did you leave there?" asked the woman, and then Blanche was engaged in a series of searching questions respecting the country she had passed through.

"You can have the milk if you've anything to put it in," said the woman at last, and Blanche went to fetch the tongue and the two bottles that they had had from Aunt May.

The bottles had to be scalded, a precaution that had not occurred to Blanche, and one of the other women was sent to carry out the operation.

"Well, your tale don't tell us much," said the woman of the farm, "but we always pass the news here, now. Where are you going to sleep to-night?"

Blanche shrugged her shoulders.

"You can sleep here in the outhouses, if you've a mind to," said the woman, "but I warn you we get a crowd. Silly Londoners like yourself for the most part, but we find a use for 'em somehow, though I'd give the lot for three labourers."

She paused and twisted her mouth on one side reflectively. "Ah! well," she went on with a sigh, "no use grieving over them that's gone; all I was goin' to say was, if you sleep here you'd better keep an eye on what food you've got with you. My lot'll have it before you can say knife, if they get half a chance."

"It isn't us girls, me and my sister," explained Blanche. "It's my mother. She's bad, I'm afraid. If she could sleep in your kitchen…? She wouldn't steal anything."

After a short hesitation the woman consented.

Yet neither the glory of being once more within the four walls of a house, nor the refreshment of the milk which she drank readily enough, seemed appreciably to rouse Mrs Gosling's spirits.

The woman of the farm, a kindly enough creature, plied the old lady with questions, but received few and confused answers in reply. Mrs Gosling seemed dazed and stupid. "A touch of the sun," the farmer's widow thought.

"The sun's been cruel strong the past week," she said, "but she'll be all right in a day or two, get her to shelter."

"Ah! that's the trouble," said Blanche.

That night the farmer's widow said no more on that subject. She allowed the three Goslings to sleep in an upstair room, in which there was one small bed for the mother, and the two girls slept on the floor. Exchanging confidence for confidence, they brought their truck into the kitchen; and then the farmer's widow proceeded to lock up for the night, an elaborate business, which included the fastening of all ground-floor windows and shutters.

"It's a thievin' crowd we've got about here," she explained, "and you can't blame them or anyone when there ain't enough food to go round. But we have to be careful for 'em. Let 'em go their own way and they'd eat up everything in a week and then starve. It looks like your being hard on 'em, but it's for their own good. There's some, of course," she went on, "as you have got to get shut of. Only yesterday I had to send one of 'em packing. A Jew woman she was, called 'erself Mrs Isaacson or something. She was a caution."

Blanche wondered idly if this were the same Mrs Isaacson who had stayed too long with Aunt May.

The woman of the farm roused the Goslings at sunrise, and she, like

Aunt May, had a brisk, practical, morning manner.

She gave the travellers no more food, but when they were nearly ready to take the road again she gave them one valuable piece of information.

"If I was you," she said, "I'd make through Wycombe straight along the road here, and go up over the hill to Marlow. Mind you, they won't let every one stop there. But you look two healthy gals enough and it's getting on towards harvest when there'll be work as you *can* do."

"Marlow?" repeated Blanche, fixing the name in her memory.

The farmer's widow nodded. "There's a man there," she said. "A queer sort, by all accounts. Not like Sam Evans, the butcher at Wycombe, he ain't. Seems as this Marlow chap don't have no truck with gals, except setting 'em to work. However, time'll show. He may change his mind yet."

They had some difficulty with Mrs Gosling. She refused feebly to leave the house. "I ain't fit to go out," she complained, and when they insisted she asked if they were going home.

"Best say 'yes,'" whispered the woman of the farm. "The sun's got to her head a bit. She'll be all right when you get her to Marlow."

Blanche accepted the suggestion, and by this subterfuge Mrs Gosling was persuaded into the truck. The girl found the ruins of an umbrella, which they rigged up to protect her from the sun.

Blanche and Millie were quite convinced now that their mother was suffering from a slight attack of sunstroke.

Both the girls were still footsore, and one of Millie's boots had worn into a hole, but they had a definite objective at last, and only some ten or twelve miles to travel before reaching it.

"We shall be there by midday," said Blanche, hopefully.

Unconsciously, every one was using a new measure of time.

# CHAPTER 16

*The Young Butcher of High Wycombe*

## 1

Near Wycombe a woman rose from under the hedge as the Goslings approached, and came out into the middle of the road. She was a stout, florid woman, whose age might have been anything between forty and fifty. Her gait and the droop of her shoulders, rather than the flaccidity of her rather loose skin, gave her the appearance of being past middle age.

"Goot morning," she said as the Goslings came up. "If it iss no inconvenience I would like to come with you." She spoke with a foreign accent, thickening her final consonants and giving a different value to some of her vowels.

"Where to?" asked Blanche curtly.

"Ah! that! what does it matter?" returned the woman. "I have been living with a farmer's wife further back along the road there. But she was not company for me. She was common. Now I see that you and your mother are not common. And I do not care to live with farmers' wives. But where we go? Does it matter? We all go to find work in the fields—aristocrat as much as peasant. But iss it not better that we who are not peasants should go together?"

Millie giggled surreptitiously, and Mrs Gosling appeared conscious of the fact that some one was addressing them.

"We're goin' 'ome," she remarked, and Millie gently prodded her in the back.

"Goin' 'ome," repeated Mrs Gosling firmly.

"Ach! You are lucky. There are few that have homes now," replied the strange woman. "I had a home, once, how long ago. Now, during two months, I have no home." She was evidently on the verge of tears.

"Mother's got a touch of the sun," Blanche said in a low voice, "and we have to pretend we're going home. You needn't tell her we're not."

"Have no fear," replied the stranger. "I am all that is most discreet, yes."

Blanche hardened her heart. This woman took too much for granted. "I don't see it's any use your coming with us," she said.

"Ach! we others, we should cling together," said the stranger, with a large gesture.

"We're nobody," replied Blanche, curtly.

"It iss well to say that. I know. There iss good reason. I, too, must tell the common people that I am a nobody, I call myself, even, Mrs Isaacson. But between us there iss no need to say what iss not true. I can see what you are. Although I am not English, I have lived many years already in England, and I can see. It iss well that we cling together? Yes?"

"Oh!" burst out Blanche. "You're Mrs Isaacson, are you? I've heard of you."

For one moment Mrs Isaacson's fine eyes seemed to look inwards in an instantaneous review of her past. "Ach! so! Then we are friends already," she said cautiously.

"I heard of you from Aunt May," said Blanche, and the faint air of respect with which she pronounced the name did not escape the notice of the alert Jewess.

"Ach! the so dear and so clever Auntie May," she said. "But she iss too kind, and work so hard while her sister do always nothing. See, I will help you to draw your poor mother who has a touch of the sun. You and I at the handle and your beautiful sister to push, while we talk a little of the clever Auntie May. Yes?"

Blanche had been forewarned. She could only put one construction on the little she had heard of Mrs Isaacson. But the Jewess's manner no less than her conversation was subtly flattering. Moreover, she had made no appeal for help; finally there was a certain urgency about her, a force of will which Blanche found it difficult to resist. And as the girl still hesitated Mrs Isaacson bravely seized her side of the trolly handle and the procession moved on.

The Goslings found a use for her when they came to the drop of Amersham Hill, going down into High Wycombe. Blanche proposed that Mrs

Gosling should walk down, but the old lady did not seem to understand her. She looked perplexed and kept saying, "I don't remember this road. Are you sure we're goin' right, Blanche?"

"Ah! she must not walk in this heat," put in Mrs Isaacson. "We three can manage very well." And, indeed, although she manifestly suffered greatly from the exertion, the Jewess was of very great assistance in retarding the speed of the trolly as they made the perilous descent.

After that there could be no question of calmly telling her to go her own way.

By the time they had crossed the almost deserted town at that hour nearly all the women were either in their houses or working in gardens and fields and had found their way to the Marlow road, Mrs Isaacson had quite become one of the party, and by no means the least energetic.

"We'll have something to eat and some milk, when we get through the town," said Blanche as they faced the long hill up to Handy Cross.

"Presently, presently," replied the heaving Mrs Isaacson, as though food were of little importance to her, but accepting the admission that she had earned the right to share equally with the others.

Their first burst of energy after they had faced the ascent brought them to the gates of Wycombe Abbey, and there they decided to rest and lunch, blissfully ignorant of the long climb which lay before them.

"It will be nice and quiet here in the shade," suggested Mrs Isaacson.

## 2

The old conventions would not have suffered them to sit and eat thus under the walls, at the very gates of Wycombe Abbey. Their clothes and their boots were wearing badly, and Mrs Isaacson, at least, was not too clean. It was noticeable, however, that, despite the dryness of the weather, little dust clung to them. The surface of the roads had not been pounded and crushed into powder during the past six weeks by the constant passage of wheeled traffic, and even in the tracks frequented by farm carts the roads were stained with green. Indeed, everything was greener than in the old days, everything was more vigorous. Whether because the year had been favourable, or because it was relieved from the burden of choking dust which it had had to endure in other years from May onwards, the vegetation in hedges and by the wayside appeared to grow more strongly and with a greater self-assertion. And by contrast with this vigour and cleanness of plant life, the four women in their tumbled clothes and untidy hats, feeble and unsightly remnants of forgotten fashion, were as much out of place as if they had been set down in ancient Greece. The dowdy foolishness of their apparel marked them out from every other living thing about them, they were intruders, despoilers of beauty.

Some dim consciousness of this came to Blanche.

They had spoken little as they ate—Mrs Gosling would touch nothing but milk, and Mrs Isaacson strove desperately and with some success to control the greed that showed in the concentrated eagerness of her eyes and the grasping crook of her fingers—and when they had finished, lingering in the relief of the shade, they were still silent. It seemed as if the first word spoken must necessarily hasten the continuation of their journey.

"Oh! bother this old hat," said Blanche at last.

"I'm going to take mine off," and she drew out the solitary pin which remained to her and cast the hat into the ditch.

"That won't do it any good," remarked Millie but she, too, took off her hat with a sigh of relief.

"I'm going to chuck hats," said Blanche. "What's the good of 'em?"

Mrs Isaacson looked doubtful. "They are a protection from the sun," she said.

"Millie never wore a hat, and she didn't come to any harm," returned Blanche.

"No?" said Mrs Isaacson, and looked thoughtful.

Millie was running her fingers through the masses of her red-brown hair, loosening it and lifting it from her head.

"It *is* a relief," she remarked. "My head gets so hot."

"Ah!" said Mrs Isaacson, "and what beautiful hair! It does not seem right to hide it. I haf a comb in my bag. It is almost all I haf left. Let me now comb your beautiful hair for you."

"Oh! don't you bother," said Millie sheepishly, but she allowed herself to be persuaded. "Don't lose the hair-pins," she warned her newly-found lady's maid.

"It seems so funny out here in the open road," giggled Millie.

Mrs Isaacson's praise was fulsome.

Blanche watched without comment. Mrs Gosling was plunged in meditation. She was involved in an immense problem relating to the housekeeping at Wisteria Grove. She was debating whether the lace-curtains at the front windows could be washed at home when they went back.

Suddenly the attention of the three younger women was caught by unnatural sounds that came from the further side of the wall against which they were leaning sounds of voices, laughing and singing, the crunch of wheels and the stamping of horses.

The two girls jumped to their feet. Mrs Isaacson rose more deliberately, with a grunt of expostulation. Mrs Gosling was in a world far removed and continued to debate her problem.

Millie's hands were fumbling at her hair, and Blanche was first at the gate.

"Oh! my!" she exclaimed. "Why, whatever..."

"Goody!" squealed Millie, still struggling with her loose mane.

### 3

The centre and object of the curious crowd which moved slowly down the drive was a landau and pair. The horses were decorated as if for a May-day fête, grotesquely, foolishly decorated with roses, syringa and buttercups made into shapeless bunches and tied to the harness. Three or four women walked at the horses' heads, leading them with absurdly beflowered ropes.

Round the landau a dozen girls and young women were dancing, chattering, singing, laughing; constantly turning to the occupant of the carriage, for whose benefit the whole performance was being conducted. Some of them had their necks and breasts bare, and all appeared to be frankly shameless. They twisted and danced with clumsy eagerness, threw themselves about, screamed and shrieked, unaware of any observer but the one whose notice they were seeking to attract. They were graceless, civilized savages; Bacchantes who had never known the beauty of unconscious abandonment. There was the ugliness of conscious purpose in their every attitude, and no trace of the freedom that comes from careless rapture.

In the carriage a man and a woman were sitting side by side. The man was young, with strong claims to physical beauty—tall, broad-shouldered, swarthy, with boldly modelled features and heavily lidded eyes. But his skin was coarse; the bulk of his body was too gross for clean, muscular strength; his curly, well-oiled hair was thinning at the temples; his loose mouth leered and gaped. He was dressed in a suit of broadly-patterned tweed, his great red fingers were covered with rings, he wore a heavy gold bangle on each thick, round wrist, and a sweet, frail rose was thrust into his black and greasy hair.

The woman beside him was the typical courtesan of the ages, low-browed and full-lipped. Her eyes were eloquent with the subtleties of love, with invitation, retreat, fear and desire. Had she been dressed becomingly she would have been beautiful; but she was English and modern, and her great meaningless hat and senseless garments were of the fashion that had been in vogue just before the plague. This reigning sultana and her lover were more incongruous in that setting than the two dishevelled, travel-worn girls, who retreated timidly to let the landau pass out between the great iron gates.

The Bacchantes eyed the Goslings with obvious disfavour, but the beauty in the landau seemed unaware of their presence until her lord's attention was attracted by the sight of Millie's hair—it was all down again, rippling and spreading to her waist.

The young butcher had been lolling back in a corner of his carriage, magnificently indolent, sure of worship; but his satiety was pierced by the sight of that flaming mane. He sat up and looked at Millie with the experienced eyes which had served him so well in his judgment of cattle.

"'Ere, 'alf a jiff," he commanded the nymphs at his horses' bridles, and the carriage was stopped.

Millie, covered with shame, shrank back, and cowered behind Blanche, who threw up her chin and met the butcher's eyes with all the contempt of which she was capable little enough, perhaps, for she, too, was weak with unreasoning terror. Behind their backs the Jewess grimaced her scorn of them.

"You needn't be afraid of me—I ain't goin' to 'urt yer—" began the butcher, but his lady interrupted him.

Her fine eyes grew bright with anger. "If you stop here, I shall get out," she said, and her inflexion was not that of the people.

The butcher visibly hesitated. It may be that this chain had held him too long and was beginning to gall him, but he looked at her and wavered.

"No 'arm in stoppin'," he muttered. "Pass the news an' that."

"Are you going on?" demanded the beauty fiercely.

"All right, all right," he returned sullenly. "You needen' get so blasted 'uffy about it, old gal. Oh, gow on, you!" he added to the nymphs. "Wot the 'ell are yer starin' at?"

As the landau moved on, he looked back once at Millie.

## 4

"What a brute," said Blanche when the procession had passed on down the hill towards Wycombe.

"How he stared at my hair," said Millie, with a giggle. "I did try to get it up, but it's that stubborn with the heat or something."

"Lucky for us he had that creature with him," commented Blanche.

Millie assented without fervour. She was bold enough now the danger had passed.

Mrs Isaacson looked from one to the other and attempted no criticism of the adventure.

"You must let me do up your beautiful hair," she said to the simpering Millie.

Millie was grateful. "It *is* kind of you, Mrs Isaacson, I'm sure," she said. "My hair is a trouble. I sometimes think I'll cut it all off and be done with it..."

She appeared excited and chatted incessantly while the hair-dressing continued, and Blanche restored the remains of their meal to the trolly.

With some difficulty they succeeded in getting Mrs Gosling back into her carriage. She had taken no notice of the procession, but as they were starting again she awoke from her abstraction to ask: "When d'you expect we'll be 'ome, Blanche? I've been thinkin' about them curtains in the drawin'-room..."

"We'll be home in an hour or two, now," Blanche said, reassuringly. She did not know what a struggle awaited them before they should top the hill at Handy Cross.

Mrs Isaacson had forsaken her place at the pole. "I shall be able to push more strongly behind," she had said, but despite the theoretical gain in mechanical advantage obtained by the new arrangement, the hill seemed never-ending. They had to rest continually, and always they looked with increasing irritation at the quiet figure in the trolly, chief cause of their distress.

"I believe she could walk all right," Millie broke out at last.

"If it was for a little way, it would help," commented Mrs Isaacson.

But when Blanche put the proposition to her mother, Mrs Gosling seemed unable to comprehend it, and pity influenced them to renew the struggle.

So they toiled on with growing impatience until they reached level ground again; and presently, looking down over the long slope of the valley, saw, two miles and a half away, the spire of Marlow Church.

They rested under a hedge for a time, and when they started again Millie followed her sister's example and discarded her hat. Blanche, with a certain courage of opinion, had left hers under the walls of Wycombe Abbey, but Millie's hat found a place in the trolly.

The ease of the long descent permitted a renewal of conversation, and Mrs Isaacson and Millie talked in undertones as they made their way down towards Marlow. Blanche took little notice of them; she was struggling perplexedly with the problems of life. Mrs Gosling's presence was negligible.

"That was a very handsome fellow in the carriage," remarked Mrs Isaacson suddenly, "I think you do well not to go near that place again." Her fine eyes fixedly regarded the broad, rusty back of Mrs Gosling and the broken ribs of her umbrella.

Millie simpered. "Oh! I should be safe enough. His wife'd see to that."

"She was not his wife," returned Mrs Isaacson. "Men would not marry now that they are so few."

"Well! there's a thing to say!" exclaimed Millie on a note of expostulation, interested nevertheless.

"It iss true," continued Mrs Isaacson. "I haf heard of this handsome young fellow. He iss a butcher, and he goes every day to kill the sheep and cows, because the women do not like that work. And he iss very strong, and clever also. He teach a few of the women how to cut up the sheep and the cows. And he iss much admired, it iss of course, by all the young women; but he does not marry because he is one man among so many women, and it would not be right that he should love only one, for so there would be so few children and the world would die. Yes! But he has for a time one who iss favourite, for another time another favourite. And that iss why I warn you not to return. Because I see that he admire your so beautiful hair. And I see that if you had not been so modest and so good, and hide behind your sister, he would have come down from his carriage and put you up there beside him. And he would have said to that bold ugly woman, 'Go, I tire of you, I will haf beside me this one who iss young and beautiful and has hair of gold.' It iss not safe for you, there."

"Oh! I say," commented Millie.

"It iss true," nodded Mrs Isaacson, with intensest conviction.

"Oh! well, thank goodness, I'm not one of that sort," said Millie, warm in the knowledge of her virtue.

"Truly not," assented Mrs Isaacson. "You must not be displeased that

I warn you. It iss not your goodness that I doubt. It iss that this man iss so powerful. He iss able to do what he wishes. He iss a king."

"Goody!" was the mark of surprise with which Millie punctuated this remarkable piece of information, and for several yards they trudged on in silence.

But Millie soon revived this fascinating subject by saying thoughtfully, "Well, you don't catch me over there again."

"Truly not. It iss not wise," agreed Mrs Isaacson, and proceeded to enlarge upon Millie's dangerous beauty.

It was a topic entirely new to Millie. She simpered and giggled, disclaimed her attractions, protested that Mrs Isaacson was "getting at" her, and became so absorbed in the fascination of her disavowal that she forgot her weariness, her tender feet—naked to the road in two places—and all her discouragements. She walked with a more conscious air, straightening her back and lifting her head. The blood moved more freely in her veins, and she presently became so vivacious in her replies that Blanche was aroused to a sense of something unfamiliar. She checked the trolly and looked back at her sister, past the quiet brooding figure of Mrs Gosling.

"What is it, Mill?" she asked.

"Oh! nothing!" replied Millie. "We were just talking."

"Seem to be enjoying yourselves," said Blanche.

"We were saying that we shall soon now arrive at some place where we can rest. Yes?" put in Mrs Isaacson, and thus established a ground of confidence between herself and Millie.

"P'raps. I dunno!" returned Blanche. She sighed and looked round her.

In the fields between them and Marlow they could see here and there little figures stooping and straightening.

"Ooh!" exclaimed Millie, suddenly.

"What?" asked Blanche.

"There's another man," said Millie, pointing. "We'd better scoot!"

But they made no attempt to put such an impossible plan into action. The man had evidently seen them. He was coming towards them across one of the fields, shouting to attract their attention. "Hi! wait a minute!"

they thought he was saying.

"*Mill!*" exclaimed Blanche, with extraordinary emphasis.

"What?" asked Millie, nervously. She was flushed and trembling.

"Do you see who it is?"

"It isn't the one out of the carriage…" hesitated Millie.

"*No!* Silly. It's that young fellow who used to live with us, our Mr Fastidious. What was his name? Thrale! You remember."

"Goody!" said Millie. She was conscious of a quite inexplicable feeling of disappointment.

"He iss a friend? Yes?" asked Mrs Isaacson.

# BOOK III

## WOMANKIND IN THE MAKING

# CHAPTER 17

*London to Marlow*

1

The history of mankind is the history of human law. The larger ordinances of the universe are commonly referred to some superior lawgiver, under such names as *God* and *physico-chemical action*; names which appear mutually subversive only to the bigot, whether theologian or biologist. These larger ordinances sometimes appear inflexible, as in the domain of physics and chemistry, sometimes empirical as in the development of species, but we may believe that if they change at all, the period of change is so great as to be outside any possibility of observation by a few thousand generations of mankind.

Human law, on the other hand, is tentative, without sound precedent and in its very nature mutable. In our miserably limited record of history, that paltry ten thousand years which is but a single tick of the cosmic watch, we have been unable to formulate any overruling law to which other laws are subject. Climate, race and condition impose certain limitations, and within that *enceinte* civilizations have developed a system of rules, increasing always in complexity, and have then failed to maintain their place in the competitive struggle. It has been rashly suggested that the overriding law of laws is that rigidity is fatal to the nation. An analogy has been found in the growth of the child. Here and there some bold spirit has ventured the daring hypothesis that if a young child be confined within a perfectly fitting iron shell he will not grow. Such speculations, however, do not appeal to mankind as a whole. Perhaps the truth of the matter is that nothing appals us so much as the idea that man is capable of growth. Is it not inconceivable that any race of men could be wiser, more perfect than ourselves?

Nevertheless, out of all vague speculation one deliciously certain axiom presents itself, namely that mankind cannot live without law of some kind. The most primitive savage has his ordinances. The least primary concussion of individuals develops a rule of practice, whether it takes such diverse forms as "hit first," or "present the other cheek"; although the latter rule has not yet been developed beyond the stage of theory.

In the unprecedented year of the new plague, the old rules were thrown into the melting pot, but within three months humanity was evolving precedents for a new statute book. The concussions of these three months were fierce and destructive. Women, in the face of death, killed and stole in the old primitive ways, unhampered now by the necessity to kill and steal according to the tedious rules of twentieth-century civilization, rules that women had never been foolish enough to reverence in the letter. All those complex and incomprehensible laws had been made by men for men, and after the plague there was none to administer them, for no women and few men had ever had the least idea what the law was. Even the lawgivers themselves had had to wait for the pronouncement of some prejudiced or unprejudiced judge. Women had long known what our Bumbles can only learn by bitter experience, inspired to vision in some moment of fury or desolation.

But within three months of the first great exodus of women from the town, one dominant law was being brought to birth. It was not written on tables of stone, nor incorporated in any swollen, dyspeptic book of statutes; it was not formulated by logic, nor was it the outcome of serious thought by any individual or by a solemn committee. The law rose into recognition because it was a necessity for the life of the majority, and although that majority was not compact, had no common deliberate purpose, and had never formulated their demand in precise language, the new law came into being before harvest and was accepted by all but a small resentful minority of aristocrats and landowners, as a supreme ordinance, indisputably just.

This law was that *every woman had a right to her share in the bounty of Nature*, and the corollary was that *she earned her right by labour*.

In those days the justice of the principle was perfectly obvious; so obvious, indeed, that the law came to birth without the obstetric skill of any parliament whatever.

## 2

It is now impossible to say why such different types of male humanity as Jasper Thrale, George Gosling or the Bacchus of Wycombe Abbey escaped the plague. The bacillus (surely a strangely individual type, it must have been) was never isolated, nor the pathology of the disease investigated. The germ was some new unprecedented growth which ran through a fierce cycle of development within a few months, changed its nature as it swarmed into every corner of the earth, and finally expired more quickly than it had come into being.

If the male survivors in Europe and the East had been of one type, some theory might be formulated to account for their immunity; but so far as science can pronounce an opinion, the living male residue can only be explained by the doctrine of chances. A few escaped, by accident. In the British Isles there may have been 1,500 men who thus survived. In the whole of Europe, besides, there were less than a thousand. It seems probable that even before Scotland was attacked the climax had been reached; by the time the plague reached England the first faint evidences of a decline in virulence may be marked....

From the first, Jasper Thrale ventured his life without an afterthought. He was fearless by nature. He did not lack those powers of imagination which are commonly supposed to add so greatly to the terror of death, he simply lacked the feeling of fear. In all his life he had never experienced that sickness of apprehension which dissolves our fibre into a quivering jelly—as though the spirit had already withdrawn from the trembling inertia of the flesh. Perhaps Thrale's spirit was too dominant for such retreat, was more completely master of its material than is the spirit of the common man. For the spirit cannot know bodily fear, it is the apprehensive flesh that wilts and curdles at the approach of danger. And it is worthy of notice that in the old days, up to the early twentieth century, these rare cases of fearlessness in individuals were more often found among women than among men.

Thrale, with his perfectly careless courage, found plenty of work for himself in London during May and early June. He acted as a scavenger, and still went far afield with his burial cart long after every trace of living male humanity had disappeared from the streets of London.

Then one day, at the end of June, he realized that his task was futile, and it came to him that there was work awaiting him of more importance than this purification of streets which might never again echo to the traffic of humanity.

So he chose the best bicycle he could find in Holborn Viaduct, stripped a relay of four tyres from other machines, and with these and a reserve of food made into a somewhat cumbrous parcel, he set out to explore the new world.

He took the Bath Road, intending to make exploration of the fertile West Country. He had Cornish blood in his veins, and his ultimate goal was the county which had almost escaped urbanization. As he then visualized the problem, it appeared that life would offer greater possibilities in such places.

But before he reached Colnbrook, he had recognized that work was required of him nearer home. The exodus was then in progress. He came through armies of helpless women and children flying from starvation; women who had no object in view save that of escape to the country; "Silly Londoners" with no knowledge of how food was to be obtained when their goal was reached.

He did not stay there, however. He was beginning to see the outline of his plan, and at the same time the limitation of his own powers. He saw that enough food could not be raised near London to support the multitude, that the death of the many was demanded by the needs of the few if any were to survive, and that communities must be formed with the common purpose of tilling the land and excluding those who could not earn their right to support. In such a catastrophe as this, charity became a crime.

He intended even then to push on beyond Reading, but in Maidenhead he met a woman who influenced him to a nearer goal.

## 3

She stepped into the road and held up her hand.

Thrale stopped; he thought she was about to make the familiar demand either for food or a direction.

"Well?" he said curtly.

"Where are you going?" she asked.

He shrugged his shoulders. "To find room," he said.

"There is room for you near here," said the woman, "if you'll work."

"At what?" he asked.

"Machinery, harvesting machinery, agricultural machinery of all sorts."

"Where?" asked Thrale.

She dropped her voice and looked about her. "Marlow," she said. "It—it's an eddy. Off the main roads and by the river. There are less than a thousand women there at present, and we are keeping the others out; at least until after harvest. There is plenty of land about, and we're keeping ourselves at present. Only we *do* want a man for the machines. Will you come and help us?"

"I'll come and see what I can do," said Thrale "I won't promise to stay."

"Aren't there any other men, there?" he added after a moment's hesitation.

"One at Wycombe," said the women. "He's a butcher, but—"

"I understand," said Thrale.

"And meanwhile you might help me," said the woman. "I come over here with a horse and cart to raid the seedsmen's shops. If we leave them the women would eat all the beans and peas and things, you know; enough to feed us for the winter gone in a week, and no one any the better. Isn't it awful how careless we are?"

## 4

She was a fair, clear-eyed girl, with the figure and complexion of one who had devoted considerable attention to outdoor sports. She was wearing a man's Norfolk jacket (men's clothing was so plentiful), and a skirt that barely reached her knees, and did not entirely hide cloth knickerbockers which might also have been adapted from a man's garment. Below the knickerbockers she displayed thick stockings and sandals. Her splendid fair hair furnished sufficient protection for her head, and she had dressed a pillow of it into the nape of her neck as a shield for the sun.

Thrale looked at her with a frank curiosity as they made their way up the town to a seedsman's shop. She had left the horse and cart there, she explained, while she explored other streets of the town.

"Who are you?" he asked.

"Eileen, of Marlow," she said. "There doesn't seem to be another Eileen there, so one name's enough."

"Is that how your community feel about it?" he asked. She smiled.

"We're beginning," she said.

He pondered that for a time, and then asked, "Who *were* you?"

"Does it matter?" was the answer.

"Not in the least," said Thrale. "Never did much so far as I was concerned, but I have a memory of having seen your photographs in the illustrated papers. I was wondering whether you had been actress, peeress, scandal; or perhaps all three."

She laughed. "I'm the eldest daughter of the late Duke of Hertford," she said, "the *ci-devant* Lady Eileen Ferrar, citizen."

"Oh, was that it?" replied Thrale carelessly. "Where's this shop of yours?"

The loot was heavier than Eileen had anticipated. The shop had been ransacked, but they found an untouched store, containing such valuables as beans, potatoes and a few small sacks of turnip seed at the bottom of a yard. When these had been placed in the cart, they decided that the load was sufficient for one horse.

They took the longer road to Marlow, through Bourne End, to avoid the hill. Eileen walked at the horse's head, with Thrale beside her wheeling his bicycle, and during those two hours he learnt much of the little community which he proposed to serve for a time.

It seemed that in Marlow—and the same thing must have happened in a hundred other small towns throughout the country—a few women had taken control of the community. These women were of all classes and the committee included an Earl's widow, a national schoolmistress, a small green-grocer, and an unmarried woman of property living half a mile out of the town. These women had worked together in an eminently practical way; at first to relieve distress, and then to plan the future. They had wasted little time in discussions among themselves—none of them had the parliamentary sense of the uses of debate. When they had disagreed, they had had plenty of scope to carry out varying methods within their own spheres of influence.

Their first and most difficult task had been to teach the members of their community to work for the common good, and that task was by no means perfected as yet. Co-operation was agreeable enough to those who had nothing to lose, but the women in temporary possession of the sources of food supply were not so easily convinced. In many instances the committee's arguments had been suddenly clenched by an exposition of *force majeure*, and property owners had discovered to their amazement that they had no remedy.

But the head and leader of Marlow was a farmer's daughter of nineteen, a certain Carrie Oliver. Her father had had a small farm in the Chilterns not far from Fingest. He had been a lazy, drunken creature, and from the time Carrie had left the national school she had practically carried on the work of the farm single-handed. She liked the work; the interest of it absorbed her.

The Marlow schoolmistress had remembered her when the committee had first faced the daunting task of providing for the future. They had been more or less capable of organizing a majority of the women, but no member of the committee knew the secrets of agriculture and stock-breeding, and in all Marlow and the neighbourhood no woman had been found who was capable of instructing them in all that was necessary.

A deputation of three had been sent to Fingest, and had discovered Miss Oliver in the midst of plenty, cultivating her farm in comfort now that she had been relieved of her father's unwelcome presence.

She had been covered with confusion when requested to leave her retreat and take command of a town and the surrounding twenty thousand acres or so within reach of the new community.

"Oh! I can't," she had said, blushing and ducking her head. "It's easy enough; I'll tell you if there's anything you want to know."

The deputation had then put the case very clearly before her, pointing out that in Miss Oliver's hands lay the future of a thousand lives.

"Oh, dear. I dunno. What can *I* do?" Carrie had said, and when the deputation had urged that she should return with them and take charge forthwith, she had replied that that was quite impossible, that there were the cows to milk, the calves, pigs and chickens to feed, and goodness knew how many other necessary things to be done before sunset.

The deputation had said that cows, calves, horses, sheep, pigs and chickens might and should be transferred forthwith to the neighbourhood of Marlow.

It had taken three days to convince her, Eileen said, and added, "But she's splendid, now. It's wonderful what a lot she knows; and she rides about on a horse everywhere and sees to everything. The difficulty is to stop her getting down and doing the work herself."

Thrale understood that, exceptional male as he was, his position in Marlow would be subordinate to that of Miss Oliver.

"Does she understand agricultural machinery?" he asked.

"Oh, yes," returned Eileen. "But she hasn't time, you see, to attend to all that, and it's so jolly difficult to learn. I've been doing a bit. I'm better at it than most of 'em. But when I saw you it struck me how ripping it would be if you'd come and take over that side. Men are so jolly good at machinery. We shouldn't miss them much if it weren't for that."

## 5

After a marked preliminary hesitation the committee appointed Jasper Thrale chief mechanic of Marlow. The hesitation was understandable. Their only experience of the ways of men in this altered civilization had been drawn from observations of Mr Evans at Wycombe. His manner of life appeared representative of what they might expect. Nevertheless they did not openly condemn him, although he proved an immediate source of trouble, even to these organizers in Marlow. The youth of the place was apt to wander over the hill in the evenings; "just for fun," they said. They went in twos and threes, and occasionally one of them stayed behind. These evening walks interfered with work. "Later on I shouldn't mind so much," Lady Durham had said, commenting on the loss of a young and active worker, "but there is so much to do just now." Her comment showed that even then the situation was being accepted, and that many women were prepared to adapt their old opinions to new conditions. It also showed why the committee hesitated to accept Thrale's services.

Thrale understood their difficulty, and went straight to the point.

"You are afraid that the young women will be wasting time, running after me," he said. "Set your minds at rest. That won't last. And if you give me pupils for my machinery I should prefer women over forty in any case. I believe I shall find them more capable."

He was right in one way. When the excitement of his coming had subsided, he was not the cause of much wasted time. He adopted a manner with the younger women which did not encourage advances. He was, in fact, quite brutally frank. When the young women devised all kinds of impossible excuses to linger in his vicinity he sent them away with hot indignant faces. Among those who sought their sterile amusements in Wycombe it became the fashion openly to express hatred and contempt for "that engine fellow." It was agreed that he "wasn't a proper man." Another section, however, talked scandal, and hinted that assistant-engineer Eileen was the cause of Thrale's pretended misogyny.

The committee found their work more complicated in some respects after Thrale's coming.

Thrale, himself, was supremely indifferent to any scandal or expression of hatred. He had his hands full, his hours of work were only limited by daylight, and six hours sleep was all he asked for or desired. After a very brief introduction to the intricacies of reaper and rake at the hands of Miss Oliver—her father had never been able to afford a binder, but the days of corn-harvest were still far ahead—he set himself to learn the mysteries of all the agricultural machinery in the neighbourhood; traction engines, steam ploughs and thrashing machines, and to pass on the knowledge he gained to his pupils. He found them stupid at first, but they were patient and willing for the most part.

Then, handicapped by the lack of coal, he rode over to Bourne End and discovered two locomotives. One of them was standing on the line a mile out of the station with a full complement of coaches attached, the other was an unencumbered goods engine in a siding. He chose the latter for his first experiment, and succeeded in driving it back to Marlow. It groaned and screamed in a way that indicated serious organic trouble, but after he had overhauled it, it proved capable of taking him to Maidenhead, where he found a sound engine in a shed.

After that he devoted three days to getting a clear line to Paddington, a tedious process which involved endless descents from the cab, and mountings into signal boxes, experiments with levers and the occasional necessity for pushing whole trains out of his path into some siding. But at last he returned with magnificent loot of coal from the almost untouched London yards beyond Ealing.

London was still the storehouse of certain valuable commodities.

His passage through the surrounding country was hailed with cries of amazement and jubilant acclamation. The first railway surely excited less astonishment than did Thrale on his solitary engine. Doubtless the unfortunate women who saw him pass believed that the gods of machinery had returned once more to bring relief from all the burden of misery and unfamiliar work.

And once the points were set and the way open to London by rail he could go and return with tools and many other necessaries that had offered no temptation to the starving multitude who had fled from the town.

Marlow was greatly blessed among the communities in those days.

## 6

The harvest was early that year, and Miss Oliver decided to cut certain fields of barley at the end of July.

Thrale's energies were then diverted to the superintendence of the reapers and binders, and he rode from field to field, overlooking the work of his pupils or spending furious hours in struggle with some refractory mechanism.

One Saturday, an hour or two after midday, he was returning from some such struggle, when he saw a strange procession coming down that long hill from Handy Cross, which some pious women regarded as the road to hell.

Casual immigration had almost ceased by that time, but the sight indicated the necessity for immediate action. The immigration laws of Marlow, though not coded as yet, were strict; and only bona fide workers were admitted, and even those were critically examined.

Thrale shouted to attract attention and the procession stopped.

When he came through the gate on to the road, he was accosted by name.

"Oh, Mr Thrale, fancy finding you," said the young woman at the pole of the truck.

The meeting of Livingstone and Stanley was far less amazing.

An old woman perched on the truck and partly sheltered by the remains of an umbrella, regarded his appearance with some show of displeasure.

"By rights 'e should 'ave written to me in the first place," she muttered.

"Mother's got a touch of the sun," explained Blanche hurriedly.

Thrale had not yet spoken. He was considering the problem of whether he owed any duty to these wanderers, which could override his duty to Marlow.

"Where have you come from?" he asked.

Blanche and Millie explained volubly, by turns and together.

"You see, we don't let anyone stay here," said Thrale.

Blanche's eyebrows went up and she waved her too exuberant sister aside. "We're willing to work," she said.

"And your mother?" queried Thrale. "And this other woman?"

"Ach! I work too," put in Mrs Isaacson. "I have learnt all that is necessary for the farm. I milk and feed chickens and everything."

"You'll have to come before the committee," said Thrale.

"Anywhere out of the sun," replied Blanche, "and somewhere where we can put mother. She's very bad, I'm afraid."

"You can stay to-night, anyway," returned Thrale.

Millie made a face at him behind his back, and whispered to Mrs Isaacson, who pursed her mouth.

"Well, you do seem more civilized here," remarked Blanche as the procession restarted towards Marlow. Thrale, with something of the air of a policeman, was walking by the side of the pole.

"You've come at a good time," was his only comment.

Millie had another shock before they reached the town. She saw what she thought was a second man, on horseback this time, coming towards them. Marlow, she thought, was evidently a place to live in. But the figure was only that of Miss Oliver in corduroy trousers, riding astride.

## 7

Fate had dropped the Goslings into Buckinghamshire to fulfil their destiny. They had been led to Marlow by a casual direction, here and there, after the first propulsion of Blanche's instinct had sent them into the country beyond Harrow. And fate, doubtless with some incomprehensible purpose of its own in view, had quietly decided that in Marlow they were to stay. They had been dropped at a season when, for the first time in the long three months' history of the community, there was a shortage of labour; and Blanche and

Millie, browned by exposure and generally improved by their first six days of healthy life, were quite acceptable additions to the population at that moment. As for Mrs Isaacson, a lady of sufficient initiative and force of character to require no kindly interposition of Providence on her behalf, she arranged her own future as an expert of farm management, and incidentally as the Goslings' housemate. Mrs Isaacson was a burr that would stick anywhere for a time. She displayed an unexpected and highly specialized knowledge of the management of farms, when confronted with the expert Miss Oliver who was far too embarrassed to press her questions home. The casual remarks of Aunt May and her helpers had been retained in Mrs Isaacson's brilliant memory and she displayed her knowledge to the best possible advantage, filling the gaps with irrelevant volubility, gesture and histrionic struggles with the English language, which proved suddenly inadequate to the expression of these recondities that the German would have so aptly expressed. It was inferred that in her native Bavaria, Mrs Isaacson had farmed in the grand style.

Only Mrs Gosling, useless and ineligible, remained for consideration, and she for once took a firm line of her own, and defied the committee, Marlow generally, and the negligible remainder of the cosmos, to alter her determination.

The home at which they had finally arrived did not suit her. The tiny cottage of three rooms in the little street that runs down to the town landing stage had no lace curtains in the front window, no suites of furniture, no hall to save the discreet caller from stepping through the front door straight into the single living-room, no accumulation of dustable ornaments, not even a strip of carpet or linoleum to cover the nakedness of a bricked floor. It was not civilized; it was not decent according to the refined standards of Wisteria Grove; it was an impossible place for any respectable woman to live in, and Mrs Gosling, with unexpected force of character, chose the obvious alternative. She did not, however, make any announcement of her determination; she was wrapped in a speculative depression that found no relief in words. She had been so ordered, hoisted, dragged and bumped through the detested country during the past six days that all show of authority had been taken from her. It may be that deep in her own mind she cherished a sullen and enduring resentment against her daughters, and had vowed to take the last and unanswerable revenge of which humanity is capable. But outwardly she preserved that air of incomprehension which had marked her during the last stages of their journey, and committed herself to no statement of the enormous plan which must have been forming in her mind.

When they took her into the small, brick-paved room and deposited her temporarily on a wooden-seated chair, while they unpacked what remained to them in the accursed trolly, Mrs Gosling took one brief but comprehensive survey of her naked surroundings.

"She's a bit touched, isn't she?" whispered Millie to her sister. "Do you think she understands where we are or what we're doing?"

Blanche shook her head. "I expect she'll be all right in a day or two," she ventured, "It's the sun."

The two girls, stirred to a new outlook on life by the extraordinary experiences of the past months, were on the threshold of diverse adventures. After the toil and anxiety of their tramp through inhospitable country, and the hazard of the open air, this reception into a community and settlement into a permanent shelter afforded a relief which was too unexpected to be qualified as yet by criticism, or any comparison with past glories. They were young and plastic, and to each of them the future seemed to hold some promise; to them the silence and immobility of their mother could only be evidence of impaired faculties.

"We must get her to bed," said Blanche.

Even when Mrs Gosling asked with perfect relevance, "Are we going to stop 'ere, Blanche?" they humoured her with evasive replies. "Well, for a day or two, perhaps," and "Look here, don't you worry about that. We're going to put you to bed."

Her head dropped again and she fell back into her moody silence. Doubtless she meditated on the many wrongs her daughters had done her, and wondered why she should have been brought out to die in this wilderness?

During the nine days that elapsed before her plan matured, she made no further comment on her surroundings. She lay in the upstairs room, sleeping little, with no desire ever again to face the terror of a world which demanded a new mode of thought. Unconsciously she had adopted Blanche's phrase, "Everything's different," but to her the message was one of doom, she could not live in a different world.

And Blanche on her side was puzzled at her mother's apathy and said, "I can't understand it." Yet both the changed conditions and Mrs Gosling's unchangeable habit were fundamental things.

## CHAPTER 18

*Modes of Expression*

### 1

In Marlow that year harvesting and thrashing were carried on simultaneously. August was very dry, and the greater part of the corn was never stacked at all. Thrale took his engines into the fields, and the shocks were loaded on to carts and fed directly into the thrasher. This method entailed some disadvantages, chief among them the retarding of the actual harvest-work, but on the whole it probably economized labour. The scheme would doubtless have been impracticable in the days of small private ownership, but it worked well in this instance, favoured as it was by the drought.

The saving of labour during those six weeks of furious toil was a matter of the first importance. The work, indeed, was too heavy for many of the women who were unable to stand the physical strain of hoisting sheaves from the waggons into the thrasher; and the sacks of grain proved so unmanageable that Thrale had to devise a makeshift hoist for loading them into the carts. In Marlow, at least, machinery was still triumphant, and the committee sighed their relief in the sentence: "I don't know what we should have done without Jasper Thrale." Nevertheless it is quite certain that they would have done without him if it had not been for that fortuitous meeting in Maidenhead.

For Thrale there was no rest possible, even when the last field had been cleared and the last clumsily-built stack of straw or unthrashed corn erected. Besides the necessity for some form of thatching—or, failing efficiency in that direction, for completing the thrashing operations—he had to turn his attention to the immensely difficult problem of turning the grain into flour. He knew vaguely that the grain ought to be cleaned and conditioned before grinding, and that the actual separation of the constituents of the berry was a matter of importance; but he had no practical knowledge of the various operations, and in this matter Miss Oliver was quite unable to help him.

The mill beside the lock presented itself as an intricate and enormously detailed problem which must be solved by a concentrated effort of induction. The only person who appeared to be of real assistance to him was Eileen, and she was apt to tire and fall into despair when the detail of involved and often concealed machinery baffled them for hour after hour. Nevertheless Thrale solved this problem also. His first concern was for a head of water. The weirs had not been touched since the beginning of May, and the river was very low, but by mid-September there was enough water to work for a few hours every day, and, despite endless mistakes and setbacks, the mill was turning out a sufficient supply of fairly respectable looking flour.

Thrale had that wonderful masculine faculty for thus applying himself to a mechanical problem, and, like his predecessors in mechanical invention, it was the problem and not any promise of future reward which interested him. He became absorbed for the time in that problem of grinding corn, grudging the hours he was obliged to devote to other activities; and when he felt the throb of life running through the mill, saw the women he had taught attending each to their own appointed task in the economy, and felt the touch of the fine, smooth flour between his fingers, he needed no thanks from the committee nor promise of independence to reward him for his labour. The sight of this thing he had created was sufficient recompense. He loved this beautiful efficient toy that changed wheat into flour, and oats into meal, it was his to father and to fight for; the perfect child of his ingenuity and toil.

But if Thrale's time was tremendously occupied the women found that they had more opportunities for leisure after harvest. They were still employed in field and garden, and there was still much to be done, but their hours were shorter and the work seemed light in contrast with the heroic labour that had been necessary at the harvest.

And with this first coming of comparative ease, this first opportunity for reflection since the terrible plague had thrust upon them the necessity for fierce and unremitting effort to produce the essentials of life, women began to express themselves in their various ways. Aspirations and emotions that had been crushed by the fatigues of physical labour began to revive; personal inclinations, jealousies and resentments became manifest in the detail of intercourse; old prejudices, religious and social, once more assumed an aspect of importance in the interactions of individuals. There was a faint stir in the community, the first sign of a trouble which was steadily to increase as winter laid its bond upon the storehouses of earth.

## 2

The two Goslings, working only six or seven hours a day in the mill during the latter part of September, found plenty of time for chatter and speculation. They, and more especially Blanche, had shown themselves capable workers in the harvest field, but when hands had been required in his mill Thrale had chosen the Goslings and those whom he considered less adapted to field work; and among them Mrs Isaacson and a member of the committee, Miss Jenkyn, the schoolmistress. (The education problem was in abeyance for the time being. The children had run wild for three months, and been subject only to the discipline of their mothers, but it was understood that the children were to receive attention when the winter brought opportunity.)

Blanche soon distinguished herself as a picked worker in this sphere. Her intelligence was of a somewhat more masculine quality in some respects than that of the average woman; she was slower, more detailed, more logical in her methods. And now that those male characteristics—so often deplored by women in the days before the plague—had been withdrawn from the flux of life, it had become evident that they had been an essential part of the whole, if only a part. Masculine characteristics were at a premium in Marlow that autumn, and as a natural consequence were being rated at an ever higher value. There was a tendency among some women to become more male....

Millie, however, was not among the progressives. She was not gifted intellectually; she had no swift intuitions—such as Eileen had—which enabled her to comprehend her work; she was naturally indolent, and all her emotions came to her through sensation.

When she was put to work in the mill she was secretly elated. She did not believe the stories told of Jasper Thrale's insensibility to feminine attractions, and if she believed those other stories which coupled his name with that of Lady Eileen, Millie was of opinion that such an entanglement was not necessarily final.

The first week of her association with Thrale in the work of the mill brought disillusionment.

When she looked up from her work and caught his eye as he passed her, he either stared coldly or stopped and asked in a businesslike, austere voice whether she wanted assistance. Such intimations should have been sufficient, but in this thing, at least, Millie was persistent. She thought that he did not understand—men were proverbially stupid in these matters. So she waited for an opportunity and within ten days one was presented.

A hesitation in some of the machinery she overlooked provided sufficient excuse for calling the head engineer. She looked down the stepladder which communicated with the floor below and called hesitatingly, "Oh! Please. Mr Thrale."

He heard her and looked up, "What is it?" he asked.

"Something gone wrong," she said blushing, "I've stopped the rollers, but I don't know—"

"All right, I'm coming," he returned, and presently joined her. "By the way," he remarked as he began to examine the machine, "we don't say 'Mister,' now. I thought you'd learnt that."

Millie simpered. "It sounds so familiar not to," she said.

"Rubbish," grunted Thrale. "You can call me 'engineer,' I suppose?"

"Now, look here," he continued, "do you see this hopper in here?"

She came close to him and peered into the machine.

"It gets clogged, do you see?" said Thrale, "and when the meal stutters you've just got to put your hand in and clear it. Understand?"

"I think so," hesitated Millie. She was leaning against him and her body was trembling with delicious excitement. Almost unconsciously she pressed a little closer.

Thrale suddenly drew back. "Do you understand?" he said harshly.

"Ye-yes, I think so," returned Millie; and she straightened herself, looked up at him for a moment and then dropped her eyes, blushing.

"Very well," said Thrale, "and here's another piece of advice for you. If you want to stay in the mill keep your attention on your work. You're a man now, for all intents and purposes; you've got a man's work to do, and you must keep your mind on it. If there's any foolishness you go out into the turnip fields. You won't have another warning," he concluded as he turned and left her.

"Beast," muttered Millie when she was alone. She was shaken with furious anger. "I hate you, you silly stuck-up thing," she whispered fiercely shaking with passion. "Oh, I wish you only knew how I hate you. I won't touch your beastly machines again. I'd sooner a million times be out in the turnip field than in the same mill with *you*, you stuck-up beast. I *won't* work, I won't do a thing, I'll—I'll—"

For a time she was hysterical.

Blanche coming down from the floor above found her sister tearing at her hair.

"Good heavens, Mill, what's up?" she asked.

Millie had passed through the worst stages of her seizure by then, and she dropped her hands. "I dunno," she said. "It's this beastly mill, I suppose."

"I like it," returned Blanche.

"Oh, *you*," said Millie, full of scorn for Blanche's frigidity. "You ought to have been a man, you ought."

"I dunno what's come to you," was Blanche's comment.

## 3

It was maturity that had come to Millie. Her new life of air and physical exercise had set the blood running in her veins. In the Wisteria Grove days she had had an anaemic tendency; the limited routine of her existence and all the suppressions of her narrow life had retarded her development. Now she was suddenly ripe. Two months of sun and air had brought superabundant vitality, and the surplus had become the most important factor in her existence. She found no outlet for her new vigour in the work of the mill. Something within her was crying out for joy. She wanted to find expression.

There were many other young women in Marlow that autumn in similar case, and a rumour was current among them that this was a favourable time for crossing the hill. It was said that the lord of Wycombe was seeking new favourites.

Millie heard the rumour and tossed her head superciliously.

"Let him come here. I'd give him a piece of my mind," she said.

"'E doesn't come 'ere," returned the gossip. "'E's afeard of our Mr Thrale."

"Oh! Jasper Thrale!" said Millie. "That fellow from Wycombe could knock his head off in no time."

The gossip was doubtful.

Millie was incapable of formulating a plan in this connexion, but she was seized with a desire for spending the still September evenings in the open air, and always something drew her towards the hill at Handy Cross. That way lay interest and excitement. There was a wonderful fascination in going as far as the top of the descent into Wycombe.

Usually she joined one or two other young women in these excursions. It was understood between them that they went "for fun," and they would laugh and scream when they reached the dip past the farm, pretend to push each other down the slope, and cry out suddenly: "He's coming! Run!"

But one afternoon, some ten days after Jasper Thrale had threatened her with the turnip field, Millie went alone.

She had left work early. The rain had not come yet, and Thrale was becoming anxious with regard to the shortage of water. He had the sluices of

Marlow and Hedsor weirs closed, and had opened the sluices of the weirs above as far as Hambledon, but so little water was coming down that he decided to work shorter hours for the present.

Blanche had stayed on at the mill to help with repairs. She was rapidly developing into a capable engineer. So Millie, whose only service was that of machine minder, found herself alone and unoccupied.

Every one else seemed to be working. Her friends of the evening excursions were mostly in the fields on the Henley side of the town.

Millie decided she would lie down on the bed and go to sleep for a bit; but even before she came to the cottage she changed her mind. It was a deliciously warm, still afternoon.

Almost automatically she took the road towards Little Marlow; a desire for adventure had overtaken her. Why, she argued, shouldn't she go into Wycombe? There were plenty of other women there. She would be quite safe. She only wanted to see what the place was like.

Her consciousness of perfect rectitude lasted until she reached the dip beyond Handy Cross. Farther than this she had not ventured before. Some mystery lay beyond the turn of the road.

She sat down in the grass by the wayside and called herself a fool, but she was afraid to go further. She and those friends of hers had made this place the entrance to a terrible and fascinating beyond. She remembered how they had feared to stay there in the failing light, daring each other to remain there alone after sunset. There was nothing to be afraid of, she said to herself; and yet she was afraid.

She was hot with her long climb, and the place was quite deserted. She decided to take down her hair to cool herself.

Curiously, she looked upon this simple act as deliciously daring and in some way wicked. She cast half-fearful glances at the green girt shadows of the descending road, as she shook out the masses of her hair. "If anyone should come!" she thought. "If he should come…!"

She giggled nervously, and shivered.

But as time passed, and no one came, she began to lose her fear, and presently she lay full length on the grass, and stared up into the pale blue dome of the sky until her eyes ached and she had to close them. The deep hush of the still afternoon enveloped her in a great calm.

For a time she slept peacefully, and then she dreamed that she was rushing through the air, and that some one chased her. She wanted desperately to be captured, but it was ordained that she must fly, and she flew incredibly fast. She flew through the sunlight into darkness, and awoke to find that some one was standing between her and the sun.

She lay still, paralysed with terror. She bitterly regretted her coming. She would have given ten years of life to be safe home in Marlow.

"Now, where've I seen you before?" asked Sam Evans....

It was nearly dark when Blanche accosted a knot of women in the High Street with a question as to whether they had seen anything of her sister.

One of the women laughed sneeringly. "Ah! She went over the hill this afternoon," she said. "We were in the fields that side, and saw her go."

Blanche's face burned. "She hasn't! I know she hasn't!" she blurted out. "She isn't one of that sort."

The woman laughed again.

"She's one of the lucky ones," another woman remarked. "You can expect her back in a week or two's time."

## 4

On the same evening that Millie crossed the hill, Lady Eileen Ferrar encountered the spirit of passion in another shape.

The thought of a lonely bathe tempted her, and she crossed the river, made her way through deserted Bisham, and back to the stream along a narrow, overhung lane beyond Bisham Abbey.

The sun had set, but when she came out from the trees there was light in the sky and on the water. Overhead a few wisps of cirrus, sailing in the far heights of air, still caught the direct rays of the sun. Eileen paused on the bank, rejoicing in the glow of colour about her; but as she gazed, the little fleet of salmon-tinted clouds were engulfed in the great earth-shadow, and the delicate crisp rose-leaves were transfigured into flat stipples of steel grey.

A slight chill had come into the air, but the water was deliciously soft and warm. Eileen swam a couple of hundred yards up-stream, towards the gloom of shadows that obscured the course of the river. The after-glow was fading now, and though the surface of the water seemed to catch some reflection of light from an unknown source, the near distance loomed dark and mysterious. She trod water for a few moments, but could not decide whether the river turned to right or left. To all appearances, it terminated abruptly fifty yards ahead....

A new sound was forcing itself upon her attention—a low, steady booming. She stopped swimming, and, keeping herself afloat by slow, silent movements of hands and feet under water, she listened attentively. The dull boom seemed changed into a low, ceaseless moan.

She remembered then the recently opened sluices of Temple Weir, but quite suddenly she was aware of fear. She thought she saw a movement among the reeds by the bank. She thought she heard laughter and the thin pipe of a flute.

Were the old gods coming back to witness the death of man, as they had witnessed his birth? Now that machinery and civilization were being re-absorbed into the nature-spirit from which they had been wrung by the force of man's devilish and alien intelligence, were the old things returning for one mad revel before the creatures of their sport disappeared for ever, these representatives of a species which had failed to hold its own in the struggle for existence?

Night was coming up like a shadow, and in the east a red, enormous moon was rising, coming not to dissipate, but to enhance the mysteries of the dark, coming to countenance the wild and blind the eyes of man.

Eileen, almost motionless, was floating down with the drift of the sluggish stream. She was afraid to intrude upon the natural sounds of the night, the stealthy trickle of the river, and the furtive rustle of secret movement whose origin she could not guess. And again she thought that she heard the trembling reed of a distant flute.

She touched bottom near her landing-place, and waded out of the river, crouching, afraid even in the black shadow of the trees to exhibit the white column of her slim body. She dried and dressed hastily, and when she felt again the touch of her familiar clothes about her, she knew that she was safe from the wiles of nymph or satyr. She had come out of the half-world that interposes between man and Nature; her clothes made her invisible to the earth-gods, and hid them from her knowledge.

But she was still trembling and afraid. The flesh had terrors great as those of the spirit.

A little uncertain wind was coming out of the south-west, and the trees were stirred now and again into hushed whisperings. A dead leaf brushed her face in falling, and she started back, thrusting at an imaginary enemy with nervously agitated hands.

The thought of her remoteness from life terrified her. She was alone, face to face with implacable, brutal Nature. Man, the boastful, full of foolish pride, was vanishing from the earth. He had been an alien, ever out of place, defiling and corrupting the order of growth. Now he was beaten and a fugitive. All around her, the representative of this vile destructive species, was the slow, persistent hatred of the earth, which longed to be at peace again. There was no god favourable to man, now that he was dying; the gods of man's creation would perish with him. Only a few women were left to realize that they were strangers in the world of Nature which hated them. The world was not theirs, had never been theirs; they were only some horrible, unnatural fungus that had disfigured the Earth for a time....

She moved cautiously and slowly under the darkness of the trees, and even when she came back to the road she could not shake off her fear. On her right she could see the black cliff of the woods, transfigured by the light of the moon. In the day she knew them for woods; now they were strange and threatening; they menaced her with invasion. She knew that they would march down from the hills and swarm across the valley. In a hundred, two hundred years, Marlow would be a few heaps of brick and stone lost in the heart of the forest.

Ashamed of her race, she hurried on stealthily towards the bridge.

But before she reached it, she heard the sound of a firm, defiant step coming towards her. She paused and listened, and her fear fell from her. In the old days she would have feared man more than Nature, feared robbery or assault, but now, man was united in a common cause; the sound of humanity was the sound of a friend.

"Hullo!" she called, and the voice of Jasper Thrale answered. "Hullo! Who's that?" he said.

"Me—Eileen," she replied. "I've been for a bathe."

He paused opposite her, and they looked at one another.

"Jolly night," he remarked.

"I've seen the great god Pan," said Eileen. "Those sailors in the Ionian Sea were misinformed. He's not dead."

"Why should Pan die and Dionysus live?" returned Thrale. "I hear that Dionysus has claimed one of our hands, by the way."

"Millie?"

"Yes."

"Are you angry?"

"Yes. Not with Millie. If *you* saw Pan, why shouldn't *she* see Dionysus? No, I'm angry with the Jenkyn woman. She's saying that we ought not to have Millie back if she wants to come."

"How silly!" commented Eileen.

"Oh! if that were all!" replied Thrale. "The real trouble is that the Jenkyn woman is proselytizing. She wants to revive Church services and Sunday observances. We're going to have a split before the winter's over, and all the old misunderstandings and antagonisms back again."

"Why, of course we are," returned Eileen, after a pause. "We are going to divide into those that are afraid and those that aren't. It's fear that's got hold of us, now we've time to think. It's all about us to-night; I've seen it, and Millie has seen it; and Clara Jenkyn and all those who are going with her have seen it; and we've all got to find our own way out." She hesitated for a moment, and then said: "And what about you? Have you seen it?"

"Yes, for the first time. Within the last ten minutes," said Thrale.

The moon was above the trees now, and she could see his face clearly. "Have you?" she asked. "I can't picture it. It can't be Pan or Dionysus, or fear of the Earth or of humanity. No; and it can't be the most terrible of all, the fear of an idea. What are you afraid of?"

"I'm afraid of you," said Thrale, and he turned away quickly and hurried on in the direction of the river.

"I *did* see Pan," affirmed Eileen, as she returned, happy and unafraid, towards Marlow.

## 5

That mood of the night had suggested to Eileen the idea of a single cause which seemed sufficient to account for the revivalist tendencies of Miss Jenkyn and certain other women in Marlow. Fear was presented as a simple explanation, and Eileen, like many other philosophers who had preceded her, was too eager for the simple and inclusive explanation.

At first the revivalist tendency was feeble and circumscribed. Twenty or thirty women met in the schoolroom and talked and prayed by the light of a single, tenderly nursed oil-lamp. The absence of any minister kept them back at first; the less earnest needed some concrete embodiment of religion in the form of a black coat and white tie.

But when the rain came in early October, came and persisted; when the beeches, instead of flaring into scarlet, grew sodden and dead; when the threat of flood grew even more imminent, and the distraction of physical toil almost ceased, this little nucleus of women was joined by many new recruits, and their comparatively harmless prostrations, lamentations and worshippings of the abstract, developed into an attempt to enforce a moral law upon the community.

Millie Gosling, returning to Marlow in mid-October, gave the religionists splendid opportunity for a first demonstration.

Millie returned with a bold face and a shrinking heart. She had fled from Wycombe because she could not meet the taunts of the women who had so lately envied her as she rode, prime favourite for a time, in the Dionysian landau. A great loneliness had come over her after she was dethroned; she needed sympathy, and she hoped that Blanche might be made to understand. Millie came back from over the hill prepared with a long tale of excuses.

She found her sister perfectly complacent.

Blanche was a fervent disciple of Jasper Thrale and machinery, and Thrale had anticipated Millie's return and in some ways prepared for it. At odd moments he had preached the new gospel, the tenets of which Blanche had begun to formulate for herself.

"It's no good going back to the old morality for a precedent," had been the essential argument used by Thrale; "we have to face new conditions. If a man is only to have one wife now, the race will decline, probably perish. It is a woman's duty to bear children."

Eileen, Blanche and a few other young women had wondered that he made no application of the argument to his own case, but his opinion carried more weight by reason of his continence. Even Miss Jenkyn could not urge that his opinion was framed to defend his own mode of life, and, failing that casuistical support, she had to fall back on the second alternative of her kind, namely, to assert that this preacher of antagonistic opinions was either the devil in person or possessed by him—a line of defence which took longer to establish than the simple accusation of expediency.

So Millie, returning one wet October afternoon, found that no excuses were required of her. Blanche welcomed her and asked no questions, and Jasper Thrale and Eileen came to the little cottage in St Peter's Street at sunset and treated the prodigal Millie with a new and altogether delightful friendliness. It was understood that she would return at once to her work in the Mill. But in the school-house opposite another reception was being prepared for her.

The more advanced of the Jenkynites were for taking immediate action. Prayer, worship, and the acknowledgment of personal sin fell into the background that evening, Millie appeared not as a brand to be saved from the burning, but as an abandoned and evil creature who must be thrust out of the community if any member of it was to save her soul alive. Every one of these furious religionists could stand up and declare that she was innocent of the commission of this particular sin of Millie's, and every one was willing and anxious to cast the first stone.

The meeting simmered, and at last boiled over into St Peter's Street. A band of more than a dozen rigidly virtuous and ecstatically Christian women beat at the door of the Goslings' cottage. They had come to denounce sin and thrust the sinner out of the community with physical violence. Each of them in her own heart thought of herself as the bride of Christ.

The door was opened to them by Jasper Thrale.

"We have come to cast out the evil one!" cried Miss Jenkyn in a high emotional voice.

"What are you talking about?" asked Thrale.

"She shall be cast forth from our midst!" shrilled Miss Jenkyn; and her supporters raised a horrible screaming cry of agreement.

"Cast her forth!" they cried, finding full justification for their high pitch of emotion in the use of Biblical phrase.

"Cast forth your grandmother!" replied Thrale calmly. "Get back to your homes, and don't be foolish."

"He is possessed of the devil!" chanted Miss Jenkyn. "The Lord has called upon us to vindicate his honour and glory. This man, too, must not be suffered to dwell in the congregation."

"Down with him! down with him!" assented the little crowd, now so exalted with the glory of their common purpose that they were ready for martyrdom.

Miss Jenkyn was an undersized, withered little spinster of forty-five, and physically impotent; but, drunk with the fervour of her emotion, and encouraged by the sympathy of her followers and the fury of her own voice, she flung herself fiercely upon the calm figure of Jasper Thrale. Her thwarted self-expression had found an outlet. She desired the blood of Millie Gosling and Jasper Thrale with the same intensity that women had once desired a useless vote.

Jasper Thrale put out a careless hand and pushed her back into the arms of the women behind her; but she was up again instantly, and, backed by the crowd, who, encouraging themselves by shrill screams of "Cast them forth!" were now thrusting forward into the narrow doorway, she renewed the assault with all the fierce energy of a struggling kitten.

"I shall lose my temper in a minute," said Thrale, as he took a step forward and, bracing himself against the door frame, drove the women back with vigorous thrusts of his powerful arms.

To lose his temper, indeed, seemed the only way of escape; to give way to berserk rage, and so to injure these muscularly feeble creatures that they would be unable to continue the struggle. But the babble of screaming voices was bringing other helpers to his aid, chief among them Lady Durham, and her cold, clear voice fell on the hysterical Jenkynites like a douche of cold water.

"Clara Jenkyn, what are you doing?" asked Elsie Durham.

"Millie Gosling must be cast forth," wavered the little dishevelled woman; but this time there was no response from her disciples.

"That is a question for the committee," replied Elsie Durham. "Now, please go to your homes, all of you."

Miss Jenkyn tried to explain.

Elsie Durham walked into the cottage and shut the door.

Inside, Eileen and Blanche were trying to reassure the trembling Millie. Outside, the Jenkynites were suffering a more brutal martyrdom than that they had sought. The tongues of the new arrivals, the fuller-blooded, more physically vigorous members of the community, were making sport of these brides of Christ.

## 6

But the women of Marlow were to learn afresh the old lesson that religious enthusiasm is not to be killed by ridicule or oppression. Jasper Thrale understood and appreciated that fact, but the policy he suggested could not be approved by the committee.

"This emotion is a fundamental thing," he said to Lady Durham, "and history will show you that persecution will intensify it to the point of martyrdom. There is only one way to combat it. Give it room. Let them do as they will. The heat of the fire is too fierce for you to damp it down; you only supply more fuel. Fan it, throw it open to the air, and it will burn itself harmlessly out."

Elsie Durham shrugged her shoulders. "That's all very well," she said. "I believe it's perfectly true. But they make you the bone of contention. If it were only Millie Gosling—well—she might go. We could find a place for her—at Fingest, perhaps. But we can't spare you."

"I don't know why not," returned Thrale. "I never intended to stay indefinitely. You can carry on now without me, and I can fulfil my original intention and push on into the West."

"My dear man! we can't, and we won't!" said Elsie Durham. "You are indispensable."

"No one is indispensable," replied Thrale.

"Bother your metaphysics, Jasper!" was the answer. "We are not going to let you go. 'We' is the majority of Marlow, not only the committee. We'll fight the fanatics somehow."

The majority referred to by Elsie Durham was fairly compact in relation to this issue of retaining Jasper Thrale, and included the two greater of the three recognizable parties in the community. Of these three, the greatest was the moderate party, made up of Episcopalians, Nonconformists and a few Roman Catholics, who found relief for their emotion one day in seven either in the Town Hall or Marlow Church, in which places services and meetings were held—the former by certain approved individuals, notably Elsie Durham and the widow of the late Rector of Marlow. The second party in order of size included all those who either denied the Divine revelation or were careless of all religious matters. The third party—the Jenkynites, as they were dubbed by their opponents had drawn their numbers from every old denomination. The Jenkynites were differentiated from the other two parties by certain physical differences. For instance, the Jenkynites numbered few members under the age of thirty-five; very few of them were fat, and very few of them were capable field workers; they were hungry-eyed, and had a certain air of disappointed eagerness about them; they looked as though they had for ever sought something, and, finding it, had remained unsatisfied. In all, there were some seventeen women who might have been regarded as quite true to type, and about this vivid nucleus were clustered nearly a hundred other women, many of whom exhibited some characteristic mark of the same type, while the remainder, perhaps 40 per cent of the whole body, had joined the party out of bravado, to seek excitement, or for some purpose of expediency.

Among the last was Mrs Isaacson, who was the ultimate cause of the Jenkynite defeat.

Ever since she had passed her examination in farm supervision, Mrs Isaacson had exhibited an increasing tendency to rest on her laurels. She had grown very stout again during her stay in Marlow, and complained of severe heart trouble. The least exertion brought on violent palpitation accompanied by the most alarming symptoms. The poor lady would gasp for breath, press her hands convulsively to a spot just below her left breast, and roll up her eyes till they presented only a terrifying repulsive rim of blood-streaked white, if the least exertion were demanded from her, and yet she would persist in the effort until absolutely on the verge of collapse. "No, no! I must work!" she would insist. "It iss not fair to the others that I do no work. I will try once more. It iss only fair."

At times they had to insist that she should return home and rest.

And as the winter closed in, Mrs Isaacson's rests became more and more protracted. Jasper Thrale grinned and said: "I suppose we've got to keep her"; but there was a feeling among the other members of the committee that they were creating an undesirable precedent. Mrs Isaacson's example was being followed by other women who preferred rest to work.

Heart weakness was becoming endemic in Marlow.

Then came the news that Mrs Isaacson had joined the Jenkynites. The seventeen received her somewhat doubtfully at first, but the body of the sect were in favour of her reception. Possibly they were rather proud of counting one more fat woman among them; the average member was so noticeably thin.

Even the seventeen were satisfied within a fortnight of Mrs Isaacson's conversion. She had a wonderful fluency, and she said the right and proper things in her own peculiar English—a form of speech which had a certain piquancy and interest and afforded relief and variety after the somewhat stereotyped formulas of the seventeen.

But early in December, before the floods came, Mrs Isaacson was convicted of a serious offence against the community. One of the committee's first works had been to store certain priceless valuables. Tea, coffee, sugar, soap, candles, salt, baking powder, wine and other irreplaceable commodities had been locked up in one of the bank premises. In all, they had a fairly large store, upon which they had hardly drawn as yet. It was not intended to hoard these luxuries indefinitely. After harvest a dole had been made to all the workers as acknowledgment of their services, and it had been decided to hold another festival on Christmas Day.

Mrs Isaacson, with unsuspected energy, had burglariously entered this storehouse of wealth. She had found an accessible window at the rear, which she had succeeded in forcing, and, despite her bulk and the delicate state of her heart, she had effected an entrance and stolen tea, sugar, candles and whisky.

She was, indeed, finally caught in the act; but her thefts would probably have escaped notice—she worked after dark, and with a cunning and caution that would have placed her high in the profession before the plague—had it not been for Blanche.

## 7

It seems that Mrs Isaacson had formed the habit of staying up in the evening. She pleaded that she could not sleep during the early hours of the night, which was not surprising in view of the fact that she slept much during the day; and as she was diligent in picking up or begging sufficient wood to maintain the fire, there was no reason why Blanche and Millie should offer any objection. Thrale had rigged up a dynamo at the mill now to provide artificial light, and the girls' hours of work were so prolonged that they were glad to get to bed at half-past seven.

By eight o'clock Mrs Isaacson evidently counted herself safe from all interruption.

She might have continued her enjoyment of luxury undiscovered throughout the winter if Blanche had not suffered from toothache.

She had been in bed and asleep nearly two hours when her dreams of discomfort merged into a consciousness of actual pain. She sighed and pressed her cheek into the pillows, made agonizing exploration with her tongue, and tried to go to sleep again. Possibly she might have succeeded had not that unaccountable smell of whisky obtruded itself upon her senses.

At first she thought the house was on fire. That had always been her one fear in leaving Mrs Isaacson alone; and she sat up in bed and sniffed vigorously. "Funny," she murmured; "it smells like—like plum pudding." The analogy was probably suggested to her by the odour of burning brandy.

She got up and opened the door of the bedroom.

Mrs Isaacson slept on a sort of glorified landing, and when Blanche stepped outside her own door she could see at once by the light of a watery full moon that her lodger had not yet come to bed.

The smell of the spirit was stronger on the landing, and Blanche, forgetting her toothache in the excitement of the moment, stole quietly down the short flight of crooked stairs. The door giving on to the living-room was latched, but there were two convenient knot-holes, and through one of them she saw Mrs Isaacson seated by the fire drinking hot tea. On the table stood an open whisky bottle and two lighted wax candles.

Blanche was thunderstruck. Tea, whisky and candles were inexplicable things. The thought of witchcraft obtruded itself, and so fascinated her that she stood on the stairs gazing through the knot-hole until a sudden rigour reminded her that she was deadly cold.

She did not interrupt the orgy. She crept back to bed, and after much difficulty awakened Millie.

The sound of their voices must have alarmed Mrs Isaacson, for the girls presently heard her stumbling upstairs. They stopped their discussion then, and Blanche's toothache being mysteriously cured by her excitement, they were soon asleep again.

Neither of the girls spoke of their discovery to anyone the next day, but Blanche returned to the cottage at half-past four, when Mrs Isaacson was at a meeting over the way, and explored her bedroom. She found a small store of tea, sugar and candles under the mattress—the whisky bottle had disappeared—and so came to an understanding of Mrs Isaacson's self-sacrificing insistence that she should perform all work connected with her own sleeping-place—it could hardly be called a room.

After consultation with Millie, Blanche decided that she must inform Jasper Thrale of the contraband.

"She's been stealing, of course," he said. "I suppose we shall have to bring it home to her." But he laughed at Blanche's indignation.

"She's stealing from *us*!" said Blanche, who had developed a fine sense of her duty towards and interest in the community.

"Oh, yes! you're quite right," said Thrale. "I'll inform the committee at least, the non-Jenkynites."

The five non-Jenkynites were furious.

"We must make an example," Elsie Durham said. "It isn't that we shall miss what the Isaacson woman has taken—or will take. It's the question of precedent. This is where we are facing the beginning of law—isn't it? Somebody has to protect the members of the community against themselves. If one steals and goes unpunished, another will steal. We shall have the women divided into stealers and workers."

"What are you going to do with her?" asked Thrale.

"Turn her out," replied Elsie Durham.

"The Jenkynites won't let her go," said Thrale raising the larger question.

"We shall see," said Elsie Durham, "But that reminds me that we must catch the woman *flagrante delicto*; we must have no quibbles about the facts."

Thrale agreed with the wisdom of this policy, but refused to take any part in either the detection or the prosecution of Mrs Isaacson. "They'll say its a put-up job if I have anything to do with it," he argued.

## 8

The Jenkynites blazed when Rebecca Isaacson was finally caught and denounced. The culprit, when caught in the act of entering the bank premises had made a slight error of judgment, and pleaded the excuse that she was a sleepwalker and quite unconscious of what she was doing; but she afterwards adopted a sounder line of defence. She made full confession to the seventeen, pleaded extravagant penitence with all the necessary references to the blood of the Lamb, and displayed all the well-known signs that she would become fervent in well-doing after the ensanguined ablutions had been metaphorically performed.

The Jenkynites were enraptured with so real a case of sin. They had been compelled to content themselves with so many minor failures from grace that the performances were becoming slightly monotonous.

The "Sister Rebecca" case was refreshingly real and genuine, and they meant to make the most of it. Also, this case gave them occasion to assert themselves once more against the opinions of the community.

It must not be supposed that the seventeen deliberately adopted a practical and apparently promising policy. They were not consciously seeking to obtain civil power as were the priests of the old days before the plague. The seventeen had no sense of the State as represented by the community; they were without question perfectly sincere in their beliefs and actions. Their fault, if it can be so described, was their inability to adapt themselves to their conditions. They were as unchangeable as the old lady who had died sooner than be permanently separated from the glories of a house in Wisteria Grove. She and the seventeen and many other women in Marlow were demonstrating that rigidity of opinion is detrimental to the interests of the growing State. The same proposition had been clearly demonstrated by a few exceptional individuals in the old days, but progress was so slow, the property owners so content, and the average of mankind so intensely conservative, that their arguments received no attention. For every man who believed in the broad principle of maintaining an open mind, there were ten thousand who were quite incapable of putting the principle into practice. With these women in Marlow the conditions were completely changed.

Moreover, women are by nature more broad-minded than men in practical affairs. Where intuition rather than the hard-and-fast methods of an intellectual logic is being brought into play, new and wonderful possibilities of adaptation may enter the domain of politics.

The Jenkynites and such individuals as the late Mrs Gosling became suddenly conspicuous in the new conditions. The type that they represent cannot persist. They are the bonds on a vigorous and increasing growth; the tree will grow and burst away all inflexible restraints.

In Marlow the new and vigorous growth was the sense of the community. The majority of the women were realizing, consciously or unconsciously, that they must work with and for each other. The Jenkynite affair served the committee as a valuable object-lesson.

Mrs Isaacson was free to do as she would while the discussion raged. Imprisonment would have been utterly futile. The committee did not wish to punish her for her offence against common property, they merely wished to rid themselves of an undesirable member and to make public announcement that they would in like manner exclude any other member who proved herself a burden to the community.

The Jenkynites were characteristically unable to comprehend this argument. They had their own definitions of heinous and venial sins, definitions based on ancient precedent, and they counted the fault of Millie Gosling in the former and that of Rebecca Isaacson in the latter category. They were not susceptible to argument. As they saw the problem, no argument was admissible. They had the old law and the old prophets on their side, and maintained that what was true once was true for all time. In their opinion, changed conditions did not affect morality.

If the need for labour had been great, the affair might have been shelved for a time as of less importance than the dominant economic demand which takes precedence of all other problems. But although the floods had not yet come, there was not enough work for all the members of the community, and this comparative idleness readied upon the importance of the Isaacson case in another and probably more influential direction than the abstract consideration of justice and humanity.

The women had time to talk, and a new and fascinating subject was given them to discuss. And they talked; and their talk ripened into action. The affair Isaacson, which included also the affair Jenkyns, was brought to a climax at a mass meeting in the Town Hall.

It was decided, noisily, but with considerable emphasis, that for the good of the community the Jenkynites must go. The seventeen were specifically indicated, but it was understood that certain of their more advanced adherents would go with them.

The Jenkynites accepted the decision in the spirit of their belief. They were martyrs in a great cause. They would leave this accursed city (their terminology was always Biblical) and cast off its dust from their feet—although the roads were deep in mud at the time. They would go forth to regenerate the world, upheld by their love of truth and their zeal for the Word.

Only Mrs Isaacson dissented, but she was compelled to go with them.

They went forth in the rain, thirty-nine of them in all, exalted with conscious righteousness and faint with enthusiasm. The women of Marlow were kind to them. They turned out and jeered the little procession as it marched out of the town by the Henley Road.

"'Oo stole the tea?" was the most popular taunt, and no doubt the exiles would have preferred that the taunts should have been cast at their faith rather than at the social misdemeanour of an obscure convert. But any form of martyrdom was better than none, and they held their heads high and sang "Glory! glory!" with magnificent fervour.

"I'm sure we've done right," commented Elsie Durham. "But we should never have had all the women with us if there had been no offence against property. That touched them—communal property. I'm not sure that it isn't become almost dearer than personal property."

## CHAPTER 19

*On The Flood*

### 1

FROM THE MIDDLE of November onwards, the river had been running nearly bank-high, and so much power was available that Thrale had been considering the possibility of lighting some of the nearer houses by electricity. He had made three journeys to London, and with half a dozen assistants he had rifled two dynamos from the power station just outside Paddington, and had brought back twenty truck-loads of coal.

The dynamos, however, were still in the truck, covered by tarpaulin. Thrale had decided that the luxury of artificial lighting could not be provided until all the grain had been thrashed and milled. The end of that work was now in sight, and the accumulated wealth of flour in Marlow was calculated to be sufficient to last the community for at least twelve months. But before the lighting scheme could be put in hand, a new trouble had threatened.

During the first week of December there was almost continuous rain, and the river began to top its banks, spreading itself over the meadowland below the lock and creeping up the end of St Peter's Street. No serious matter as yet, and a short spell of frost and clear skies followed; but before Christmas heavy rains came again, and Thrale began to grow anxious.

"The weirs down-stream ought to be opened," he explained to Eileen. "They are probably all up; we need never be afraid of shortage here; if we close our own weir we can always hold up all the water we want."

"Is it serious?" she asked.

"Not yet, but it may be," he said, looking up at the sky. "All Marlow might be flooded."

And still the rain fell, and soon the girls had to wade through a foot of water to reach the mill.

"I must go down-stream and open all the weirs," Thrale announced on Christmas Eve. "I've been looking at a steam launch over at the boat-house;

it's in quite good condition. I shall bring it up to the town landing-stage tomorrow and get enough coal and food aboard to last a week."

"You're not going alone?" said Eileen.

"No! I *must* take some one to work the engine and the locks," returned Thrale.

"I'll come!" announced Eileen, with glee.

Thrale shook his head. "You'll have to run this place," he said.

Since that night in September no reference had been made by either of them to his strange revelation of fear. They had worked together as two men might have worked. Neither of them had exhibited the least consciousness of sex. Thrale believed that he had put the fear away from him, and Eileen was content to wait. She was barely twenty.

"Blanche could run the mill," she suggested. "There isn't much to do now."

Thrale turned away from her with a touch of impatience. "Blanche had better come with me," he said.

"I *want* to come," pleaded Eileen.

"Why?" he asked.

"It'll be sport."

"I don't care to trust Blanche with the mill," he persisted.

"She's every bit as good as I am," was her reply.

He shook his head.

"Oh, look here," said Eileen, "you might let me come, or are you—are you afraid of—of what the women will say?" She was standing by one of the flour-encrusted mill windows and she began to scratch a clean place on it with her nail.

Thrale did not answer for a moment and then he came and stood near her. "What is it?" he asked. "Are you sick of your work here?"

"I shouldn't mind a change," she said, intent on enlarging her peep-hole.

"One forgets that you are women," said Thrale. "I suppose women are never content with work for work's sake."

"If you like," returned Eileen inconsequently. "I can see out now. Why don't we have these windows cleaned sometimes?"

"You can have them done while I'm away," he suggested.

"I'm coming with you," said Eileen.

"Oh! you can come if you like," he said. He thought he was perfectly safe, despite this unusual display of femininity.

"You'll have to run the engine," he concluded.

"Oh! I'll run the engine," she agreed and looked down at her capable, frankly dirty little hands.

## 2

The weirs at Marlow and Hedsor had been roaring open-mouthed for ten days before Thrale and Eileen began their journey; but the water had been piling up from below and the floods were working back up river. The fact that none of the weirs above Henley was closed had served to protect Marlow in some degree. There were great floods above Sonning, and from Goring to Culham the country was a vast sheet of water. This water, however, only came down comparatively slowly owing to the dammed condition of the main channel, and a greater proportion of it was absorbed. If the upper weirs had been open, Marlow would have been under water by the middle of December.

Not until the launch had been manoeuvred with some difficulty through Boulter's Lock did Thrale begin to realize the full significance of the situation.

He had had very great difficulty first in reaching and second in raising the paddles of the Taplow weir. In one place the force of the flood had broken away the structure, but even with the relief this passage had afforded the pressure of water on the paddles was so great that he had been working for more than two hours before the last valve was opened.

Eileen had been waiting for him with the launch warped up just below the lock where the force of the stream was not so great.

"I don't know whether we shall be able to carry out this job," remarked Thrale when he rejoined her.

"Oh, but we must," she expostulated.

"Do you see what has happened?" he explained. "All the water is piled up below us. We shall probably find the next locks flood-high, which means that we sha'n't be able to open them."

"We must navigate," said Eileen. "Steam round them; shoot the weirs."

"Oh, well," said Thrale, "I'm wondering how far our responsibility goes. If we don't open the river right down to Richmond, we shall only be increasing the flood in the lower reaches, and there may be women living there. After all, Marlow isn't the only place on the river. And there is another thing; we may never get back. It's a risky thing we are proposing to do. No one could swim against this current. If we were upset and carried into a weir, we should be smashed to pieces in no time. Do you think the community can spare us?"

"Bother the community!" replied Eileen.

The community and its activities were already in the background of her mind. Marlow had receded into a little distant place with which she was no longer connected. The world of adventure and romance lay open before her. She wanted only to explore this turbulent river, widened now into a miniature Amazon, from which arose the islands of half-submerged houses and trees that composed the strange archipelago of Maidenhead.

"Oh, well," said Thrale again. "We'll try. It's no use waiting for the stream to go down. We'd better go on now."

"Shall I cast off?" asked Eileen.

"Steady, steady," Thrale warned her. "The next quarter of a mile is simply a rapid. You must be ready to get the engines going full ahead the moment we start, or I sha'n't be able to steer her. And, now, we must both cast off together or we shall be across the stream in two ticks. Just loosen the rope round the cleats and let go, and then start the engine. Let the loose end of the rope drag till we've time to pick it up. Are you ready? All right—cast off!"

The little launch swept out into the current with a bound the instant she was released from her moorings, and almost before the engines began to revolve she was caught in the rapids that surged down from the newly-opened weir. She was only a light draught pleasure-boat, designed to navigate the placid surface of the summer Thames, and when she entered the curling broken water below the island she threw up her nose and plunged like a nervous mare.

"Full steam ahead," shouted Thrale at the toy wheel. Eileen nodded, crouching over her little engine; the roar of the stream had drowned Thrale's voice, but she guessed his order.

Her eyes were bright with excitement. She had no sense of fear. She was exhilarated by the sense of rapid movement. The launch, indeed, was travelling at a remarkable pace. In the narrow channel between the islands and the town, the river must have been running at nearly ten miles an hour, and the engines were probably adding another eight. In the wide spaces of the ocean eighteen miles an hour may appear a safe and controllable speed, but this little launch was running down hill, she could not be stopped at command, and the restricted course was beset with many and dangerous obstacles.

Thrale, handling the little brass wheel forward, was conscious of uneasiness. The launch steered after a fashion, but he had little control of her. The trees on the banks appeared to be flying upstream at the pace of an express train, and ahead of him was the town bridge.

He decided instantly that they could not pass under it, and put the wheel over, intending to shoot out of the stream into the calm of the flood water over the new open bank. But as the launch turned and came across, the current took her stern and turned her half round. For a moment her lee rail was under water, and she trembled and rocked on the verge of capsize. Then her engines drove her out of the stream and she righted herself again and began to cut through the almost still, shallow flood water.

"Stop her!" roared Thrale.

"I say, what's up?" replied Eileen, coolly, as she obeyed the order.

"No room to pass under the bridge," said Thrale. "I suppose we'll have to navigate, as you call it. Go dead slow, and be prepared to stop her at a moment's notice."

They spent over an hour in finding a passage round the approach to the bridge. They had laboriously to pole the launch through the tops of hedges, and in one place they were aground for ten minutes. But after they had returned to the stream once more they had a rapid and easy passage down to Bray. They shot the great arch of the Maidenhead railway bridge triumphantly. Eileen said it was "glorious."

The weir at Bray proved even more difficult to negotiate than the one above, and by the time it was fully opened the dull December afternoon was closing in.

They spent that night moored to two of the elms that ring the isolated little church in the meadows by Boveney.

"At this rate," remarked Thrale as they settled themselves for the night, "it'll take us a week to get to Richmond. We've done two weirs out of thirteen, so far."

### 3

Thrale's estimate proved excessive. They reached Richmond on the fourth day out from Marlow, having opened another nine weirs—the one at Old Windsor had been swept away, and the one below Richmond Bridge Thrale opened that afternoon.

During those four days they had seen few signs of life. They had moved, keeping to the main stream for the most part, in the midst of a wide expanse of water; exploring a desolate and wasted country. Once they had been hailed by three women, who looked out at them from a house in Windsor, and shouted something they did not catch; and a woman had been standing on Staines Bridge as they careered intrepidly through the centre arch—they had no time even to distinguish her dress. But with these exceptions they might have come through the land of an extinct civilization, devoid of life; a land in which deserted houses and church towers stood up from the silver sheet of a vast lake, that was threaded by this one impetuous torrent of swelling river.

Richmond, also, was deserted. The emigrants had passed on over the river or southwards to Petersham and so into Surrey.

"Well!" said Eileen, wiping her oil-blackened hands on a bunch of cotton waste, "that job's done. We've fairly drawn the plug of the cistern now. And how are we going to get back?"

"We'll find a couple of bicycles somewhere here," said Thrale.

It had been a clear day, and there was a suggestion of frost in the air. The sun was setting very red and full behind the bare trees across the river. Save for the gurgle and hiss of the eddying flood, everything was very still. The little launch which had served them so well, and bore the marks of its great adventure in broken rails and bruised sides, was run aground by the side of the bridge. Thrale was standing in the road, but Eileen still sat by her engine.

"I hate to leave the launch," she said, after a long pause.

"We can come back and fetch her up when the flood goes down," returned Thrale.

"We've done pretty well, the three of us."

"Yes, the three of us," he echoed.

"It has been great fun," sighed Eileen.

Thrale did not reply. He was thinking himself back into the past. He saw a street in Melbourne on a burning December evening, and the figure of a gaily-clad little brunette who spoke purest cockney and asked him why he looked so glum. "We ain't goin' to a funeral," she had said. Yet afterwards he had believed that something had been buried that night. He had faced his own passion and the sight of it had disgusted him. He had seen the shadow of a demon who might master him, and he had grappled with it; he believed that he had slain and buried lust in Melbourne ten years ago. It had not risen up to confront him when the plague had put a world of women at his command. He had not been forced to fight, he was not tempted—surely the thing was dead and buried. Only once, on that warm September night, had he felt a sudden furious desire to take this girl into his arms and fly with her into the woods. The desire had come and gone, he was master of it, and in any case it bore no resemblance to the brutal thing he had faced in Melbourne.

Nor, as he stood now by Richmond Bridge watching the vault of the sky deepen to an intenser blue, did the feeling that possessed him in any way resemble that old cruel passion which had flared up and died—surely it had died. He could not analyse his feeling for this brave, clear-eyed companion, who had faced with him all the dangers of the past four days without a sign of fear. She had made no advances to him, they were friends, she might have been some delightfully clean, wholesome boy. And then his thought was pierced and broken by a horrible suggestion.

A picture of the hill to Handy Cross flashed before him, and he saw a little lonely figure creeping furtively away from Marlow. He drove his nails into his palms and suddenly cried out.

"What's up?" said Eileen, turning round and looking up at him. "Have you forgotten anything?"

He stepped into the boat and sat down beside her. "I want to know—I must know," he said.

She looked at him and smiled. "All right, old man," she said. "Fire away."

"I told you once that I was frightened of you," said Thrale. "I want to know if you have ever been frightened of yourself—or—of me?"

"I could never be frightened of you," she replied, and looked away towards the rising darkness of the shadows across the hurrying river, "and I haven't been afraid of myself—yet. I don't think—"

"Wouldn't you be frightened of me if I picked you up and ran shouting into the woods?" he asked, fiercely.

Her eyes met his without reserve. "Dear old man," she said. "I should love it. I'm so glad you understand. That was the one thing that prevented our being real friends. I've wanted so much to be frank and open with you. It's all these silly reserves that make love abominable. Now we can be two jolly, clean human beings who understand each other, can't we? And we shall be such ripping good friends always; quite open and honest with each other."

He drew a deep, sighing breath and put his arms round her, drew her close to him and laid his face against hers. "I've been such an awful ass," he said. "I've always thought that love was unclean. I've been like that Jenkyn woman. I've been prurient and suspicious and evil-minded. I've been like the people who cover up statues. But there was an excuse for me—and for them, too. I didn't know, because there was no woman like you to teach me. All the women I've known have been secretive and sly. They've fouled love for me by making it seem a hidden, disreputable thing. Oh! we shall be ripping good friends, little Eileen—magnificent friends."

"This is a jolly old boat, isn't it?" replied Eileen, inconsequently. "Don't smother me, old man. And, I say, do you think we'll be able to raid some soap from somewhere? Do look at my hands! You couldn't be friends with a chap who had hands like that!"...

"There's one thing I'd like to remark," said Eileen the next morning. There had been a frost in the night, and there was every promise of an easy ride back to Marlow.

"Yes?" said Thrale, examining the deflated tyres of two bicycles they had chosen from a shop in the High Street.

"We'd never have understood each other so well if we hadn't worked together on the same job," said Eileen.

"Well, of course not," returned Thrale. His tone seemed to imply that she had stated a truth that must always have been obvious to sensible people.

"That and there being no footle about marriage," concluded Eileen.

## 4

A third factor that had contributed to the perfection of that complete understanding was not realized by either until they were descending the hill into Bisham.

"I rather wish we weren't going back," said Eileen. "Let's stop a moment. I want to talk. We've never thought of what we're going to do."

"Do?" said Jasper, as he dismounted. "Well, we've just got to make an announcement and that's the end of it. The Jenkyns lot have all gone."

"It isn't the end, it's the beginning," replied Eileen. "Don't you see that we can't even explain?"

"We sha'n't try."

"We shall. We shall have to—in a way. It'll take years and years to do it.

But the point is that they won't understand, now, none of them, not even Elsie Durham. We aren't free any longer."

"We aren't alone," she added, bringing the hitherto unacknowledged factor into prominence.

Thrale frowned and looked up into the thin brightness of the frosty sky. "Yes, I understand," he said. "It's public opinion that compels one to regard love as shameful and secret. Alone together, free from every suspicion, we hadn't a doubt. But now, we have to explain and we can't explain, and we are forced against our wills to wonder whether we can be right and all the rest of the world wrong."

"We *are* right," put in Eileen.

"Only we can't prove it to anyone but ourselves."

"And we shouldn't want to, if we hadn't got to live with them."

For a moment they looked at one another thoughtfully.

"No, we mustn't run away," Jasper said, with determination, after a pause. "Look, the flood has begun to go down already. That's our work. There's other work for us to do yet."

For a time they were silent, looking down on to Marlow and out over the valley.

"We didn't go over *that* hill," said Eileen, at last, pointing to the distant rise of Handy Cross.

"No," replied Jasper, and then, "we won't hide behind hills. Damn public opinion."

"Oh, yes, damn public opinion," agreed Eileen. "But we won't stay in Marlow always."

# CHAPTER 20

*The Terrors of Spring*

## 1

THE FROST GAVE way on the third night, and for ten days there was a spell of mild weather with some rain. Carrie Oliver began to contemplate the possibility of getting forward with such ploughing as still remained to be done. She proposed to have an increased acreage of arable that year, and less pasture, less hay and less turnips; the arable was to include potatoes, beans and peas. For the community was rapidly tending towards vegetarianism. They had no butcher in Marlow, and the women revolted against the slaughter of cattle and sheep. They were hesitating and clumsy in the attack, and so inflicted wounds which were not fatal, they turned sick at the sight of the brute's agonies and at the appalling spurts of blood, and finally when the animal was at last mercifully dead, they bungled the dissection of the carcase.

"I'd sooner starve than do it again," was the invariable decision pronounced by any new volunteer who had heroically offered to provide Marlow with meat, and even Carrie Oliver admitted that it was a "beastly dirty job."

"Only," she added "we'll 'ave to go on breeding calves or we won't get no milk, an' what are we goin' to do with the bullocks?"

The committee wondered if some form of barter might not be introduced. Wycombe and Henley might have something to offer in exchange, or, failing that, might be urged to accept these superfluous beasts as a present, returning the skins and horns, for which there might be a use in the near future. Sheep must be reared for their wool—the clothes of the community would not last for ever. The subjects of tanning and weaving were being studied by certain members of the now enlarged committee. Neither operation presented insuperable difficulties.

Now that a certain supply of food was provided for, the community was already turning its energy towards the industries. Many schemes were being planned and debated. Marlow was well situated, with such abundance of water and wood at its gates; and the question of attracting desirable immigrants had been raised.

Time was afforded for the consideration of all these schemes by the great frost which began on New Year's Day and lasted until the end of February.

The frost came first from the south-west, and for three days the country was changed into a fairy world built of sharp white crystals, a world that was seen dimly through a magic veil of mist. Then followed a black and bitter wind from the north-east, that bought a thin and driving snow, and when the wind fell the country was locked in an iron shell that was not relaxed for six weeks.

The flood had nearly subsided before the first frost came, but the river was still high, and presently the water came down laden with ice-floes, that jammed against the weir and the mill, and formed a sheet of ice that gradually crept back towards the bridge.

All field and mill work was stopped, and Thrale and Eileen spent two or three days a week making excursions to London, bringing back coal and other forms of riches.

## 2

Their fear of being misunderstood had proved to have been an exaggeration. In that exalted mood of theirs, which had risen to such heights, after four days of adventurous solitude, they had come a little too near the stars. In finding themselves they had lost touch with the world.

Elsie Durham had smiled at their defensive announcement.

"My dear children," she had said, "don't be touchy about it. I am so glad; and, of course, I've known for months that you would come to an understanding. And there's no need to tell me that your—agreement, did you say?—was entirely different to any other. I know. But be human about it. Don't apologize for it by being superior to all of us."

"Oh, you're a dear," Eileen had said enthusiastically.

Nevertheless there were many women still left in Marlow who were less spiritually-minded than Elsie Durham. Comparative idleness induced gossip, and there was more than one party in the community which regarded Thrale and Eileen with disfavour.

The old ruts had been worn too deep to be smoothed out in a few months, however heavy had been the great roller of necessity. And, strangely enough, the life of Sam Evans at High Wycombe was regarded by many of the more bigoted with less displeasure than this perfectly wholesome and desirable union of Thrale and Eileen. The prostitution of Sam Evans was a new thing outside the experience of these women, and it was accepted as an outcome of the new conditions. The other affair was familiar in its associations, and was condemned on both the old and the new precedents.

The mass of the women were quite unable to think out a new morality for themselves....

## 3

Relief from all these foolish criticisms, gossipings and false emotions came when the frost broke. A warm rain in the first week of March released the soil from its bonds, and as the retarded spring began to move impatiently into life there was a great call for labour.

But as the year ripened the temperament of the community exhibited a new and alarming symptom.

There was a terrible spirit of depression abroad.

All Nature was warm with the movement of reproduction. Nature was growing and propagating, thrusting out and taking a larger hold upon life. Nature was coming to the fight with new reserves and allies, a fruitful and increasing army, eager for the struggle against this little decreasing band of sterile humanity. Nature was prolific and these women were barren.

And in some inexplicable way the consciousness of futility had spread through the Marlow community. Some posthumous children had been born since the plague, a few young girls—Millie among them—were pregnant, but death had been busier than life during the winter, and from outside came stray reports that in other communities death had been busier still.

What hope was there for that generation? They were too few to cope with their task. Grass was growing in their streets, their houses were in need of repair, and after their day's labour in the fields to provide themselves with food, they had neither strength nor inclination to take up the battle anew.

Moreover, the spice was gone from life. Some inherent need for emulation was gone. They were ceasing to take any pride in their persons, and in their clothes. They wore knickerbockers or trousers for convenience in working, and suffered a strange loss of self-esteem in consequence. Many of the younger women still returned in the evenings to what skirts and ribbons they still possessed, but the habit was declining. The uselessness of it was growing even more apparent. There were no sex distinctions or class distinctions among them. Of what account was it that one girl was prettier or better dressed than her neighbour? What mattered was whether she was a stronger or more intelligent worker.

Above all, the woman's need for love and admiration could find no outlet. They realized that they were becoming hardened and unsexed, and revolted against the coming change. Something within them rose up and cried for expression, and when it was thwarted it turned to a thing of evil....

The mind of the community was becoming distorted. Hysteria, sexual perversions, and various forms of religious mania were rife. Young women broke into futile and unsatisfying orgies of foolish dancing, and middle-aged women became absorbed in the contemplation of a male and human god.

Even the committee did not escape the influence of the growing despair. They looked forward to a future when such machines and tools as they possessed would be worn out, and they had no means of replacing them.

Thrale had reported that the line to London was becoming unsafe for the passage of his trucks. Rust was at work upon the rails; rain and floods had weakened embankments; young growths were springing up on the permanent way, and it was hopeless to contemplate any work of repair. In the old days an army of men had been needed for that work alone. The country roads needed re-metalling, and the houses restoration; they had not the means or the labour to undertake half the necessary work. There were breaches in the river bank and a large and apparently permanent lake was forming in the low meadows towards Bourne End. All about them Nature was so intensely busy in her own regardless way, and they were helpless, now, to oppose her.

The age of iron and machinery was falling into a swift decline. All that the community could look for in the future was a return to primitive conditions and the fight for bare life. Every year their tools and machines would grow less efficient, every year Nature would return more powerful to the attack. In ten years they would be fighting her with rude and tedious weapons of wood, grinding their scanty corn between two stones, and living from hand to mouth. In the bountiful South such a life might have its rewards, but how could they endure it in this uncertain and cruel North?

So while the sun rose higher in the sky and the earth was wonderfully reclothed, the women of Marlow fell deeper and deeper into the horrors of mental depression. What had they to work for, and to hope for, save this miserable possession of unsatisfied life?

# CHAPTER 21
*Smoke*

1

One bright morning, at the end of April, Jasper and Eileen sat on the cliffs at the Land's End and talked of the future.

Ten days before, they had left Marlow on bicycles to make exploration. They intended to return; they had explained they would be away for a month at the outside, but in view of the growing depression and the loss of spirit shown by the community, they considered it necessary to go out and discover what conditions obtained in other parts of England. It might be, they urged, that the plague had been less deadly in other districts.

"We should not know, here," Jasper had argued. "There may be many men left elsewhere; but they might not have been able to communicate with us yet. Their attention, like ours, would have been concentrated upon local conditions for a time. Eileen and I will find out. Perhaps we may be able to open up communication again. In any case we'll come back within a month and report."

His natural instinct had taken him into the West Country.

They had left Elsie Durham slightly more cheerful. They had given her a gleam of hope, given her something, at last, to which she might look forward.

Their own hopes had quickly faded and died as they rode on into the West. By the time they reached Plymouth they were thinking of Marlow as a place peculiarly favoured by Providence.

At first they had passed through communities conducted on lines resembling their own, greater or smaller groups of women working more or less in co-operation. In many of these communities a single man was living—in some cases two men—who viewed their duty towards society in the same light as the Adonis of Wycombe. But the unit grew steadily smaller as they progressed. It was no longer the town or village community but the farm which was the centre of activity, and the occupied farms grew more scattered. For it appeared that here in the West the plague had attacked women as well as men. Another curious fact they learned was that the men had taken longer to die. One woman spoke of having nursed her husband for two months before the paralysis proved fatal....

And if the depression in Marlow had been great, the travellers soon learned that elsewhere it was greater still. The women worked mechanically, drudgingly. They spoke in low, melancholy voices when they were questioned, and save for a faint accession of interest in Thrale's presence there, and the signs of some feeble flicker of hope as they asked of conditions further north and east, they appeared to have no thought beyond the instant necessity of sustaining the life to which they clung so feebly.

Thrale and Eileen rode on into Cornwall, not because they still hoped, but because they both felt a vivid desire to reach the Land's End and gaze out over the Atlantic. They wanted to leave this desolate land behind them for a few hours, and rest their minds in the presence of the unchangeable sea.

"Let us go on and forget for a few days," Eileen had said, and so they had at last reached the furthest limit of land.

Cornwall had proved to be a land of the dead. Save for a few women in the neighbourhood of St Austell, they had not seen a living human being in the whole county.

And so, on this clear April morning, they sat upon this ultimate cliff and talked of the future.

## 2

The water below them was delicately flecked with white. No long rollers were riding in from the Atlantic, but the fresh April breeze was flicking the crests of little waves into foam; and, above, an ever-renewed drift of scattered white clouds threw coursing shadows upon the blues and purples of the curdling sea.

Eileen and Thrale had walked southwards as far as Carn Voel to avoid the obstruction to vision of the Longships, and on three sides they looked out to an unbroken horizon of water, which on that bright morning was clearly differentiated from the impending sky.

"One might forget here," remarked Eileen, after a long silence.

"If it were better to forget," said Jasper.

Eileen drew up her knees until she could rest her chin upon them, embracing them with her arms. "What can one do?" she asked. "What good is it all, if there is no future?"

"Just to live out one's own life in the best way," was the answer.

She frowned over that for a time. "Do you really believe, dear," she said, when she had considered Jasper's suggestion, "do you really believe that this is the end of humanity?"

"I don't know," he said. "I have changed my mind half a dozen times in the last few days. There may be a race untouched somewhere in the archipelagos of the South Seas, perhaps—which will gradually develop and repeople the world again."

"Or in Australia, or New Zealand," she prompted.

"We should have heard from them before this," he said. "We must have heard before this."

"And is there no hope for us, here in England, in Marlow? There are a few boys—infants born since the plague, you know—and there will be more children in the future—Evans's children and those others. There were two men in some places, you remember."

"Can they ever grow up? It seems to me that the women are dying. They've nothing to live for. It's only a year since the plague first came, and look at them now. What will they be like in five years' time? They'll die of hopelessness, or commit suicide, or simply starve from the lack of any purpose in living, because work isn't worthwhile. And the others, the mothers, that have some object in living, will fall back into savagery. They'll be so occupied in the necessity for work, for forcing a living out of the ground somehow, that they'll have neither time nor wish to teach their children. It seems to me that we are faced with decrease, gradually leading on to extinction.

"And I doubt," he continued, after a little hesitation, "I doubt whether these sons of the new conditions will have much vitality. They are the children of lust on the father's side, worse still, of tired lust. It does make a difference. Perhaps if we were a young and vigorous people like the old Jews the seed would be strong enough to override any inherent weakness. But we are not, we are an old civilization. Before the plague, we had come to a consideration of eugenics. It had been forced upon us. A vital and growing people does not spend its time on such a question as that. Eugenics was a proposition that grew out of the necessity of the time. It was easy enough to deny decadence, and to prove our fitness by apparently sound argument, but, to me, it always seemed that this growing demand for some form of artificial selection of parents, by restriction of the palpably unfit, afforded the surest evidence. Things like that are only produced if there is a need for them. Eugenics was a symptom."

Eileen sighed. "And what about us?" she asked.

"We're happy," replied Jasper. "Probably the happiest people in the world at the present time. And we must try to give some of our happiness to others. We must go back to Marlow and work for the community. And I think we'll try in our limited way to do something for the younger generation. Perhaps, it might be possible for us to go north and try our hands at making steel, there are probably women there who would help us. But I don't think it's worth while, unless to preserve our knowledge and hand it on. We can only lessen the difficulty in one little district for a time. As the pressure of necessity grows, as it must grow, we shall be forced to abandon manufacture. The need for food will outrun us. We are too few, and it will be simpler and perhaps quicker to plough with a wooden plough than to wait for our faulty and slowly-produced steel. The adult population, small as it is, must decrease, and I'm afraid it will decrease more rapidly than we anticipate, owing to these causes of depression and lack of stimulus...."

"Oh, well," said Eileen at last, getting to her feet, "we're happy, as you say, and our job seems pretty plain before us. To-morrow, I suppose, we ought to be getting back, though I hate taking the news to Elsie."

Jasper came and stood beside her, and put his arm across her shoulders. "We, at any rate, must keep our spirits up," he said. "That, before everything."

"I'm all right," said Eileen, brightly. "I've got you and, for the moment, the sea. We'll come back here sometimes, if the roads don't get too bad.

And, already, the briars are creeping across the road from hedge to hedge. The forest is coming back."

"The forest and the wild."

He drew her a little closer and they stood looking out towards the horizon.

## 3

In the south-west the clear line had been wiped out and what looked like mist was sweeping towards them.

"There's a shower coming," said Thrale.

They stood quietly and let the sharp spatter of rain beat in their faces, and then the shadow of the storm moved on and the horizon line was clear again.

"That's a queer cloud out there," said Eileen. "Is it another shower?"

She pointed to a tiny blur on the far rim of the sea.

"It *is* queer," said Thrale. "It's so precisely like the smoke of a steamer."

For a few seconds they gazed in intent silence.

"It's getting bigger," broke out Eileen, suddenly excited. "What is it, Jasper?"

"I don't know. I can't make it out," he said. He moved away from her and shaded his eyes from the glare of the momentarily cloudless sky.

"I can't make it out," he repeated mechanically.

The blur was widening into a grey-black smudge, into a vaguely diffused smear with a darker centre.

"With the wind blowing towards us—" said Jasper, and broke off.

"Yes, yes—what?" asked Eileen, and then as he did not answer, she gripped his arm and repeated importunately. "What? Jasper, what? With the wind blowing towards us?"

"By God it is," he said in a low voice, disregarding her question. "By God it *is*," he repeated, and then a third time, "It *is*."

"Oh! what, what? Do answer me! I can't see!" pleaded Eileen.

But still he did not answer. He stood like a rock and stared without wavering at the growing cloud on the horizon.

And then the cloud began to grow more diffused, to die away, and Eileen could see tiny indentations on the sky line, indentations which pushed up and presently revealed themselves as attached to a little black speck in the remotest distance.

"Oh, Jasper!" she cried, and her eyes filled with inexplicable tears, so that she could see only a misty field of troubled blue. "It's a liner," said Jasper at last, turning to her. He looked puzzled and his eyes stared through her. "And its coming from America. Do you suppose the American women—"

The boat was revealed now. They could see the shape of her, the high deck, the two tall funnels and the three masts. She was passing across, fifteen miles or so to the south of them, making up Channel.

For a moment they felt like shipwrecked sailors on a lonely island, who see a vessel pass beyond hail.

"Oh, Jasper, what can it be?" Eileen besought him.

"It's a White Star boat," he said, and he still spoke as if his mind was far away. "Is it possible, is it anyway possible that America has survived? Is it possible that there is traffic between America and Europe, and that they pass us by for fear of infection? How do we know that vessels haven't been passing up the Channel for months past? Why should we think that this is the first?"

"It *is* the first," proclaimed Eileen. "I feel it. Oh, let us hurry. Let us ride and ride as fast as we can to Plymouth or Southampton. I know they'll be coming to Plymouth or Southampton. Men, Jasper, men! No women would dare to run a boat at that pace. See how fast she is going. Oh hurry, hurry!"

He caught fire then. They ran back to find their bicycles. They ran, and presently they rode in silence, with fierce intensity. They rode at first as if they had but ten miles to go, and the lives of all the women in England depended upon their speed.

And though they slackened after the first few miles they still rode on with such eager determination that they reached Plymouth at sunset.

But they could see no sign of the liner in the waters about Plymouth. They saw only the deserted hulks of a hundred vessels that had ridden there untouched for twelve months, futile battleships and destroyers among them; great, venomous, useless things that had become void of all meaning in the struggle of humanity.

"It's not here. Let's go on!" said Eileen.

Jasper shrugged his shoulders. "It's well over a hundred miles to Southampton," he said. "Nearer a hundred and fifty, I should say."

"But we must go on, we must," urged Eileen.

It was evident that Jasper, too, felt a compelling desire to go on. He stood still with a look of intense concentration on his face. Eileen had seen him look thus, when he had been momentarily frustrated by some problem of mill machinery. She waited expectant for the solution she was sure would presently emerge.

"A motor," he said, speaking in short disconnected sentences. "If we can find paraffin and petrol and candles—light of some sort. The engines wouldn't rust, but they'd clog. It must be paraffin. We daren't clean with petrol by artificial light. It's possible. Let's try...."

That night Jasper did not sleep, but Eileen, as she sat beside him in the softly moving motor, soon lost consciousness of the dim streak of road and black river of hedge. The moon, in her third quarter, had risen before midnight, and when they started was riding deep in the sky, half veiled by a vast wing of dappled cirrus. And that, too, merged into her dream. She thought she was driving out into the open sea in a ship which became miraculously winged and soared up towards an ever-approaching but unincreasing moon. She woke with a start to find that it was broad daylight and that a thin misty rain was coming up from the sea.

"The Solent," said Jasper, pointing to a distant gleam below them.

On the common they stopped and stood up in the car, watching a distant smear of smoke that stained the thin mist.

"She'll be coming up Southampton Water with the lead going," said Jasper, trying desperately to be calm.

# EPILOGUE

## THE GREAT PLAN

# 1

On the evening of that day Jasper and Eileen dined on board the "Bombastic," that latest development of the old trans-Atlantic competition in shipbuilding, the boat that had made her first journey to New York carrying fugitives from England in the days when the threat of the plague grew hourly more imminent. The "Bombastic" had not justified her name, she had fled from Southampton without ceremony, and she had not returned for over a year. The "Apologetic" would have been more apt.

And on this evening of her return, the demeanour of that crowd of quiet serious men in the huge over-decorated saloon, gave no hint of bombast. As they listened intently to the rapid story of their two travel-stained and somewhat ragged guests, there was no hint of brag or boast among them all. They came not as conquerors but as friends.

"But oh, it's *your* story we want to hear," broke in Eileen at last.

She had been strangely quiet so far, she had become suddenly conscious of the defects of her dress. The old associations were swarming about her. Eighteen months ago she had sat in just such another saloon as this, courted and flattered, the daughter of a great aristocrat, a creature on a remote and gorgeous pedestal. Now it seemed that she was neither greater nor less than any man present. She was one of them, not set apart. She looked down at her hands, still oil-stained by her struggles with the motor on the previous night.

Jasper had been more patient. He was not less eager than Eileen to hear the explanation of this wonderful visit, of the resurrection of these twelve hundred men from a dead and silent world. But he had restrained his impatience and told his story first. He knew that so he would be more quickly satisfied. He would be able to listen to men who were not tense with an anxiety to ask questions.

They were sitting now at one end of a long table in the saloon, after eating a meal that had provided once more the longed-for satisfaction of salt.

"Well," said an American at the head of the table, turning to Eileen in answer to her protest, "we've maybe been selfish in putting all these questions but we're looking ahead. We aren't forgetting that we've a big work to do."

"But how did you get here?" asked Eileen impetuously. "How is it that you're all alive?"

"Well, as to that, you'd better ask the doctor, there," replied the American. "He's a countryman of yours, and he's been in the thick of it and knows the life story of that plague microbe like the history of England."

The doctor, a bearded, grave-eyed man, looked up and smiled.

"Hardly that," he said. "We shall never know now, I hope, the history of the plague organism. It was never studied under the microscope—we were too busy—and now we trust that the bacillus—if it were a bacillus—has encompassed its own destruction. What interests you, however, is that this sudden, miraculously sudden, development of its deadly power as regards humanity ran through a determinable cycle of evolution. From what you've told us, already, it seems clear, I think, that even in England the bacillus was losing what I may call its effectiveness. The men in the West Country you've described, probably died from starvation and neglect."

He paused for a moment and then continued: "Now in America both men and women were attacked. There was certainly a greater percentage of male cases, but I suppose something like half the female population was infected as well. As far as one can judge the bacillus was simply losing power. But for all we know it may have developed, it may be entering on a new stage of evolution, and in some apparently haphazard way now be beneficial to man instead of deadly. Such things may be happening every day below the reach of our knowledge. The little world is hidden from us, even as the great world is hidden....

"However," he went on more briskly, "the thing we do know is that the symptoms of the new plague in America differed materially from our expectation of them, gathered from the accounts that had reached us from the Old World. In England the paralysis lasted, I believe, some forty-eight hours and ended in death. In America the paralysis rarely ended fatally, but it lasted in some cases for six months. 'Paresis,' we called it. The patient was perfectly conscious but practically unable to move hand or foot."

"That paresis gave us time to do some very clear and consecutive thinking, I may remark," put in an American. "I had four months to study my ideas of life."

The doctor nodded thoughtfully. "America is no less changed than England," he said, "but it is another change. Well, you understand that we did not all get the plague over there; the thing was less deadly in attack and about ten per cent of us were left to look after the patients."

"And find food," interpolated one of the listeners.

"That was a time we won't ever forget," agreed another.

"Sure thing," said some one, and a general murmur of assent ran round the table.

"And all the machines were idle, of course," continued the doctor, "and even when the tide of recovery began to flow we had to turn our attention first to the getting of food."

"If it hadn't been for that we'd have been here before this," said a young man. "I feel we owe England and Europe some kind of an apology, but we just had to get busy on food growing right away. We couldn't spare a ship's crew till three weeks ago."

"And the others are hard at it over there still," put in another. "This is just a pioneer party."

"It's all so comprehensible now," said Thrale after a silence, "but we had no idea, we never thought there could be any one living in America. We thought that somehow we must have heard. One forgets..."

"We tried to get on to you," said one of the party, "by cable and wireless. We kept on tapping away for months, but we got no reply. We thought you must be all dead too."

"Well, we guessed you were having a real bad time anyway," amended another. "You see we knew the way that plague had taken Europe but we kept hoping and trying to get on to you all the same."

*

"We've got a message for Elsie, after all," Eileen said to Jasper the next day. "There's hope for us yet."

"Yes, there's hope," said Jasper.

They had been up at the town railway station assisting a party of Americans to investigate the condition of the rolling stock and the permanent way. Neither could be pronounced satisfactory. A few women had come in from the neighbouring country that morning attracted by the sight of an inexplicable pillar of smoke, and their report of local conditions had been equally uninspiring. They had spoken of famine and failure, but their faces had been lit by a new brightness at the sight of this miraculous little army of men. There had been hope in the faces and bearing of these toil-worn women, faith in the promise of support and succour.

Now Jasper and Eileen stood looking down towards the harbour. The tide was creeping in to efface the repulsive ugliness of the mud flats, and the sluggish water rippled faintly against the foul sloping sides of small boats that had lain anchored there for more than twelve months. Behind them, across the line, was a row of unsightly houses, hung with weather-slating.

"Oh, there's hope," repeated Jasper.

He was thinking of all the work that lay before them, and yet he had faith that a new and better civilization would arise. "We must get things going again," had been the Americans' phrase, and they apparently faced the future without a qualm.

But Jasper's mind was perplexed with the detail of the mechanical work that must be faced, detail so intricate and confused that he was bewildered by its complexity. It appeared to him that the crux of the whole problem lay in the North, in the counties of coal and iron. Coal and steel were the first essentials, he thought. They must begin there in however small a way, and America must send out more men, continually more men. To-morrow he was going back in the motor, with two experts, to the cable hut in Sennen Cove. They were going to test the cable and hoped to re-establish communication with America, and then more ships would come and more men, ever more men.

And, even so, they could do little at first, and beyond lay the whole of Europe and still further the whole of Asia. Were women there, also, maintaining the terrible fight against Nature in the awful struggle to find food? Steel and coal we must have, was the burden of his thought, and in his imagination he pictured the waking of factories and mines, he had a vision of little engines running....

Eileen's thought had flown ahead. With one magnificent leap she had passed from the contemplation of present necessity to a realization of the dim future. And her thought found words.

"Hope, lots of hope," she said. "Hope of a new clean world. We've got such a chance to begin all over again, and do it better. No more sweated labour, Jasper, and no more living on the work of others. We've just got to pull together and work for each other. If we can get enough food, and we can now with all these dear men come to help us, we can do such wonderful things afterwards. There'll be lots of children growing up in a few years' time, and we shall teach them the things we've had to learn by the force of necessity. They'll begin so differently because, although we have had the experience of all history, we sha'n't be bound by all the foolish conventions that grew out of it. Such a silly incongruous growth, wasn't it? But I suppose it couldn't be helped in one way. We were so penned in. We all had our rotten little places to keep and that took all our time. We never had a chance to consider the broad issues, the real fundamental things. But you've got to consider the fundamental things when you start clean away from a new beginning.

"And, oh! Jasper, surely we have all learnt certain things to avoid, haven't we? I mean class distinctions and sex distinctions, and things like that. Women won't trouble any more about titles and all that rot now, and anyway there aren't any left to trouble about. And social conditions will be so different now that there won't be any more marriage. Marriage was a man's prerogative; he wanted to keep his woman to himself, and keep his property for his children. It never really protected women, and anyway they were capable of protecting themselves if they'd been given a chance. I know the children were a difficulty in the old days, but they won't be now. It'll be everybody's business to see that the children get looked after, and a woman won't starve just because she hasn't got a husband to keep her. She'll get better wages than that. The women who have children will be the most precious things we shall have. They'll live healthier lives, too, and they won't be incapacitated as they used to be. They'll work and be strong instead of spending all their time either in doing nothing or pottering about the house in an eternal round of cleaning the stupid, ugly things we used. We shall have to have all new houses, Jasper, when we get things going again.

"Oh, it *will* be splendid," she broke out in a great burst of enthusiasm, "and we begin to-day. We have begun."

Jasper nodded. "It's a wonderful opportunity," he said.

"Wonderful, wonderful," repeated Eileen. "We all, men and women, start level again. Equality, Jasper, It's a beautiful word—Equality. Of course I know how unequal we all are from one point of view, and there must come a sort of aristocracy of intellect and efficiency. But underneath there will be a true equality for all that, and we shall see to it that no man or woman can abuse their powers by making slaves again. What a world of slaves it used to be, and we weren't even slaves to intellect and efficiency, only to wealth and to money, and to some foolish idea of position and power."

"Well, we've got *our* work to do, here and now," said Jasper after a long pause.

"Work? Of course, and I love it," returned Eileen, "and while we work we've got to think and teach."

The tide was coming in steadily, and near them an old boat that had been lying on the mud was now afloat once more and had taken on some of its old dignity.

Eileen pointed to it. "We're afloat again," she remarked.

"Embarked on the greatest plan the world has ever known," added Jasper.

"Oh, it's all part of the great plan," concluded Eileen.

THE END